PANTHER

Also by Melvin Van Peebles

The Big Heart

Un Ours Pour le FBI (A Bear for the FBI)

Le Chinois de XIV

La Permission (Story of a Three Day Pass)

La Fête à Harlem (Dont Play Us Cheap)

Aint Supposed to Die

Un Americain en Enfer (The True American)

Sweet Sweetback's Baadasssss Song

Just an Old Sweet Song

Waltz of the Stork

Becky

Bold Money

Champeeen

No Identity Crisis

PANTHER

A NOVEL BY

MELVIN VAN PEEBLES

THUNDER'S MOUTH PRESS ■ NEW YORK

Copyright © 1995 by Melvin Van Peebles
All rights reserved

First edition
First printing, 1995

Published by
Thunder's Mouth Press
632 Broadway, 7th Floor
New York, NY 10012

This novel is a work of historical reconstruction. Any references to historical events; to real people, living or dead; or to real locales are intended only to give the fiction a setting in historical reality. Other names, characters, places, and incidents either are the product of the author's imagination or are used fictitiously, and their resemblance, if any, to real-life counterparts is entirely coincidental.

Library of Congress Cataloging-in-Publication Data
Van Peebles, Melvin, 1932–
Panther : a novel / by Melvin Van Peebles. — 1st ed.
p. cm.
ISBN 1-56025-096-8
1. Black Panther Party—Fiction. 2. Afro-Americans—History—20th century—Fiction.
3. Black power—United States—History—Fiction.
4. United States—Race relations—Fiction.
I. Title.
PS3572.A52P36 1995
813'.54—dc20 95-14085
CIP

Printed in the United States of America

Distributed by Publishers Group West
4065 Hollis Street
Emeryville, CA 94608
(800) 788-3123

To my eldest son Mario for prodding me
into turning my novel into a movie

To Preston Holmes for holding the fort
on the West Coast

&

To Isabel Helton for holding the fort
on the East Coast and to her husband George
for being such a wonderful artist

Author's Note

> J. Edgar Hoover and the FBI engaged in lawless tactics against the Black Panther Party and responded to deep-seated societal problems by fomenting violence and unrest.
>
> —Senate Select Committee investigating domestic intelligence operations, 1976

Foremost, this novel is an attempt to read between the lines—the above lines, to be precise. First, how was it that a supposedly ragtag group of young hoodlums managed to survive and even flourish against such formidable governmental repression? Second, was the rise of militancy in the ghettoes and the rise of drug usage there pure coincidence, or is there a more sinister explanation?

This story is fiction based on fact, using real and composite characters and a historical backdrop. Yes, artistic liberties have been taken, but the story is by no means sheer fancy.

The truth, as one of the witnesses in the book puts it, is coming out in the wash. Seepage from the toxic barrel of unofficial reality, loose tongues, memos, and files have begun to provide pieces. Things only suspected back then, things routinely ridiculed and dismissed as paranoid fantasies seem closer to reality than they once did.

Personally, I view the reaction to the Black Panthers as a living, breathing, All-American Rorschach test. I suppose it depends on how experiences group themselves in your memory. The late 1960s were no more than a blip in time, and the heyday of the Panthers didn't last all that much longer. But their appearance was an atomic explosion, the flame so ferocious, the heat so intense, that the fabric of the American dream is still smoldering and shit is still falling out. Heroes, creeps, bystanders—guilty and innocent alike—are still rushing to get into the act and establish their position of importance in the scheme of things. Ask anybody and what do you get? Lectures, legends, dissertations, half-alibis, three-quarters alibis, anything and everything to justify their own action or inaction. And why not? Hope, treachery, tragedy, arrogance, altruism . . . all the big themes were there. Heck, there have been lots of courageous eyewitnesses willing to step up and testify about the details. But I feel the truth isn't in any individual tree, it lies in the forest itself and that's what I have attempted to convey here.

MVP, NYC/LA 1995

THE TEN-POINT PROGRAM OF THE BLACK PANTHER PARTY FOR SELF DEFENSE

■ ■ ■

1. We want freedom. We want the power to determine the destiny of our black community.

2. We want full employment for our people.

3. We want an end to the robbery by the white man of our black community.

4. We want decent housing, fit for shelter of human beings.

5. We want education for our people that espouses the true nature of this decadent American society.

6. We want all black men to be exempt from military service.

7. We want an immediate end to police brutality and murder of black people.

8. We want freedom for all black men held in federal, state, county, and city prisons and jails.

9. We want all black people when brought to trial to be tried in court by a jury of their peer group or people from their black communities.

10. We want land, bread, housing, education, clothing, justice, and peace.

1

TESTING, ONE-TWO-THREE . . . Witness #1. Name: Refused (target of opportunity) . . . "Leroy's Lounge," pool hall, Oakland. . . Skinny black man, pointed shoes, very large ring . . . Obviously a hustler waiting for a pigeon . . .

PARDON ME, BUT ARE YOU FROM THESE PARTS, BROTHER?

All my life, brother. You wanta shoot a game?

NOT EXACTLY. MY THESIS IS THAT THERE IS SOME AS YET UNDISCOVERED CORRELATION AND THEREFORE SOME EQUATION WHEREBY ONE CAN PREDICT WHEN A DISSIDENT VOICE WILL IGNITE A SPARK IN A DOWN-TRODDEN GROUP, A LA JOAN OF ARC. I CALL MY HYPOTHESIS "THE LAST STRAW" . . .

Uh-hunh, yeah . . .

WELL, ACTUALLY, I'D LIKE TO TAPE AN INTERVIEW WITH YOU ABOUT THE BLACK PANTHER PARTY, ESPE-CIALLY ITS INCEPTION. YOU KNOW, ITS START.

I know what the fuck inception means. Inception, hunh? How'd it start, hunh? I mean shit, you ask

> anybody about the Panthers and they got a different story, you know? But maybe there ain't no big mystery to it. Maybe folks can just get tired of other folks fucking them over. Back then, just like now, we was what they call "second-class citizens." Just a fancy title for slave—they got lots of words to go masquerading the slave fact...serf, peasant, disenfranchised and stuff. Shit . . . still means slave—human nature works that way. Second-class my ass! Second-class equal no-class if you ask me . . . It was like you said, the last straw.

Emboldened by the chill in the late night air the fog crawls in off the bay, up the rotting pilings, across the cobblestones, and proceeds to take over the entire warehouse district.

A car comes slowly out of the fog. The rangy black man at the wheel peers out the window searching through the mist. Judge doesn't know if he can find the garage in the dark, but he is a dead man if he doesn't and . . .

Check—there it is! He has picked up the trail . . . Ancient oil stains from thousands of weary engines limping back to the roost, the asphalt so soaked with grease that after all the years the streak in the road leading to the abandoned garage still points like an arrow—a glistening, malevolent arrow that thickens as it gets closer to its destination, finally veering off and disappearing underneath the rusty corrugated doors of the garage.

But maybe the garage isn't the warehouse in the first place . . . *No, it is* the warehouse all right, it had to be!

Judge can feel the sweat dripping off his face. He isn't so afraid for himself, it's the mission. Huey had said in the visiting room, leaning so close that his breath fogged up the glass partition separating them, that the whole future of black people depended on the success of the mission . . .

Bingo!. . . This had to be it. They had to be using the garage for a warehouse. What else would two goons be doing pulling sentry duty in front of a peeling old door in this deserted rundown industrial part of town in the middle of the night?

There they stand, positioned about twenty feet apart, smug not even trying to look innocuous, arms folded above their guts in a don't-fuck-with-me-buddy style.

Steady now, not too fast not too slow, Judge cruises past. One of the two thugs glances over as the car passes. He grunts and lets it go, probably figuring it's just a bunch of sloppy drunk Mexicans trying to find their way back to the casa.

Judge continues down the street three more blocks to be sure he is out of sight before making a U-turn. Then he tromps on the gas and heads back.

Grudgingly, the old jalopy starts to pick up speed. They're flying by the time they reach the middle of the second block. Judge keeps the pedal to the metal. Then just as he comes abreast of the garage he yanks the wheel to the left. The car spins ninety degrees and barrels across the road. Judge hurtles the heap straight for the garage doors, using the hood ornament as a crosshairs—like the one formed by the intersection at Fifty-Fifth and Market in Oakland where it all began . . .

2

TESTING, ONE-TWO-THREE . . . Witness #2. Name: Anthony Wheatstraw . . . Living room, neat . . . Older black male, collar frayed.

JUST IGNORE THE TAPE RECORDER, PLEASE, MR. WHEATSTRAW. IN YOUR OWN WORDS, WHAT CAN YOU TELL ME ABOUT THE BEGINNINGS OF THE BLACK PANTHER PARTY FOR SELF DEFENSE? THE MOVEMENT OFTEN REFERRED TO AS THE SPARK THAT IGNITED THE GHETTO...

Spark my ass. When them two boys started out, as far as I can tell everybody thought they was farting in the wind. Nobody 'cept maybe three, four other youngsters was even listening to them with all that "any means necessary" talking. One thing you gotta remember, the Panthers started up before Dr. King got murdered, so most colored folks was still hoping they was gonna be able to pray themselves to freedom. Hell, until that vigil thing happened the Panthers couldn't barely get themselves arrested . . . Shit, wouldn't been no Panther movement if it hadn't been for that intersection.

■ ■ ■

Oakland, 1967. Tiny-the-Daredevil is flying down the middle of the rust-encrusted railroad tracks clickety clackety clickety clackety barely able to control his bike (a hand-me-down, you'll-grow-into-it job). He pedals for all he is worth to keep his balance—plus he has to make up the time taking his favorite unsanctioned way home from school cost him.

Leering up at him between the railroad ties is the gravel-turd-rag-glass-wire rubble just waiting for him to skid and take a tumble. But Tiny, relishing the challenge, stand-stoops over the handlebars, his skinny going-on-ten legs churning the pedals.

The tracks suddenly curve around a forgotten factory and down to an abrupt, undignified end in a piss-stained alley. Before the dip, the Daredevil takes off, jumping the bike in a twisting, death-defying leap to the concrete. At the end of the alley he hits the street, hangs a right, and heads into the ghetto.

Concentrating, Tiny blurs along. Cars and trucks, using the ghetto streets as a speedway, roar past, close enough so the wind they kick up could topple Tiny, and fast enough so that they would flatten him if he fell in their path. City Hall didn't give a fuck.

Now the boy glides along "the projects," the squat, featureless government-funded apartment buildings, once upon a time a grand gesture, now Oakland's own Mason-Dixon line. A posse of bums shaking themselves up a bottle of Bitter Dog—a mixture of white port and lemon juice—watch him pass and shout well-intentioned platitudes at him.

"Yeah, you stay in that school, youngblood! Getcha self some education," hollers Rose, king of the winos, wearing a hairnet for a crown.

McStick, Rose's tall, emaciated sidekick, chimes in, "You get that education, boy . . ."

Tiny waves back respectfully and zooms on. Just as the projects give way to threadbare but tidy private homes, he slams on the brakes and fishtails to a halt. A huge semi, having missed its exit on the freeway, comes barreling through making up time.

As the massive truck roars past him, Tiny gapes in heart-pounding admiration. The tires are taller than he is! An idea leaps into his young mind, and he sees his future. His dad was always telling his mom that things were gradually opening up for colored people, and if he was a young man again he'd drive a truck. That's what he'll be when he grows up. He imagines pulling his rig up to the house, climbing down from the cab of his truck, and handing his folks his paycheck.

Tiny's eyes follow the truck down the street, and then he is slammed by the following wind. The gust also hits a woman waiting for the bus at the corner. She grabs her wide-brimmed hat with both hands, holding onto it for dear life even though the fluttering hem of her dress is whipped up above her waist. Tiny's eyes open wider.

Miss Juicy Thighs sees him. "Yeah, I see you getting an eye full, son, but ain't no way I'm letting go this hat. It's practically brand new, and these hips you staring at's two-three times older than you."

"Yes ma'am," Tiny mumbles, embarrassed to be caught ogling, and he takes off blushing.

Watching Tiny burn rubber, Judge, the Vietnam vet, shakes his head and chuckles to himself, remembering his own escapades.

Baking under a hot sun imported up from L.A., the Oakland ghetto isn't up to its normal teeming self. So the few folks moving about on missions stand out like sore thumbs...

There's Tyrone, a tough-looking young guy, new to the ghetto since Judge had left for the Marines, trying to hand out pamphlets without much success. Tiny averts his eyes when he passes him.

There are the white cops scanning the street like soldiers scouting hostile territory for signs of the enemy.

There's Reverend Slocum, a man esconced in middle-age, his saintly appearance enhanced by a dramatic, flecked-with-gray beard and a justa-humble-disciple-of-our-father demeanor, walking up and down the street pressing the flesh. Recruiting, he calls it, for God's army. The Reverend, pastor of the second-largest church in the ghetto, considers the entire neighborhood his congregation. Just like Avis, he tries harder.

And near the end of the block, there is Sabu. Sabu, a bow-legged, fast-talking young hustler, has set up a three-card monte game on a box and is practicing his con.

"Queen of Spades, Queen of Spades, folks," he announces to a semicircle of locals, waving the card in the air.

Sabu points to the two other cards on the box. "That's right—the Queen of Spades and a coupla friends," he proclaims. He flips all three cards face down in a line and starts switching them on the box top.

"That's right, folks, watch the lady." The neighbors crowd around. "Keep your eye on the lady. Round and round she goes and where that bitch lands no one knows."

Done with his quick-hand shuffle, Sabu steps back. "Okay okay okay... where is the bitch? For five dollars who wants to give it a guess?"

Cy, another stumpy guy with a patch over his left eye, slaps a five-dollar bill down and taps a card. "That one!"

Sabu has to turn the card over. It's the Queen of Spades.

The neighbors laugh.

"You better woodshed your game some more, Sabu, before you go trying your con on folks downtown," Cy teases, "'cause you're the sorriest hustler I ever saw. Now gimme my five dollars!"

Humiliated, Sabu retaliates. "Who the fuck you calling a sorry hustler?" Tiny glides towards the corner. He waves as he pedals past, ducking his head to hide his grin.

Sabu is calling Cy an "ugly, one-eyed mothafucka... " A squad car going in the other direction rolls past—past Tiny, Sabu, Reverend Slocum, Rose and McStick, and the rest of them. Tyrone turns and glares at the smirking cops, but it takes sticks and stones to hurt bones, and the squad car disappears unharmed down the block and around the corner.

Tiny starts across the intersection...

A horn blares. There is the piercing screech of tires clawing asphalt, then *WHUMP!*... a sickening thud as Tiny is broadsided by a late-model Buick flying across the intersection.

The impact launches boy and bike skyward.

Rita, Judge's gray-haired, soft-hearted, hard-working mother, sees the whole thing. She is hurrying across her lawn with her arms flung wide to greet her precious son coming through the gate. Beyond Judge's shoulder, Tiny's lifeless body is hurtling towards heaven.

"No!" Rita screams. "Oh lord . . . Not again . . ." Her arms, still outstretched, hang forgotten, starched stiff by the tragedy on the corner.

Judge whirls around just as the bike and Tiny come crashing down on the Buick. They shatter the windshield, bounce off the hood, and roll into the street.

Hollering bloody murder, neighbors rush towards the scene as the car attempts to flee.

"MUTHAFUCKA HEY!! HEY!! WHAT THE HELL! MUTHAFUCKA MUTHAFUCKA MUTHAFUCKA . . ."

The residents swarm around the automobile, attacking with sticks, bricks, and feet. The battered Buick manages to burst free of the vengeful mob. Accelerating, it recedes into the distance, trailing curses and tears in its wake.

Rose throws his wine bottle after the car, Rev Slocum goes down on one knee, and Tyrone sprints off to get Huey and Bobby.

A thin red stream moves down the boy's leg. Judge's eyes begin to sting as the blood trickles past Tiny-the-Daredevil's small sneakered foot into the gutter . . .

3

TESTING, ONE-TWO-THREE . . . Witness #3. Name: Withheld.

Anyway. . . the way I got it, Bobby Seale had climbed up on this chair out in front of this sidewalk cafe and was running down some poetry about the Man, cop comes over and starts going upside his head and Huey Newton jumps in to help the brother out. Well they both get thrown in jail . . .

WHAT FOR?

What the fuck you think for? For being uppity! Shit, outside the ghetto people use to believe if the cops kicked your ass you musta had it coming. What they caught the cops doing to that brother Rodney King on video wasn't anything compared to the way they treated folks in the ghetto on a regular basis back then. Anyhow, that's how Bobby and Huey got to really know each other, sitting in a goddamn jail. They was pretty fucking mad . . . wouldn't you be?

YES, I SUPPOSE I WOULD. I WOULD LIKE TO QUOTE YOU DIRECTLY. WOULD IT BE POSSIBLE FOR YOU TO USE LESS PROFANITY?

Look, motherfucker, nobody asked you to come around here asking your white boy questions in the first place. You want the truth, or don't you?

I DEFINITELY WANT THE TRUTH . . . IN YOUR OWN WORDS.

Well, listen up then. I suppose they started talking about black folks oughta stand up for themselves. They start hanging out together, woofing about it always being open season on black behinds. They didn't have no master plan or nothing, just two more bloods bitching about having to eat shit. Except this time, well, it was an idea whose time had come . . . and BOOM! . . . Next thing you know we got the Panthers.

PA PA PA . . . Lamplight illuminates a patch of concrete. A basketball comes dribbling across the cement. A friendly little three-on-three game is going on, scrambling sneakers zigzagging around the court. Rhythm and blues blaring from the halfass transistor rigged over the fence mingles in the ghetto dusk with wisecracks from the brothers hooting and hollering while they wait to get a shot at the winners.

It's Judge, his one-eyed buddy Cy, and a reprobate named T-Bone against Rose the Head Wino (who "could have almost made it to the NBA"), his sidekick McStick, and another guy named Jamal. Jamal considers himself a black cultural nationalist and he is wearing a dashiki and sporting a goatee to prove it.

Judge, driving for the rim, puts a move on McStick and banks one in. Impressed, Rose says, "Hey! You supposed to be a wounded vet, motherfucka. What you do in Vietnam anyway, shoot gooks or shoot hoops?"

Judge struts. "All of the above my man . . . and then some."

Judge takes the ball out. Moving up to guard him, Rose spots Tyrone and a kid with his hat cocked to one side approaching. Tyrone's partner turns out to be Little-Bobby, a gangly teenager with elfin features trying to look older with a cool stare and a gray stingy-brim hat.

Judge zips a pass across court to Cy, but Tyrone, muscular and athletic, shoots out a hand and grabs the ball.

The game stops dead.

Tyrone, his shaven head adding to his natural ferocity, eyes the players. "Tell me," he challenges. "Don't you fine black men got anything better to do than play games?"

"Sure I do," Rose snaps back. "But your sister's busy tonight . . . Give us the damn ball!"

"Here, take it!" Tyrone bounces the ball back viciously. "We just thought you righteous brothers might like to help us out, but I guess the job might be a little too strenuous for you."

Jamal thrusts out his chin. "Help who? With what?"

"The community, brother, that's who! Maybe you didn't hear about it, but another kid got killed on Fifty-Fifth and Market!"

"That's three this year. Same spot!" Little-Bobby volunteers.

"Damn straight," Tyrone adds. "And old Reverend Slocum's having another vigil, trying to get a stoplight put in. What we're asking for is some of you able black asses to come down and be 'observers'—help us watch the cops. Take down badge numbers if they get out of line. They don't like pulling shit with too many eyes on 'em."

"The police!" McStick cackles. "Hell, the cops ain't gonna bother to bother no niggers praying. The community been praying and begging the powers that be to put up a stoplight before dirt was invented. City Hall don't care about niggers holding another prayer vigil at some church."

"This is different," Tyrone insists. "This ain't just about no praying. It's about organizing doing something . . . this is political! They ain't gonna stay in church. They're gonna march to the intersection."

"I think my Mom's gone to that," Judge remarks.

T-Bone is skeptical about the whole thing. "Political? That don't sound like Rev Slocum to me."

"Well," Rose proclaims, "tell you one thing. This black ass ain't fucking with no cops. One thing the man don't like you to be messing with is nothing political!"

The others mumble agreement.

Then Jamal lays out his view. "Look, brother, some of us feel that we should not interact with the white man. We are African, brother! And Mother Africa is our only salvation!"

"No, you look, you phony-ass boojie nigger!" growls Tyrone, starting to get pissed off. "We ain't in Africa, we're in Oakland. And we got the white cops interacting their billy clubs up against the black man's head." He leans close to Jamal. "Now if that don't bother you . . . well, then take your skirt-wearing ass back to Africa, you Uncle Tom!"

Jamal takes a step towards Tyrone, and Tyrone takes one towards him. They stand toe to toe, ready to go to war.

Rose pushes between the two antagonists.

"Cool it, y'all. And brother, why don't you just go on and leave us be. We're trying to have a little game here in peace. If you wanta play, get in line with them other chumps over there." Rose nods at the brothers waiting on the sidelines. "Guarantee ya it won't be long before we finish these bums," he says, cocking his thumb towards Judge and his team. "We only got two points to go."

Instead of answering Rose, Tyrone turns to Judge. "How about you? You were there. You saw that kid get hit."

"Yeah," Judge admits, "but . . . "

"But nothing!" Tyrone cuts in fiercely. "You do live here, don't you?!"

Judge stares back at Tyrone, sizing him up. "Yeah, I do," he replies evenly.

"Well, act like it then! Come on with us, brother. I'm not asking you to break the law." Without waiting for an answer from Judge, Tyrone turns to Cy. "How about you? You're not gonna chicken out, are you?"

Cy's one eye shoots daggers at Tyrone.

Taking advantage of all the distraction, Rose dribbles for the hoop and sinks a basket.

McStick lets out a triumphant whoop. "We won!" He slaps Rose on the back. "Next!"

Three more homeboys leap up to play.

Tyrone and Little-Bobby take one more look around, and then leave the court in disgust. "Chickenshit boojies," Little-Bobby grumbles.

PA PA PA... Rose dribbles around while the challengers sort themselves out. He makes an awesome shot from downtown.

Cy turns to Judge and says, "Aw, what the hell, maybe we oughta go."

"Yeah," Judge agrees, "what the hell." The two buddies head out after Tyrone and Little-Bobby.

Feeling pumped after his swisher, Rose yells a warning to Judge and Cy. "You muthafuckas better cool it! The Man don't play that shit! He's gonna come down on your ass like a ton of bricks."

4

"All right, just remember to be cool," Tyrone chides Judge and Cy as they head for Fifty-Fifth and Market. "Don't let 'em provoke you," Tyrone continues. "We're only there to watch and take badge numbers." His stride is confident and purposeful.

"Who is we?" Judge asks. "And who exactly are you?"

Little-Bobby shakes his head. "Brother where you been?" He gives Judge a proud grin. "We're the Black Panthers!"

"The Panthers?" Cy repeats. "That's that new gang, ain't it?"

"We ain't no gang. We're revolutionaries!" Little-Bobby answers.

Cy, amused, gives Little-Bobby a skeptical glance. "How old are you, anyhow?" he asks.

"Shit, I was the first one to sign up," Little-Bobby says with pride. "A couple of months ago it was only Huey, Bobby Seale, and me."

Tyrone chuckles. "He's just sixteen. Huey and Bobby Seale made him get his mom's permission before they'd let him join."

"He's just a kid," Judge observes.

"Yeah, well, cops kick the shit out of kids too," Tyrone retorts.

"You a big motherfucka," Cy says to Tyrone, "but you ain't no more than a kid yourself, maybe eighteen."

"Nineteen," Tyrone corrects him, drawing himself up to his full six-foot-three-inches.

"How about Bobby Seale and Huey, are they out of nursery school yet?"

"They're old," Little-Bobby affirms, "like you guys . . . twenty or something."

As the quartet passes Beulah's Tamale Parlor, a fat-mouthing hard-hat standing out front gives them a piece of his colonized mind. "You young niggas crazy! You gonna get us all killed. The Cau-Caucasian race don't like to be pushed, specially by no niggers. He'll put a stop-light in when he gets good and ready."

"Come on, brothers," Tyrone says, ignoring the man and speeding up. "Let's hit it. Freedom don't wait for nobody!"

The quartet turns the corner, and two more young men emerge from the shadows and fall in step. "See you got some more observers," one of them says.

"Yeah," Little-Bobby boasts, "two! How about you guys?"

Making a joke on himself, Cy says, "Yeah. But one of 'em only got one eye."

"Wouldn't nobody come with us," the second newcomer grumbles. "Most of the motherfuckers just cop some lame-ass plea when we ask for help. Some of 'em don't even bother to do that. We don't even believe in ourselves!"

"Yet, brother, yet!" Tyrone instructs him. "We don't believe in ourselves yet. But we will, we will! Rome wasn't built in a day."

In the distance, they hear singing—that old spiritual "We Shall Not Be Moved." Reverend Slocum and his congregation are converging on the intersection.

Judge pulls up alongside Tyrone. "What's the deal? I thought all the Panthers were gonna meet us."

"What you see is what you got. We're all here 'cept for Bobby and Huey, waiting up ahead at the intersection, on watchout."

"Hell, that only makes six of y'all in all," Cy butts in.

Tyrone nods. "Six . . . that's two more than there was last week! Shit, a couple of months ago it was just Huey and Bobby Seale, then . . . " pointing over his shoulder, "Little-Bobby back there made it three."

As they come to the end of the block, Little-Bobby tries to lower his voice to a manly baritone. "Look alive, we're almost there!"

There is a growing feeling of apprehension as they approach the crossroads of Fifty-Fifth and Market. The intersection smells of trouble. It is deserted except for the two brothers waiting in the pinkish-gold cone of the streetlight on the far side.

Tyrone waves and they nod back.

"That's Huey Newton," Tyrone says, pointing to the shorter of the two—the solid, broad-shouldered, light-skinned one.

"And that's Bobby Seale," Little-Bobby says, indicating the wiry, dark-skinned one.

There they are, the co-founders of the Black Panther Party for Self Defense. There they are, side by side, leaning slightly forward almost as if bracing themselves against the current of history, poised for action, pads and pencils at the ready. Two ordinary, handsome sorta, but nothing-in-particular-looking dudes, Judge thinks.

Reverend Slocum and his congregation are coming up from one end of the street—around three hundred people in all. Most of the men are older, with a few preteen boys clinging to their mommas. There are women of every size and shape, from skinny girls through pregnant-again mothers to bosomy matrons. Here they come, ten-fifteen marchers across and twenty-thirty deep, with pounding hearts but unswerving feet. What seems like a battalion of cops backed up with squad cars and paddy wagons is advancing from the other end of the street. They're all heading for the X someone chalked in the intersection—the X that marks the spot where Tiny was run down. In the middle waits the tiny band of observers to guarantee democracy.

Everyone in Reverend Slocum's group is holding a flickering candle and singing with determination as if to say that the black community is a family, a force to be reckoned with. And despite himself, despite his intention not to get sucked into anything that wasn't his business, Judge feels a tingle of admiration, maybe even pride. The ghetto was never heaven, he thinks, it had its crooks and drunks and the establishment doing its exploitation bit, but as long as it suffered in humble silence the authorities let it be. But maybe that silent suffering shit was about to change . . .

The congregation reaches the fateful X and blocks the intersection.

"WE SHALL NOT BE MO-OVED," they continue to sing.

The army of police takes up battle formation. Shreck, the sergeant in charge, grabs a bullhorn from his command car and lays down the law. "Listen up . . . Listen up, people . . ."

The congregation falls silent.

"You have thirty seconds to disperse and return to your homes. Failure to obey will result in your immediate arrest."

The seconds tick by, but the parishioners don't move. The first line of cops begins to advance. Undaunted, the congregation stands fast and starts to sing again. Glowering, the cops try to stare them into obedience.

WE SHALL NOT, WE SHALL NOT BE MOVED
WE SHALL NOT, WE SHALL NOT BE MO-OVED
JUST LIKE A TREE
PLANTED BY THE WA-A-TER
WE SHALL NOT BE MOVED.

TESTING, ONE-TWO-THREE . . . Witness #4. Name: Mrs. Abernathy . . . Purple robe outlined in the doorway of the church . . . Squat figure lumbers down the steps towards me.

MRS. ABERNATHY?

Yes, I'm Sister Abernathy.

PLEASE, JUST IGNORE THE MIKE.

God bless you, but I'm usta microphones. I'm alternate leader of the choir. Our minister said I was to talk to you, but I don't have long though, I gotta get back to choir practice.

I APPRECIATE YOUR TAKING THE TIME. "THE LAST STRAW" IS THE NAME OF A SOCIAL THEORY I HAVE. AS YOU PROBABLY KNOW, MOST ANTHROPOLOGISTS AND SOCIAL SCIENTISTS ARE IN AGREEMENT AS TO THE INNATE AGGRESSIVENESS OF THE HUMAN SPECIES . . .

The Devil's work.

...BUT, ON THE OTHER HAND, HISTORY SHOWS US THAT LARGE GROUPS OF PEOPLE WILL PASSIVELY ENDURE PERSECUTION FOR YEARS, EVEN CENTURIES. IN OTHER WORDS, IT APPEARS THAT EN MASSE HUMANITY IS MORE INCLINED TO ENDURE HARDSHIP THAN REBEL, THAT IS, UNTIL THE LAST STRAW.

It's about the two boys, ain't it? Well, to tell the truth I don't think nobody took them two boys seriously when they started out. And to tell the truth all that talk about standing up to the police and defending yourself by any means necessary scared me. Bothered most other folks too, at first... lying if they say it didn't. Anyhow, the Good Book says, "And children shall lead them." So since us older folks hadn't been able to budge them white folks none, the flock decided, you know, to have a different kinda meeting, to go along with the Panthers to hold a vigil, hoping maybe we'd get that traffic light we'd been begging for... Amen, His will be done...

"WE SHALL NOT BE MOVED!"

"This is your last warning!" Sergeant Shreck shouts through the bullhorn. "One... Two... Three!"

Frightened, frozen in the glare of the headlights but filled with holy conviction, the parishioners continue singing. Shreck lowers the bullhorn and motions for the attack.

The police cover their badges and wade in, shoving people and brandishing their nightsticks.

"Get their numbers! Get their numbers!" the Panthers yell to each other, charging into the fray, trying to scribble numbers.

The congregation manages to keep singing.

Exasperated, Shreck motions a full onslaught. Police reinforcements leap from their cars and charge the congregation. Defenseless, the congregation finally turns to flee, but the detachment that Shreck had sent to outflank the marchers comes up from behind and blocks any escape. The clubbing begins . . .

"You are resisting arrest!" Shreck bellows into the bullhorn.

The parishioners start to stampede, and chaos reigns. The police are slapping and snatching black folks right and left. *THUD!* . . . the sound of nightsticks cracking skulls . . . moans of the wounded. The cops shoving and shouting, the congregation scurrying and screaming. *Move when you're told! . . . Get their badge numbers! . . . She's pregnant! . . . Get 'em in the wagon . . . Help! Somebody . . . My brother's hurt . . . Nigger . . . Savior . . . Jesus . . . Coon.*

"Oh my God! Oh my God!" Rita is screaming.

Judge twists, recognizing his mother's voice, and his eyes go wide with horror. Rita is running across a lawn, a cop and his billy club right on her ass.

"Oh shit! Moms!" He sprints towards his mother.

Just as the policeman lifts his nightstick to strike, Judge reaches him. In a single motion he grabs the cop by the collar, whips him around, and punches him square in the mouth. The blow knocks the cop straight off his feet. He tumbles back flat on his butt out cold.

Suddenly another nightstick comes flashing out of nowhere connecting with Judge's skull . . .

"Oh, my God," Judge moans, slowly coming around on the filthy jailhouse floor. He has nasty bruises on his face and a lump on the side of his head. Cy hovers over him protectively. A strident, high-pitched voice is coming from a circle of prisoners over in the corner.

". . . The power structure locks the black man up. That's right. We move from chains to cells with bars and locks. Kangaroo courts put brothers in jail. No jury of our peers. No jury of black folks. How do we stop this insanity? It's simple. Organization. That's the key. We must organize. We must maintain discipline. Without that we're at his mercy . . . So we organize, we put the power into the hands of the people, where it belongs . . . "

Ignoring the lecture, Judge staggers to his feet and over to the bars of the cell and starts yelling down the corridor. "Hey, I'm not supposed to be in here. Hey, goddamnit, somebody out there! People have rights!"

"Yeah!" a drunk shouts back, "we got the right to get some goddamn sleep."

"Quit all that yelling," somebody else gripes.

"Yeah, shut the fuck up!"

Judge keeps right on hollering. "Hey, goddamnit! Hey, you ever hear of the Constitution? Hey, people have rights! I'm a veteran . . . "

Three drunks gang up on Judge. They wrestle him away from the bars and shove him to the floor.

Cy kneels next to his buddy. "Are you okay?"

Judge is still smoldering. "Yeah, I'm all right," he lies. "But my Moms—I'm worried about her."

"She's okay," Cy reassures him. "They got all the ladies over in the women's section."

Tyrone glances over at them, amused.

Cy notices him grinning. "What so fucking funny?" Cy snaps. "We're in jail and we haven't done anything."

"Don't act so surprised, brother," Tyrone says. "You musta been black before."

Over in the corner the high-pitched voice is still orating in its strange mixture of legalese, street, textbook, and hip. "Organization is the key, you dig. It is imperative that we organize and we must maintain discipline . . . "

"So why the hell doesn't somebody make whoever that is shut up?" Judge grumbles.

"Listen, brother!" Tyrone answers, his voice full of admiration. "Listen and learn, brother. That's Huey!"

". . . The Black Panther Party for Self Defense, realizing that America has historically reserved the most barbaric treatment for nonwhite people since the beginning of this country, feels that it is time for black people, who have suffered so much for so long, to finally draw the line. There are always antagonistic contradictions and non-antagonistic contradictions existing between the masses and the power structure. We as black people must realize that our destiny is in our hands."

Little-Bobby raises his hand to speak. Huey nods.

"Well, uh . . . ," Little-Bobby clears his mind, then spits it out, "uh . . . speaking of hands, Huey, this observer stuff ain't working. The cops cover their badges with one hand and beat the shit out of you with the other. Even when we do get a number and make a complaint nothing ever happens."

Tyrone seconds the motion. "I know we need to stay disciplined, Huey, but I didn't join this motherfucker just to get my ass kicked."

Reverend Slocum raises his voice to admonish one and all. "We must turn the other cheek. Remember, the meek shall inherit the earth. Pray for their forgiveness, for they know not what they do."

"No offense Reverend," Huey responds, "but they know exactly what they're doing. They've been practicing for four hundred years."

"Amen to that!" Bobby Seale agrees. "Malcolm said we need to stop singing and start swinging!"

"Yeah, pray, brothers, pray," a sarcastic drunk chimes in. "Yeah, y'all better listen to the Reverend over there, 'cause pray is about all you can do long as the police got the guns. That's right, the white man got all the guns!"

"Just as well that we don't got any," another jailbird mumbles. "Niggers don't respect each other. Shit, if we had guns all we'd do is end up shooting each other."

Reverend Slocum looks heavenward, although he seems to be beseeching the overhead sprinklers. "Lord, why don't they show us no respect?"

"Because they don't have to," Huey cuts in. "We must organize. As citizens we have the right to defend ourselves. We must find the means."

"All you negroes full of shit!" It's the resident jailhouse lawyer. "I get so tired of niggers sniveling 'bout how they cain't do nothing 'cause the cops got the guns. This is California, ain't it? This ain't Illinois, this ain't New Jersey, or most of them other states neither. No, this is California and in California you got the right to carry a gun and that's according to the California law!"

Huey turns to Bobby. "You hear that?"

Bobby smiles, reading Huey's mind.

Huey turns to the jailhouse lawyer, a thick-set, balding black man wearing what was once a suit. "You sure about that?"

"Damn right, boy. In California you got the right to carry a gun and that's according to the California law. Look it up!"

The co-founders of the Black Panther Party nod at one another with a what-we-got-to-lose-but-our-chains grin. So Huey throws his shoulders back and announces to the members, "We are going to start carrying guns. The establishment doesn't listen when we sing or pray or beg for our rights, but believe me if . . . no, make that when . . . when they see disciplined brothers with guns they'll know that the Black Panther Party for Self Defense is serious about defending the rights of black people!"

Little-Bobby is confused. "You mean we gonna get some guns and go shoot up some cops?"

"It's not about shooting cops," Bobby Seale explains. "It's about getting the Man's attention and showing our community that they don't have to take this shit!"

Over in the corner, Reverend Slocum, disturbed by the turn of events, clutches his Bible and calls on the Savior again.

"Oh Lord, why don't they show black people respect?"

"They're going to Reverend," Huey promises, "they're going to!"

BLANG BLANG BLANG BLANG Just as the Panthers are taking the quantum leap from "problem" to "solution," a white cop comes strutting down the corridor banging his billy club on the bars to remind the negroes who's boss of the universe.

Bobby makes the black power sign. "All power to the people." The rest of the Panthers return his salute.

At the sight of the band of young men with their fists clenched in the air, the Reverend's congregation cringes and the jailhouse drunks laugh.

6

TESTING, ONE-TWO-THREE . . . Witness #5. Name: Felix Shreck . . . Office, oak paneling, framed photos of dignitaries.

Wallick is it? So they tell me you want to talk about the Black Panthers. Mind if I sit? I saw you admiring the photographs on the wall as I came in. Take a look at that one on my desk . . . Go ahead, look at it! Notice anything about that picture? Hunh? Bullshit you don't! Or maybe you think it's just some oriental kid me and my wife went fishing with. That's not just any kid, that's my son. He's Korean. My wife and I adopted him. Fine kid too, graduated from Cal Tech with honors. If you're looking for a redneck bigot, you got the wrong guy because I'm not a racist. Just so we got that straight. I suppose you want to know about that so-called vigil. Yes, I was with the department then. I was there, I don't deny it. I'm proud of it. A policeman's job is to keep the peace and that's what I always did. It is equally well known that to keep said peace you must be firm. Now this is not some secondhand bullshit I'm telling, these are the facts. Like I said, I was there. I was a sergeant back then. In fact, I can still fit into my old uniform if anybody is interested. Little tight, but I can still make it. Anyhow what had happened was a few troublemakers were trying to seize on an unfortunate accident to make trouble. This occurs in all communities, so I don't see how this could be construed as a racial thing. Plus action was under serious consideration concerning a traffic control device at the intersection. What followed was directly in the line of duty. Hell—we let 'em out the next morning. We just wanted to remind them who was in charge, that's all.

Blinking at the morning sun, the Panthers and the parishioners pour out of the jailhouse. They pause at the top of the steps, old comrades for a moment, then wearing a collective grin of relief they start down the steps .

"We're free!" Reverend Slocum declares. "The miracle has come to pass. God has delivered us from the lion's den!"

"No, Reverend," Bobby says somberly. "We're not free. We're just right black where we started."

"They couldn't hold us anyhow," Tyrone says. "They were just harassing our ass. We weren't breaking any law."

"Well, then be thankful for the Lord's fresh air," Reverend Slocum beams, reassured in his faith by their release. "I prayed for deliverance all night. As the Good Book says, 'God helps those who help themselves.'"

"Well," Bobby snaps, "we still don't have a stoplight."

But Huey nods towards the minister, acknowledging the wisdom of his statement. "The Reverend's got a point, Bobby. 'He helps those who help themselves.' We'll control the traffic ourselves."

"Yeah," Bobby says, reading Huey's mind, then they recite in unison, ". . . learn by observation and participation!"

"We'll be our own stoplight!"

Huey turns to Tyrone. "Assemble the men."

The mighty Panther army of six men falls in and marches towards

Fifty-Fifth and Market. And since they are heading in the same direction, Cy and Judge tag along at a safe distance.

When they reach the intersection the Panthers strut out into the middle of it. Amid screeching brakes and cursing drivers, they start directing traffic.

Cy and Judge stand on the curb watching.

Cy, full of admiration, says, "Look at that. Great, hunh? They're controlling traffic!"

Judge sneers. "What's that gonna do?"

"You gotta start somewheres!" Cy says enthusiastically.

"I'm gonna start by getting back on my feet," Judge explains. "Then I'll work on things from inside the system. You can be more effective from the inside."

"The 'inside' ain't in the system," Cy says. "It's right there, man," poking Judge in the chest, "inside each one of us!"

Judge defends his position. "You can't help yourself, or anybody else, when you're flat on your back. That's why I volunteered for the Marines, to get the GI Bill so I could pull myself up."

"Bullshit! You joined to beat that joy-riding rap." Immediately regretting his harsh words, Cy hurries on. "Come on roomie. Let's get to the pad. Tell you what, brother, you smelling a little funky, so I'm gonna let you use the shower first."

"You don't smell like any bed of roses yourself," Judge grins, then nods towards his mother's house in the middle of the block. "You go ahead. I want to stop in and see about my Moms."

Judge turns to go, but Cy grabs his arm. Looking back, Judge notices the proud-but-embarrassed look on his buddy's face. "What's up—you okay?"

"Yeah, man, I'm okay. I just wanta tell you something."

"Sure, go ahead."

"I think I'm gonna join up."

Judge looks at Cy hard, and Cy returns his gaze, steady. Not quite knowing what to say, Judge hugs his friend. "Be careful—good luck," he mumbles.

■ ■ ■

After hurrying straight home from prison, Rita has been anxiously watching for her boy. When she sees him coming up the walk, she flies out the door and down the porch steps to meet him.

Throwing her arms around him, she asks, "You all right, son? I bet I've been back ten minutes." Satisfied that he is in one piece, she catches up on her hugs.

Regaining his breath, Judge asks how she is.

"I'm fine," Rita says, pulling back a bit to get a good look at her son. Her handsome face creases with concern. "But you don't look all right, not with that lump on your head."

"Yeah. Cop hit me . . . "

They sit on the steps.

"You was whipping up on that policeman like you were crazy."

"That policeman was trying to hurt my Moms. You know I can't have that."

"Lord," Rita sighs, "I never thought I'd live to see my boy in prison."

In mock horror, Judge says, "You! How about me? Never thought I'd see my Moms in jail."

"Your daddy would turn over in his grave," she chuckles, "if he saw us locked up like a couple of jailbirds."

"I think daddy would have understood, Moms."

Rita lowers her eyes. "I went because I thought we'd be praying, doing the Lord's work. I didn't know we were going to be doing something we weren't suppose to."

Judge puts his arm around his mother's shoulders and hugs her. "You weren't doing anything illegal, Moms."

"Must have been, or they wouldn't have put us in jail," she says with unquestioning acceptance. She glances towards the intersection, at the Panthers busily directing traffic. "I hear them boys, those Black Panthers, they're communists. Don't even believe in God."

"It's not like that, Moms. They're all right. We've been praying for four hundred years. Maybe it's time somebody tried something else."

Rita, shocked, raises her eyebrows at Judge. "You believe that?"

"Well, at least they're out there trying."

Mother and son sit quietly for a minute, watching the Panthers. "I can tell you one thing," Rita finally says. "Them boys gonna bring down a mess of trouble they keep this up."

7

TESTING, ONE-TWO-THREE . . . Witness #6. Name: Mr. T-Bone . . . Pier, tackle-box, bamboo fishing pole, lawn chair, jogging suit.

IF I UNDERSTAND CORRECTLY, MR. T-BONE, THE PANTHERS STARTED DIRECTING TRAFFIC AT THE INTERSECTION IN AN EFFORT TO REDEEM THEMSELVES WITH THE COMMUNITY AND RECOVER FROM THE MISTAKE THEY HAD MADE IN ENCOURAGING THE VIGIL . . .

What mistake? Where did you hear anything about some fucking mistake!

THE OBVIOUS MISTAKE OF ENCOURAGING THE PROTEST MARCH. THE PANTHERS OVERREACHED THEMSELVES WITH THE PRAYER VIGIL, THEREBY BRINGING DOWN THE WRATH OF THE POLICE ON THE COMMUNITY.

That wasn't no goddamn mistake! You white people think you always got everything figured out, don'tcha? Just like my friend Rose use to say. Me, I believe Huey knew that shit was gonna blow up in his face the whole time. Sometimes you gotta smoke the truth out, snatch the wool off folks' eyes, stick their nose in the shit, like you do a puppy. The cops

> going upside the congregation's head while they was carrying their candles and singing their hymns didn't turn the community against the Panthers, it just made folks around here mad. That's what they wanted! Get everybody mad, even the good church folks. That's whatcha call "solidifying the community." Churchgoing niggers couldn't go around lying to themselves that police brutality was reserved just for us riffraff. Naw, talking ole Rev Slocum into holding that vigil was a stroke of pure-D genius if you ask me. Made the cops show they true colors.

At headquarters of Oakland police, Dorsett, in charge of Special External Affairs, surveys the mountain of paperwork accumulating on his desk, and then, with a sinking feeling, refocuses on Tynan, the smooth, just-this-side-of-sleazy mouthpiece seated across from him.

"Okay?" Tynan says. "We got a deal?"

Dorsett is in his mid-fifties, not too far from retirement. Except for the slack, conniving mouth, he is a gone-to-pot version of the fat kid used for comic relief in some silent film. But he is far from funny now.

"Not okay!" Dorsett bursts out, waving his hand in emphasis. "There is no deal!"

Tynan takes Dorsett's refusal graciously. He looks down at his manicured fingernails and smiles. He can afford to, for he's holding all the aces. Time, he feels, is on his side, and Dorsett would eventually be coming to him.

The door behind Tynan opens and Dorsett's secretary pokes her head into the room.

"Excuse me, sir, but Mr. Rodgers is here."

"Rodgers?" Dorsett blinks, trying to remember.

Positioning herself behind Tynan's back, the secretary mouths "FBI" to refresh her boss's memory.

"Oh, yeah, yeah," Dorsett nods, getting the message. "We're just winding up. I'll buzz you in a minute."

Tynan takes his cue and rises to leave. Dorsett points him to the side door. "Use that one."

At the door, Tynan gives it one last shot. "Now is the time, with all the shit going on, to make our move. Like I keep telling you, we'd be doing everybody a favor. Two birds with one stone."

Dorsett frowns at him, and Tynan shrugs and exits. Dorsett pops a Tums in his mouth, but doesn't quite get the jar back in the drawer before Agent Rodgers enters, all buzz cut and horn-rimmed glasses on a slippery nose.

"Come in, Agent Rodgers, sit down . . . always good to see you." Dorsett says, trying to sound friendly.

"You should give up those pills, Dorsett, they don't help," Rodgers answers gruffly, with no hint of actual caring.

"How can we be of help to you?" Dorsett asks as solicitously as he can.

"The question is, can we be of any help to you?" Rodgers says, taking a chair. "Mr. Hoover has sent a memo directing all field agents, including yours truly, to reiterate that the FBI will be more than happy to assist local authorities in any way we can."

"The Oakland Police Department appreciates your offer, but . . . " Dorsett begins.

Rodgers cuts him off. "As you know, the Bay Area is infested with radical groups trying to foment resistance to the war in Vietnam."

Dorsett has to backpedal. "Well outside of them, I mean. Outside of them, I believe we have our community under control."

Rodgers persists. "No new subversive activity?"

"Not really, just the same kooks you guys already have under surveillance, still doing a lot of yelling and pot-smoking but not much else."

Rodgers glances at his notepad. "And the Black Panther Party for Self Defense. What can you tell me about them?"

"Who, them!" Dorsett can't help smiling. "A bunch of shines running around waving their fists about some streetlight and talking about defending themselves. It won't amount to anything, it never does. They don't have a political thought in their kinky heads. SDS or some other commie fronts maybe you gotta worry! But the Panthers, we'll have 'em out of business in another week."

Rodgers leans forward. "Can you make a deal with them?"

"Naw, they're idealists, practically kids," Dorsett shakes his head reassuringly. "There's not much to them, although they think they're for real."

"As you know," Rodgers replies, inflexible as ever, "the Bureau and Mr. Hoover are particularly sensitive to anything that might agitate or unify the coloreds with the left."

Dorsett sighs. "We'll keep that in mind."

Rodgers rises and holds out his hand to Dorsett. After a moment, Dorsett accepts it. "Look, Rodgers," Dorsett offers, "you want me to put a man on it?"

"Good idea," Rodgers smiles and pushes his glasses back up on his nose. "Make sure that for the moment he keeps a low profile."

8

Early morning, Fifty-Fifth and Market, and the ghetto is just beginning to pull itself out of bed. There is no traffic to speak of, but Little-Bobby in his white gloves is on duty in the middle of the intersection. He entertains himself by working on some hip James Brown traffic-directing moves.

Meanwhile, Dorsett's man Brimmer, a hulking, permanently rumpled detective, is slouched in his unmarked police car spying on the proceedings.

Kisha, a nubile high school girl, starts across the street.

"Hey, Sugar!" Little-Bobby greets her. "How about coming on down to Panther headquarters with me?"

Kisha puts her nose in the air and swishes on past. Playing the grown-up, Little-Bobby shouts after her, "Or how about going to dinner with me?"

Up the street comes Cy, sleepily pulling on his white gloves. Behind him staggers Rose and McStick, wending homeward after a hard night of boozing. Down the street Sabu, the early-bird entrepreneur, beckons a cruising white hippie couple in a painted Volkswagen bus over to the curb.

"So what can I do for you?" Sabu asks, trotting up to the VW with a confident grin. "You name it. Panama Red or some sinsemilla? How about some chocolate hash? Get you high as a motherfucking monkey."

"Uh, man, uh," the white kid stammers, dropping his voice. "Can you score us some cocaine?"

"Coke?" Sabu is all accommodating smiles. "Shee-it. No problem. It's dangerous, but I'll do it for you, man. Gimme twenty dollars and meet me back here in an hour. Don't fuck around, this is serious shit."

The girl hands her boyfriend a twenty.

"Okay, uh, an hour?" the longhair doublechecks. "You'll be here, right?"

"Sure, sure," Sabu promises, grabbing the twenty. "I'll be right here."

The van pulls away. Sabu watches it go, chortling. "Now that was one dumb mother—"

Out of nowhere, Cy is on him. He grabs Sabu by the front of his imitation silk shirt and slams him against the wall.

"Sabu, what the fuck you doing?" Cy growls. "Ain't no more pushing poison on this street."

Sabu squirms. "I was just running my scam! And fuck you anyhow! All that Panther shit don't get it with me. I ain't doing nothing to you anyhow."

"Watch yourself, brother," Cy warns him, "or you will bring down much grief on your sorry ass."

Sabu snatches himself free and scurries down the street. "You motherfucking Panthers worse than the police."

Brimmer watches the confrontation with indifference. But when Cy relieves Little-Bobby, he goes on the alert. Stubbing out his cigarette, the detective fumbles under a coffee cup for the pencil and notepad he's using to count Panther heads. Just then, Kisha passes his car, and Brimmer looks up to admire her.

From the other side of the street, Rose notices the big white guy sitting in his car. He nudges McStick and points across the road. They grin at one another, finish off the bottle, and veer off towards the car.

Brimmer, all absorbed in checking out the schoolgirl, doesn't see them coming.

WHAM WHAM WHAM... Rose and McStick bang on the car. "What's the matter Casper, you lost or something?"

Brimmer whirls, then seeing it's only a couple of winos he tries to ignore them. But Rose stays on his case. "Hey! I'm talking to you," he shouts.

Rolling his eyes in exasperation, Brimmer pulls out his gold detective's badge and holds it up to the window. Rose nudges McStick. "Ooh-weeee! Looky here . . . it's a cop!"

"You couldn't be no plain ole white man, could ya?" McStick wisecracks.

"Fuck!" Brimmer fumes, starting the car and putting it in gear. So much for keeping a low profile. Rose and McStick giggle and wave the flushed-out detective au revoir.

Brimmer drives down the block, turns the corner, and hightails it. He passes a squad car gliding malevolently in the other direction.

The two cops inside scan the street, looking for trouble. They spot a woman with enormous earrings and stiletto-heeled shoes wavering down the block.

"She's high," the driver says. "Gotta be. Just a kid."

"Yeah, damn shame," his partner agrees. "A looker too."

The cops smile at each other and the driver turns the wheel sharp right. The cruiser leaps the curb, blocking the woman's escape, and the officers jump out and confront the woozy woman.

"You dealing dope, sister?" the passenger cop asks.

The young woman stands frozen, frightened and befuddled.

The driver cop ogles her curves and her tie-dyed peasant skirt and nods towards the alley. "She's high . . . Better search her for evidence."

The passenger cop grabs her arm and tugs her towards the alley. "C'mon sugar, we don't find nothin' maybe we'll let you go." When the cops lift up her skirt, she tries to scream, but one of the cops clamps a big hand over her mouth.

Walking to her bus Alma, a tall student nurse with a close-cut Afro, hears the woman's muffled cries. She peers into the alley, then turns and bolts down the street, yelling for help.

Cy and Little-Bobby run up. "What's the matter, sister?"

"Cops . . . got a sister in the alley," Alma points down the street, trying to catch her breath. "They're molesting her!"

"Let's go!" Cy says.

By the time the three of them get there, a small group of early-rising ghetto folks are standing at the entrance of the alley. The group is cursing the cops; the cops have their guns out. Behind them, the young woman is sobbing hysterically as she tries to pull her clothes back on.

"Stay back!" the passenger cop orders. "This is police business. You niggers can't come in here. Move on!!"

Cy steps into the alley. "Police business, hunh?" He points to the sniffling woman picking up her panties. "That what you call it, hunh!"

Alma steps in beside Cy. "I call it rape!"

Little-Bobby pulls out his notebook. "What's your badge numbers?"

"Yeah," Cy repeats, "what's your damn badge numbers?"

The passenger cop's mouth drops open, and his eyes flit nervously across the trio. "We . . . We were conducting a lawful search of her person," he stammers out, running the official duty bullshit. "We suspected this woman of transporting drugs."

"Where, in her pussy?" someone in the crowd jeers.

"Look, we didn't find anything during our lawful search so we are letting her go," the driver cop says, switching to the appeasement approach. "C'mon, lets roll," he says to his partner.

The cops shoulder their way through the crowd towards their car. But Alma won't let it rest. She is right on them, furious and defiant. She scoots around in front of the driver to block his path.

"We want your badge number," Alma says.

"Outta my way!" the cop barks. "You're lucky we don't take you in for disturbing the peace."

"No, I'm lucky I wasn't the black woman you tried to rape in that alley!" Alma retorts. "Is that the only way a pig like you can get any?"

"Look, you little cooze," the driver snarls, snatching at Alma's arm. She's too fast for him and he misses. The crowd begins to close in, and the officers jump back into their car.

"You're nothing but goddamn pigs!" Alma screams at them as they flee. "Nothing but goddamn pigs! PIGS!"

In a daze, Tyrone hears pounding on the door of his top-floor tenement apartment. Sleepy and rumpled, he gets up to answer, leaving his date asleep on the pullout sofa. When he opens the door, Cy and Little-Bobby dash in with Alma in tow.

"Cy, Little-Bobby, what's up?" Tyrone asks, trying to work the sleep out of his eyes.

"The cops were down on Market bullying some nookie off some poor chick."

"Limp-dick, cocksuck—" Tyrone catches himself mid-curse, remembering his manners. "'Scuse me, sister." He nods towards Alma. "Who is this?"

"My name is Alma."

"She's the one who alerted us to what was going down," Cy explains.

"She's baaad, Tyrone," Little-Bobby adds. "You shoulda seen her get up in those cops' faces." He lowers his voice. "Watcha doing sleeping on the couch, Tyrone?"

Tyrone whispers, "Huey stayed over . . . We got lucky."

The bedroom door opens and Huey comes out. Behind him, a girl is still asleep on the bed. He is shirtless, and Alma is a little awestricken by his appearance.

"Cops?" Huey jumps right into the conversation. "You get their badge numbers?"

"They covered 'em soon as we asked for them."

Tyrone grimaces. "Huey, like Little-Bobby said, this observer shit ain't working. Even when we get their numbers and report them, not a damn thing happens, not even a reprimand."

Alma speaks her mind. "They're bleeding the pride out of us. The community is hemorrhaging."

"Right on!" Tyrone nods. "The sister is telling it like it is!"

"The cops had their guns out," Cy is frustrated and disgusted, "calling everybody 'nigger' and stuff like they always do."

"Acting like pigs!" Alma says.

Little-Bobby laughs. "Pigs! . . . That's what we oughta call 'em. They always calling us out of our names."

Tyrone tries it out. "Pigs? . . . oink oink . . . Pigs!"

"Yeah," Huey grins, "I like that." Then he turns to Alma and gives a little bow. "And thank you for your help, sister."

Alma grins. "My pleasure, I'm sure."

"Sister," Huey continues, "we're gonna have a little fund-raising lawn party. Would you like to come to that as our guest?"

"Sure," Alma says, deeply flattered.

9

TESTING, ONE-TWO-THREE . . . Witness #7. Name: Sidney Walton Graham . . . Lockerroom/lounge, municipal bus depot . . . Black, handsome, bus driver uniform.

HI, BROTHER, I'D LIKE TO TALK TO YOU.

And why may I ask is that?

YOU'RE RELATED TO CY GRAHAM, AREN'T YOU? ONE OF THE EARLY PANTHERS.

He was my cousin, but you probably already knew that. So what's the government up to after all these years? What branch are you snooping for, the FBI?

I'M NOT WITH THE GOVERNMENT, BUT I'VE DONE MY HOMEWORK. WHAT'S THIS ABOUT THE FBI?

If you don't know, then you obviously have got some more homework to do.

WHAT CAN YOU TELL ME ABOUT YOUR COUSIN?

We weren't really close. I was five years younger and that's a big difference when you're young. He was really tight with another guy named Judge.

JUDGE? I'VE STUDIED THE HISTORY OF THE PANTHER PARTY, AND THAT NAME DOESN'T SOUND FAMILIAR.

History, hunh. "History is the past written by the winners."

I'D BE GRATEFUL FOR ANYTHING YOU CAN TELL ME.

Well, first let me say—so there is no misunderstanding—I believe in calling it like it is . . . I'm referring to your being white. Everybody talks about how they all loved the Panthers from day one. But the truth is, it was pretty lucky those brothers didn't know the meaning of the word quit! The ghetto being the ghetto, the Panthers had two big obstacles to overcome: the "big L's" as they called 'em—Laziness and the Lord . . .

Judge stares out of the classroom window down onto the Berkeley campus, the green lawns, the strolling students. The professor drones through some minutiae of structural engineering. Judge's mind drifts away from the tensile strength of steel, free associating to scenes he's seen strolling the streets of the ghetto. Panthers trying to organize the black community. Food programs, medical programs, legal aid . . . they are everywhere . . . on the corners, inside the two-bit bars, underneath beat-up cars . . .

The fund-raising party is in full swing on the scraggly front lawn of a rambling, weathered Victorian. Neighbors are milling around with food and drink. Jamal, the brother in the dashiki who almost got into it with Tyrone on the basketball court, has Huey off in a corner.

"Betty Shabazz is coming to the Bay Area for a visit," Jamal is saying, "and we need to provide security for her. So if you brothers are interested . . ."

Huey gets very excited. "Interested! We are trying to practice what Brother Malcolm preached. Stay here while I check it out with the chairman of the party."

Chairman Bobby Seale is busy barbecuing. Huey spots him and rushes over.

"Where you been Bobby? I've been looking . . . "

Bobby laughs. "Where have I been?" He flips one of his specialty hamburgers sizzling on the grate. "I been right here, slaving over this grill, making sure our guests get some decent food. But before that I was over in Chinatown. Now listen to this, Huey, you're gonna love this . . . "

Huey signals time-out. "Hold it a second. We've got a decision to make."

"What? What kinda decision?"

"You know those brothers over in San Fran, the ones that go around calling themselves Black Panthers too?"

"Sure, those boojie jokers don't do anything except print up a lotta paper saying 'Black is Beautiful.'"

Tyrone walks up. "Shit, they ain't nothing but Punk Panthers."

"Yeah, maybe, but . . . " Huey points out Jamal. "Anyway, he's one of them and he says they're bringing Malcolm's widow Betty Shabazz to town. She's gonna speak at a rally and do an interview for *Ramparts* magazine. They want to know if we want to help with security."

"Well," Bobby says, "If anyone's gonna protect Malcolm's legacy it best be us. All power to the people!"

"Damn straight," Huey agrees. "Let's go check it out.

Looking street and very tough, Bobby, Huey, Tyrone, Little-Bobby, and Cy stride through the foyer of a private home in one of the classier sections of San Francisco. Bobby's rundown Chevy sits down the block, looking like its owner—out of place, almost an affront to the neighborhood.

The Oakland Panthers step into a spacious living room lined with African artifacts. At the far end of the room a line of brothers in tribal garb—the San Francisco Panthers—are standing at attention awaiting their leader.

Larkin, who has been peeping from an adjoining room, pats his

Afro, smooths his flowing gown, and makes a dramatic entrance, strutting in like some potentate. He takes a seat directly in front of his men and turns his eyes on the brothers from the Oakland ghetto. He grimaces with distaste. A sister in African garb appears and begins to massage his shoulders.

"Greetings African brothers from across the bay," Larkin begins. "We understand you would like to assist us with Sister Betty Shabazz's security."

"Fucking boojie," Tyrone mutters into Bobby Seale's ear.

Huey speaks up, businesslike. "That's right. We'd be proud to serve as escort for Malcolm's widow."

"Could you supply us with, say, ten men?" Larkin asks, then adds condescendingly, "or would that put too much of a strain on your resources?"

"No problem," Huey responds, not batting an eyelash. "More, if you need 'em."

Larkin, not sure if Huey is bluffing, ups the ante. "Of course, I mean armed."

Huey doesn't flinch. "Yes, armed, of course. Now let me ask you a question."

"Certainly, brother," Larkin says. But first he turns to the sister kneading his shoulders and orders, "Get our Oakland brothers some libation, sister, and me too while you're at it."

"No thank you, sister," Huey says, courteously declining for the group, and then looking straight at Larkin. "How many men and how many guns have you got?"

Larkin and his men grin pompously.

The sister returns with Larkin's tea in a carved wooden cup. Larkin raises the chalice—"Here is to you, brother Duey, and your men."

"Huey."

"Yeah . . . Louie . . . uh . . . whatever." Larkin dismisses it with a flick of his hand and begins his speech. "Let me assure you that we as the revolutionary vanguard of San Francisco are serious with our shit. When the time comes we will rise to the occasion in full effect.

You just make sure you're on time . . . dig?"

With the Punk Panthers peeping through the curtains at them, the Oakland Panthers march back to Bobby's Chevy in military formation.

While Bobby fishes for his keys, Tyrone offers his opinion. "Those rinky-dink, dashiki-wearing motherfuckers ain't fit to go around calling themselves Panthers."

"That's not our concern," Huey reminds. "Right now we got to worry about protecting Sister Shabazz. Those phonies sure as hell can't. Have we got enough men to hold up our end?"

"Sure," Little-Bobby brags, "we have almost that many brothers already."

Tyrone injects his dose of reality. "But all we got is two pistols."

"Yes, we need guns too," Huey agrees.

"And guns take money," says Bobby Seale.

"Yeah, guns take money," Tyrone echoes. "We need money first."

Bobby Seale starts giving Huey a hard time. "The ball is in your court, Mr. Defense Minister! So now tell us, Brother Huey, where are we gonna get the money to buy all them guns you told them Punk Panthers we had?"

Huey puts the ball back in Bobby's court. "You're the Chairman, Brother Seale. I'm just the Minster of Defense—you're supposed to figure that out."

With a sly smile, Bobby hops to the trunk of the Chevy. "I already did! That's what I was trying to tell you at the party. I had this idea, you dig. The college kids always talking that revolution shit, right?"

"Yeah? So?" Nobody has a clue what Bobby is up to.

Bobby turns the key in the trunk's lock. "So . . . check it out! Now they can get it straight from the horse's mouth."

The trunk pops open. It is stuffed with boxes of small crimson books.

The Panthers are stunned. "Books!!"

"Not just any ole book my friends. Chairman Mao's Little Red Book," Bobby grins, very pleased with himself. "I bought every copy in Chinatown. Got us a discount too—thirty cents apiece."

■ ■ ■

Sather Gate, the entrance to the Berkeley campus. The Panthers have strategically positioned themselves in the stream of students, calling out their wares. Chairman Mao is selling like hotcakes.

"Only a dollar!" Bobby pitches, waving a book in the air. "Get the lowdown straight from Comrade Mao's mouth!"

Two earnest-looking white students approach Tyrone. "One dollar—cost you less than a coupla joints," he points out to them. "Your own personal guide to the revolution. China's Number One brother tells it like it is."

"You guys revolutionaries?" one of them inquires. "We'd like to join up."

"Huey, come here a couple of guys want to join," Tyrone yells, uncertain of what to do.

"Sorry fellows," Huey explains as he approaches. "We don't take whites because at this juncture in history we feel it is important for black people to do for themselves. But if you're down with what we're up to, go organize some righteous white folks. We need their support."

A psychedelic truck with a loudspeaker on top, advertising a rock concert at the Fillmore, goes past blasting "Heard It Through the Grapevine," drowning out the students' reply. But obviously they understand, because they buy a couple of books. The Panthers go back to hawking.

"One dollar . . . exclusive Bay Area distribution right here!" Cy shouts.

Little-Bobby is having trouble pronouncing the product's name. "Chairman Mayo," he pipes. "Chairman Mayo, only a dollar."

Tyrone gives him a playful shove. "Mah-O, brother. This ain't mayonnaise."

Little-Bobby tries again. "Ma . . . May . . . Mayooow! Ahh, who the hell cares! Red Book! Red Book. Get you Red Book, only a dollar!" Everybody laughs.

Judge on his way to class turns to see what is so funny and catches sight of Cy. "So this is what you do on your day off from work?" he challenges.

"The party needs the bread, brother," Cy answers tersely.

A student eyes a book and Cy pounces. "Be hip to the struggle, comrade. Only a dollar!"

The would-be scholar fingers the book. "Only a dollar? Far out! Is it authentic?"

"Comrade, this is the real deal, direct from Revolution HQ."

Cy makes the sale and the student goes off happy.

Peeved, Judge starts in on his friend. "What the fuck is that book supposed to do for these college freaks? And what the fuck is it supposed to do for you?"

Cy's response is more pleading than angry. "Don't go putting me down, man. I believe in this—I bet I believe in it a whole lot more than you believed in Nam."

Judge refuses to lighten up. "Well, that don't say shit!" But seeing the hurt in his buddy's face, he apologizes. "Hey, man . . . I'm sorry."

Cy is still wounded. "Man, wasn't it you who told me sorry was just a word in the dictionary between spit and sympathy?"

A polite student approaches, holding out two bucks. "Gimme a couple, please."

Cy obliges cheerfully.

"Long live the revolution, brother," the student shouts over his shoulder as he leaves.

"Right on!" Cy yells to him, then turns back to Judge, his good humor restored. "That's what we got here, man, a revolution." He shoves one of the books at Judge. "Read it, brother."

Judge keeps his hands at his sides. "I already read it," he admits, shamefacedly, "while I was waiting to ship out to Nam."

"Yeah? Then you know the bread is gonna help, but what the party needs even more than money is brothers like you. And . . . " Cy lowers his voice, "on the personal tip I could use some help with these books, I gotta learn to become a full-fledged Panther. You down with giving me a hand?"

Judge is pleased. "Sure. Be glad to help you out with your studying, my man. But I gotta skip the revolution this afternoon. I got class. Look, I was thinking about checking out Cloud Nine later tonight. We could hang out like old times. What do you say?"

"I'm gonna be passing out leaflets, but thanks for asking."

"Sure, Cy, see you at the pad."

Judge turns to split, but Cy detains him. "They're having a PE meeting at headquarters tonight. Maybe you could come with me?"

"PE? What's that—they got you guys doing gym class?"

"Naw man," Cy chuckles, "'PE' is 'political education.' Come on down and check it out."

Tyrone struts over and horns in on the conversation.

"Yeah, c'mon. You're a smart brother . . . you'd dig what Huey and Bobby got to say."

Judge smiles and hedges. "Maybe."

"Fuck 'maybe,'" Tyrone's face goes hard. "Be there!"

Judge isn't intimidated. "Like I said . . . maybe."

10

Panther headquarters is a run-down storefront that used to be a bakery or a grocery or something like that in the heart of Oakland's ghetto. Judge brushes past two Panthers posted outside who are trying to convince the curious and the evening strollers to come in. Including these two sentries, the Black Panther Party for Self Defense is now up to eight members.

Bobby is standing at the front of the room addressing a small assembly of people fidgeting in an assortment of seen-better-days folding chairs. An upraised black fist is painted on the wall. Piles of pamphlets bearing titles like "What We Want" and "What We Believe" are stacked on one side of the room. Judge is surprised to see Jamal, dashiki and all, leaning against the wall checking things out.

Judge takes a seat in one of the rickety chairs.

Bobby is down to earth yet eloquent, gesturing as he speaks. "Plain and simple we want a government that serves black people and we want to be rid of the thousands of enemy troops occupying our communities. What troops? you say—this isn't Vietnam." Bobby jabs a finger towards the world just beyond the storefront window. "The police, that's who! They are not here to serve and protect, they are here to patrol and control."

Judge finds himself applauding along with the rest. Huey joins Bobby on the platform as Bobby winds up his talk.

"Whether a brother is in a dashiki or a pimp suit, whether a sister's hooking or teaching kids to read, the police will murder you because you're black."

"The police are pigs," Alma calls.

"Yes they are, sister! Pigs," Huey says. "The sister is telling it like it is. That's a good idea . . . that's what we are gonna call them from now on. Pigs!"

The community folks grin, but they squirm too, and it is plain that they are afraid to stand up to the police.

Huey tries to reassure them. "Look, it's all right to call a cop a pig, dig! Not just because that's what they are, but because it's legal. If you call him a dirty motherwhatever or something like that he can have you arrested for cursing him. But pig is not a curse word, so there isn't anything he can do."

Bobby gives a signal, and Tyrone picks up a stack of leaflets and begins handing them out. Just then a burly young brother with a couple of stooges strolls in. They lean up against the wall, checking things out.

Tyrone explains the regulations as he passes around the leaflets. "First, to become a member of the Black Panther Party for Self Defense you must not only know their laws but ours too."

One of the stooges has a bottle in a bag. As smooth as you please, Tyrone walks over and relieves him of his booze. He passes the bag to one of the sentries outside and continues his rap. "Like I was saying, our laws must be kept—like no drinking or getting high on Panther premises, or while carrying out Panther duties."

The stooge glares. Tyrone gives him a friendly grin. "Stay cool, brother," he says softly. "Your refreshments will be outside waiting for you. You'll get your bottle back as soon as you pass the threshold."

"When do I get a gun?" the burly ringleader asks as Tyrone hands him a pamphlet.

"We don't have no guns yet," Tyrone explains, raising his voice again. "And no one gets one from us until they've gone through the proper training . . . including knowing the Ten-Point Program."

"That's right!" Bobby Seale concurs, backing Tyrone up. "People, we need to educate ourselves . . . know our history."

The burly brother starts bellyaching. "Shit, I done took history in school!"

"No! Not the colonial slavery bullshit they want you to know," says Bobby, holding up a handful of books. "But our history, the real history, from Mao to Fanon to Malcolm X. And if anyone is a little behind on their reading we've got tutors to help you study. We best get it together, organize, learn our history, and put the power in the hands of the people!"

"You Panther brothers better slow your roll," the burly brother says. "You gonna get the Man mad at you. You must be crazy. You ain't even got no guns or nothing. You better check your shit out before its too late. I'm outta here. Like I said, all y'all niggas crazy!"

The burly brother and his entourage stomp out, and most of the people in the room seem to share his sentiments. They start for the door.

"Brothers, sisters," Huey moves forward, trying to stem the tide. "We can control our own destiny . . ." But his efforts are in vain. Shaking their heads and mumbling excuses as they leave, most even refuse to take the leaflets to read.

"Damn," Little-Bobby sums up in a whisper to Tyrone. "They act like we trying to feed 'em rat turds or something."

The only people remaining besides the Panthers are a couple at the front of the room chatting with Bobby, and Judge still in his seat near the back.

Despite the negative reaction of the crowd, Cy is overjoyed to see his pal. "Glad you made it, man."

"I figured by now you'd be doing the lecturing," Judge teases.

"One of these days," Cy answers, dead serious.

Huey comes over and squats down so that his mouth is next to Judge's ear. "So why do think that is, brother?"

"Why what is?" Judge says.

"Why every time a black man goes to raise his head another one comes along and calls him crazy?" Before Judge can answer Huey presses on, "You're Cy's Vietnam friend, correct?"

Judge nods.

"Maybe you could give us a hand."

Shadowing Huey as usual, Tyrone offers an opinion. "Huey, I don't think that's a good idea. We ain't even checked the brother out."

"Well I do," Huey snaps. He resumes talking to Judge. "You were in the infantry, right?"

"Yeah."

"So I guess it's safe to say you're an expert on firepower."

"I suppose."

Huey comes to the point. "We need to buy some guns."

Bobby Seale walks over.

Tyrone tries to get back in the conversation. "If you know all about weapons," he quizzes, "where would you say we could get the best deal?"

"You can get whatever you want out on the street," Judge shrugs. "That shouldn't be . . . "

"We're talking legit shit," Bobby cuts in. "And at a price."

Judge shrugs again. "Sorry, I wouldn't know. Uncle Sam supplied me, remember?"

"How about that white guy you used to hang around with, Judge?" Cy asks. "You know—Stone, or something like that, he might be able to help us out."

"You mean Brick?" Judge is surprised Cy even remembers him. "I haven't seen much of him since I got back. But he's into electronics these days, just like me."

"Yeah, just like you," Cy smirks. "He always tried to copy you! For a while there after you went into the military he turned into a gun freak."

"I didn't know that."

"Well he did. That's why I thought maybe he could help us score."

Judge chugs up the winding driveway to Brick's house in Cy's jalopy, borrowed for this trip to the suburbs. He gets out and ambles up the flagstone walk.

SCREECH . . . *Sputter* . . . *Sssscrunch* . . . The sounds of an amplifier trying to wheeze back to life greet Judge, and he smiles at the incongruity of such a grundgy noise in such a palatial setting. He knows where the noises are coming from—the workshop—and makes his way around the side of the house, passing the garage. A door is up, revealing Brick's Harley next to a Jeep. The Jeep has a puddle of oil underneath.

Not bothering to knock, Judge steps into the workshop, a converted handyman's shed. The room is filled with speakers and amplifiers in various stages of disrepair. Bending over his current victim, Brick is wearing a bandanna over his wheat-colored hair, a greasy t-shirt, tie-dyed painter's pants, and combat boots. He is a little shorter than Judge, stocky and well-muscled.

"Try reversing the polarity," Judge advises by way of a greeting.

Brick glances up and then turns away, smiling. "So where the fuck you been, Judge?" he asks, sounding more angry than he really is. He reverses the polarity on the speaker.

"Just school."

"Well, it's about time you paid your old buddy a visit!" The amplifier quiets down. "All right! It works." Brick stands up and turns to face Judge. They shake hands warmly.

"You would have gotten it yourself a couple of minutes more. You're getting good."

"Maybe. So what's this 'just school' bullshit? What else?"

"Well . . . I went to jail."

"Jail?" Brick guffaws. "If you don't watch your step, my man, your mother is gonna have to enlist you again."

Brick's big mouth has opened an old wound. "The fuck she will," Judge snarls, remembering. "Anyway, there's nobody left to accuse me of stealing his damn car! Your father's dead, or have you forgotten?"

"Dad didn't know it was us who took his car or he wouldn't have called the police."

"Yeah maybe, but he got your ass turned loose and left mine to face the music."

Recognizing his mistake, Brick trys to change the subject. "So what they get you for this time, jaywalking?"

"Being black," Judge snaps.

"Never knew you noticed," Brick snaps back. "Look, you're not gonna try some 'poor-downtrodden-colored-folks' routine on me are you? You must have been talking to Sarah."

Brick's older sister Sarah. Judge blinks. "Sarah. Wow—I haven't even seen her since I got back. How is she?"

"Okay, I suppose. She's up north, some kinda urban commune. She's out to save the planet."

"Somebody has to. Anyhow, since you asked, they arrested every ebony behind in sight just for having a demonstration to get a traffic light installed."

"Surprise, surprise. What did you expect? Like Sarah would say, we live in a fascist state." Brick needles, "You're the born-again-capitalist. What's your beef? Look at you! You're gonna be a big-time engineer. Ghetto boy making good in the land of the free."

"I'm just staying out of the line of fire—I never said anything about free."

Brick takes it as a big joke. "Yassuh, Boss! In the meantime, how about helping me get this other speaker working."

"Brick, why don't you go back to school, or something like that. You can afford it."

The question troubles Brick, so he goes glib. "It ain't about the money, it's about getting back to basics."

The two friends set to work. After a while, Judge says, "I was sorry to hear about the accident and your folks getting killed."

"Both of them?"

"Yeah, your dad, too. He had his moments."

"Well," Brick nods in memory, "you're a better man than I am if you really feel that way. I owe you, brother. I owe you big-time."

"Actually, I could use a favor. Some Panthers I met would like to buy some guns."

"No shit!" Brick is impressed. "You been hanging out with the Panthers? Guns, hunh? Sounds like serious action to me."

Judge frowns. “Not too serious, I hope.”

Brick thinks for a moment. “I might know someone.”

“Solid!”

“You down for hanging out sometime?” Brick asks, trying to sound nonchalant. “You know, like we did when we were kids and you used to stay with us in the summer.”

“Sure,” Judge laughs, “Now we’ve even got real IDs? But first things first.”

“Meaning?”

“The guns, my man, the guns.”

11

Yang's Hardware is situated on a hill in a seedy section of San Francisco. The surroundings are of dubious distinction, but the view is spectacular. Judge and Brick lounge against the Harley, silent, overwhelmed by the night, the sight—the black bowl of sky overhead, the twinkling necklace of the Bay Bridge skipping over the dark water of the harbor, and on the far side the ominous mass of Oakland.

The Panther contingent pulls up in a newly donated, freshly painted but still run-down van. Tyrone is at the wheel, with Huey riding shotgun. While Huey goes around back to let the others out, Tyrone stomps over to Judge.

"Where'd you get the white guy?" Tyrone glares.

Brick returns Tyrone's scowl with an unperturbed smile.

"He's an old friend. I used to stay with his family a couple of weeks every summer. Brick, this is Tyrone. Tyrone, this is Brick. He's our connection."

"Yeah." Tyrone is unappeased. "What kind of kickback is he getting?"

Judge smiles, "Well actually, brother, he doesn't need the money."

The other Panthers approach.

"Huey," Tyrone says, "Judge vouches for this dude, claims that we can trust the guy."

"Well," Huey nods, "that's good enough for me. Let's do it."

Brick leads them past the front of the store, already shuttered for the night, to a gate at the side of the building, then down along a narrow passageway to a rear door.

Yang, a youngish oriental man with a perpetual cigarette, eyes the group warily as Brick, Judge, Tyrone, Cy, Huey, and Bobby cram into the cluttered back room of his store. He shows them his stock of armaments. Judge starts to sort through the weapons. "You want only the legal stuff, right?" Judge asks, checking a .38.

"Just the legit shit," Bobby replies. Judge nods and sets the revolver aside.

"Nothing's wrong with that revolver," Yang insists.

"Yeah," Cy agrees. "That is one fucking beautiful cannon."

Judge holds the piece close to Cy's one good eye. "See that? The serial number's been filed. If the cops catch you with this piece, they'll bust your ass seven ways to Sunday."

Huey smiles slightly. "Brother Judge certainly is an expert."

Yang speaks up. "I don't want no trouble with the cops," he says, nervously lighting a new cigarette with the old.

"Who the fuck does?" Judge replies.

"Suppose the FBI requests information or something?" Yang persists.

Huey pushes forward. "Give it to them. I'm Huey P. Newton, Minister of Defense. You have a permit to sell . . . "

". . . and we're buying!" Bobby counts out the cash under Yang's nose. "All by the book, registered and perfectly legal."

Yang studies the pile of money. "What your 'expert' has selected is worth a lot more than this."

Bobby points to Mao's portrait on the wall. "Brother, you supposed to be a revolutionary, or what? We can't afford your merchandise if you don't cut us some slack. But you treat us right and I promise you we'll be doing a lot of business."

Yang considers the tip of his cigarette for a long time, then takes a puff. "All right, deal!"

Outside again, Huey thanks Judge and Brick while the other Panthers load the guns in the van.

Brick shakes Huey's hand and heads for his motorcycle. "We appreciate your help with this," Huey calls after him.

"Anytime," Brick grins back, straddling his machine. He sits there, waiting for Judge and Huey to sign off.

"Good guns," Judge explains. "Clean and oil them up and you're in business." He lowers his voice. "What's the deal, Huey?"

"Freedom," Huey replies, with deep sincerity. "We're gonna test some of the words in those law books of theirs."

Bobby, who has swiped Huey's front seat, leans out the window and yells to Judge. "Hey, man! You oughta join the Panthers!"

"Count us in!" Brick volunteers, totally psyched up by the smell of action.

"Speak for yourself, Brick," Judge cautions his friend, as he climbs on the back of the motorcycle. "My joining days are over."

"Sorry, Brother Brick," Huey begs pardon. "We don't take white people. But thanks for helping on the guns."

"Hey, Brick is righteous," Judge says, defending his friend. "I can vouch for him."

"I'm sure he is," Huey agrees politely, "but that's not the question. Right now the Party feels its important for black people to do for themselves."

Brick starts to steam. "What kinda racist bullshit is that!"

Huey goes into his spiel. "Hey, if you're so down with what we're doing, brother, go organize the white . . . "

"Organize, my ass!" Brick fumes. "Fuck you guys!" Having heard enough, he kick-starts the engine. "Come on, Judge. Let's roll."

Tyrone watches Judge warily as he and Brick roar off on the Harley.

Although the ride back to Oakland is serene, with the bright lights of the bridge popping past and the twinkling hills of San Francisco receding in the distance, the warm wind rushing past reminds Judge of the war—like being in the helicopter with the doors open.

As they pass an all-night grocery near his house, Judge tells Brick to stop—a sudden craving for ice cream.

"I'll wait," Brick says.

Judge declines. "I . . . I'll walk. I need to stretch my leg."

Halfway home, a squad car pulls abreast of Judge. The cops flick on their searchlight and shine it in his face, blinding him. They glide slowly past, sizing him up.

When he finally gets to his place, Judge eats a couple of spoonfuls of the pecan-fudge and shoves the rest in the freezer. Exhausted, he tosses himself onto his bed, still feeling the weapons in his hands, the rushing wind, the searchlight in his eyes . . .

FULL LOAD! . . . WE GOT A FULL LOAD!. . . RETAIN CONTROL OF THE PERIMETER . . . REPEAT, CONTROL PERIMETER! The chopper's loudspeaker clamors at him. Judge is standing in the clearing, watching the helicopter struggling to lift off . . . leaving him and four of his men behind.

"You lousy, motherfucking racist bastards!" Winston, a black corporal, curses the helicopter. He gives it the finger as it claws its way skyward.

As the chopper swoops towards the horizon, the five stranded soldiers flee for cover. They regroup amongst a pile of tree trunks blown into the clearing.

"Can you fucking believe that?!" Winston yells. "They pick up all the honkies, then split. What the fuck we suppose to do?"

In answer to Winston's question, a burst of Cong machine gun fire from the edge of the perimeter kicks up dirt at their feet.

Judge shoves a fresh clip into his M-16 and returns fire. "What we're supposed to do is keep this pad clear so they can land when they come back for us."

"Don't go getting fucking paranoid on us," chips in Mark, a big grunt sporting a khaki bandanna on his head instead of the regulation helmet. "Picked up all the honkies, hunh—what the fuck am I, chopped liver?"

"Aw, fuck off, Goldstein," Winston snaps back. "You're Jewish—that don't count as full white."

"Shut up! That's an order! Save your bullshit for the gooks. Shoot

your gun instead of your damn mouth!"

"Don't let them stripes go to your head, Sarge," Winston warns Judge, "or . . . "

"Or what? You wanta try my ass!?" Judge twists to face Winston, his body rising for the confrontation. "Make your move or shut up."

PUNG! A Cong slug spraying golden slivers of wood tears into a log a few inches from Judge's head. Everybody fires a burst in the direction of the sniper.

Winston sidesteps the challenge, "Just 'cause some cradle-robbing draft board scraping the bottom of the barrel done snatched your ass, don't come jumping salty with me!"

Judge rolls on his back to dig for a fresh clip in his vest. "Shows what the fuck you know. I volunteered."

Fab jumps on that bit of information. "Jesus, Judge! I didn't know that! You vola-fucking-teered? After what they did to Malcolm—what are you, some kinda Uncle Tom?"

"Quit the shit," says Judge, squeezing off a couple of rounds into the jungle. "Let's just concentrate on getting our asses out of here in one fucking piece."

BLOOOM! A mortar, searching for the range, explodes ten yards off, sending a geyser of elephant grass into the air.

"Maybe we wanta know what kind of brother we gonna die with," Fab says. "We're suppose to be a fuckin' team."

"Screw that team bullshit," Mark spits. "You wanta stay alive out here, you look out for number one."

"You illiterate assholes ever heard of the GI Bill?" Judge replies. "That's why I enlisted. I'm not gonna spend the rest of my life . . . "

WHOOOM! Another mortar round, closer. "What makes you think," Mark deadpans, "there's gonna be some fuckin' rest of your life? Who cares about this shit, anyhow?"

But Fab is dumbfounded. "You bought into that house-nigger American dream shit? Serves you right, now that you're gonna die out here in this Asian shithole for it."

"They're back!" Mark shouts, pointing skyward. "Here comes the cavalry."

A helicopter roars in over the jungle, overshooting the old landing site and coming down on the far side of the field.

"That asshole," Winston gripes. "Couldn't the motherfucker get no closer?" But without waiting, he vaults the tree trunks and dashes full-out for the chopper.

Judge barely has time to shout "Keep low!" before POW!... A Cong sniper takes advantage of Winston's exposed back. Winston falls, disappearing in the grass. From the cursing, the others know he's alive, but hurt bad.

"Okay, listen up!" Judge barks, "No more bullshit! We're gonna do this by the numbers. Fab you go first." Then he points to big Carl, the silent soldier. "Carl, you next. You help Winston when we reach him. I'll cover you, and Mark, you bring up the rear... Let's move it!"

The four of them crawl from the protection of the logs and creep-crouch across the field towards salvation.

"Watch your step," Judge warns. "Single file... Maybe we got booby traps."

When they reach Winston, he is lying quietly clutching his shoulder, with his eyes rolled back in pain. Carl hoists him on his back and they start off again.

Fab makes it to the chopper. Then BLOOM!... Carl trips a mine. He and Winston disintegrate in a red spray of blood and guts.

The explosion tosses Judge into the sky, into the clouds, into the very heart of the universe. A magnificently attired black man in a red and green robe with gold and silver trim catches him and they soar towards the stars, but the regal apparition evaporates and Judge crashes to earth.

Helpless, Judge lies in the grass clutching his leg. Mark looks down at him, and then darts towards the chopper. But with one foot on the landing gear, he turns around and comes back. He drags Judge to the helicopter and lifts him aboard.

"Thanks, brother," Judge says, reaching down to hoist Mark in. Mark winks back and starts to say something about how he never was good at taking advice, even his own... BLAM!... a VC bullet

catches him in the back of the skull splattering his brains all over Judge's outstretched hand. The helicopter starts to rise. Judge peeks downward, the fetid air whooshing in through the wide open chopper door tearing at his face. Mark's body, its head half gone, sprawled in the elephant grass, begins to recede. The helicopter starts to vibrate violently.

Judge wakes up in a cold sweat. Cy, concern etched on his face, is leaning over his bed shaking him.

"You okay, brother?"

"What? . . . Oh . . . Yeah, yeah, just resting my eyes. Musta dropped off in a bad position or something," Judge alibis. "I'm okay. Want some ice cream?"

Cy is not convinced. "No, thanks."

"Well, don't say I didn't ask you. Come on, roomie, let's get to work on those books."

Cy stacks a pile of books on the desk. "Look, I got . . . let me see . . . I got Brother Malcolm, Frederick Douglass, Mao, Fannon . . . Fan . . . Fa . . . "

"Fa-*nyon*," Judge pronounces. "Who's up first?"

Cy beams with excitement. "Shit, man, you choose."

"Okay, Fanon. The deal is we're gonna do this for a half hour every evening, rain or shine," Judge says, laying down the law. "You up for that?"

"Does a bear shit in the woods?" Cy gives him the raised fist salute.

Judge salutes back. "Right on, brother!"

"Power to the people!"

12

TESTING, ONE-TWO-THREE . . . Witness #8. Name: Valerie Vitello . . . Women's shelter, dormitory, drab . . . Anorexic woman sitting on cot.

Yeah, I was around then, but I wasn't singing any of that folk bullshit. I had my own band by then. I did a little folk singing at the very beginning of my career. That's how everybody started out back then. They were too sanctimonious for me, but I know all about its roots and shit if that's what you're after. Pete Seeger, ever hear of him? He was the first to go along with the peace movement and since he was everybody's role model all the folkniks started tagging along, Dylan, Joan Baez, Odetta, Peter, Paul, and Mary, and all the wannabees. Seeger came out of the populist folk singing tradition where you would support the people trying to organize and stand up for them by providing the entertainment at their union meetings and stuff. They sorta used the music itself to teach and tell the people what was happening besides keeping their spirits up. The coffeehouses were our incubators. They became sorta a USO of the counterculture, the student free speech protests, civil rights, resistance to the war in Vietnam, fund-raisers for the Black Panthers. Of course harassment by the government went with the territory. Now the way you hear people babbling about the peaceniks you'd think the only music at the time was some jerk with an acoustic guitar. What about Motown? What about blue-eyed soul? That's what I was. I don't have blue eyes, but I'm white. So that's what I was, a blue-eyed soul singer. As far as I'm concerned, protest songs aren't black, they're just some liberal honkie bullshit!

WHAT ABOUT THE BLACK PANTHERS? COULD YOU TELL ME ABOUT THEM?

The Black Panthers weren't really black! The Panthers were assholes. You know what black is? Black is getting down! You dig it? Freedom isn't something political, it's inside, man. You score, get high, and you're free. That simple—turn on, tune in, drop out. That's exactly what the Panthers were always running around trying to stop folks from doing. They didn't even want to let their own people get down. Can you dig that! That's what being black is! The ability to get down! That's why the best musicians use the shit, coke, smoke, smack, whatever. At the beginning, if you were hip, you could go to the ghetto and score anytime you wanted to. The Panthers wanted to put a stop to that. It got tough there for a while . . . then I don't know what happened, but suddenly it was better than it had ever been, like Christmas. Finally everybody got hip. Shit, you didn't even have to make the trip to the hood. Me and my whole band usta get down. If they didn't wanta get down, they couldn't work for me. Did I tell ya that once I had my own band?

■ ■ ■

Huey and Bobby are in the front seat of Huey's Pontiac, rolling through the ghetto night, eyes sweeping the streets and alleys. In the back seat, Cy is wedged between Little-Bobby and Tyrone.

"This is what we call our 'Panther Patrol,'" Huey explains out of the corner of his mouth for the benefit of Cy, the neophyte.

Bobby picks up the lesson. "Every time we see a brother or sister getting busted, we'll stop to 'observe'—check it out, make sure the pigs don't go beating on 'em. If they get taken downtown, we try to hook 'em up with bail and a lawyer."

"Uh-hunh, I get it," Cy says. "Like policing the police."

"Yeah," Tyrone chuckles, "It pisses 'em off, too. They sure don't like us policing them. Makes it harder for them to earn a little extra pocket money shaking down drug dealers."

Little-Bobby can't contain himself any longer. "Man, just wait till the folks get a load of us with these guns. And the threads, we look like real business! These leather jackets are great!"

"The jackets are supposed to be part of a uniform," Bobby comes back, acting like he's pissed. "How come you don't take that hat off your head and put on your beret?"

"'Cause he thinks that hat makes him look older," Tyrone guffaws.

Little-Bobby can't come up with anything hip to say.

Right in the middle of everybody laughing and admiring themselves, they spot something going down in an alley near Panther HQ. Twisting around to get a better look, Bobby tells Huey to back up.

Two cops are working over a brother. One of them looks up suddenly and sees a row of black men at the mouth of the alley carrying guns and wearing some kinda Che Guevara jackets and Lincoln Brigade berets. He stops his partner—a beefy cop named Logan—in mid-punch and points. Logan turns, and looks like he's about to shit his pants.

"Call for back-up!" Logan screeches.

Judge comes busting through the door of his shoebox apartment, feeling great. He's just gotten a test back in class—a ninety-eight.

Happily, he calls out Cy's name—once, twice—expecting to hit the books with him. The note propped on the table stops him short.

"Judge—I'm going out on my first patrol tonight. Sorry I can't study with you. P.S.—The jackets came in."

All of a sudden, Judge is at loose ends. He sits at his desk for a while, fiddling between one of his textbooks and Fanon's *Wretched of the Earth*, but doesn't make much progress in either direction. "Fuck it," he finally says. "All work and no play makes Judge a dull boy," and he looks up a phone number.

"Hey, Brick! It's Judge."

"Hey, man. What's up?"

"Are you down for a night on the town?"

"Fuckin'-A. You know the Hootenanny right off Grove? There's a new group playing there tonight I want to see. They're called the Bombers."

"Sure do. It's around the corner from Panther headquarters."

"Fuck those guys," Brick says, still smarting from his earlier encounter. "I'll see you there in half an hour."

Hootenanny is a friendly, counterculture type of joint, an urban roadhouse with a small dance floor and used-up picnic furniture. Brenda, a pretty blond with an acoustic guitar, is up on stage perched on a stool finishing a so-so version of "Blowing in the Wind." She gets polite applause as she climbs down. Judge and Brick, waiting by the door at the side of the bandstand, give her the thumbs-up.

Brenda asks Brick if he wants to give her a lift home and Brick is telling her no can do because he and Judge are gonna hang around and check out the sound equipment that the Bombers are using, when the door behind them flies open and the Bombers' emaciated drummer, Metro, comes bursting through, totally freaked.

"Get a fuckin' doctor in here! Get a doctor!" Metro screams frantically. "Help! Get a fuckin' doctor!"

A wave of rubbernecks, pushing to see what's going on, shove Judge and Brick into the back room.

A man's body is slumped on the floor, back propped against a barrel, head slumped to one side, foam drying at the corners of a gaping mouth. A needle is still hanging from the crook of his arm. Judge, an old hand at death, reaches over and checks him out.

Brick grimaces. "Who's that?"

Trembling, Metro replies, "It's our fuckin' sound engineer, K.C."

"Was!" Judge corrects him. "You don't need a doctor, you need a coroner."

Now Metro loses it. "Vanilla!" he screams at the top of his lungs. "It's your fuckin' fault, Vanilla!"

"Would you quit bitching, you sniveling reptile!" comes a throaty female voice from behind a curtain. "I'm coming!"

A toilet flushes. The curtain is shoved aside to reveal Vanilla, the group's lead singer, standing there hitching up her trousers. She is appallingly beautiful—chalk-white skin, jet-black hair, tight black jeans, cowboy boots. An angel from hell.

"Get him some coffee," she says, nodding towards the body.

"He ain't nodding out!" Metro bawls. "He's fuckin' dead, Vanilla. Dead!"

Vanilla nudges K.C.'s body with her boot, and it finally soaks in. "Shit!" she spits, annoyed. "Now what the fuck are we gonna do? Who's gonna run the sound equipment? We got three goddamn promoters out there waiting to hear us."

Brick jumps in. "My friend Judge here can run any kind of sound system that's ever been invented."

Before Vanilla can respond, one of the roadies sticks his head into the room. "Hey—looks like World War III is about to start outside! The cops and some black guys with guns and uniforms are in a big hassle down the street!"

"Come on, Brick!" Judge starts to push his way out of the room. "Let's go."

"No way!" Brick replies.

Judge's face registers surprise. Then he takes off on his own.

Metro grasps at Judge's sleeve as he passes him. "Can you really work one of these things?"

"Yeah, sure, but . . . " Judge crooks a thumb over his shoulder at

Brick. "So can he."

Vanilla grabs Brick's arm and locks his eyes with hers. "Can you handle it?" Her blood-red nails dig into his bicep, her touch like a thousand volts of electricity.

"Yeah," Brick says, snatching his arm away. "I can handle it."

Outside, the red flame of the squad car's roof light is drawing the local moths in droves to the alley down the street. Judge joins the others and hurries towards the action.

Outlined in the glare of streetlamp and headlights are the Panthers.

Judge can't help feeling a surge of pride and admiration. *They look terrific*—like real warriors with their berets, leather jackets, and guns. They stand facing the cops in a precise unflinching row, weapons at the ready.

Logan is facing Huey with a flashlight in one hand and Huey's license in the other. Recruits from Panther headquarters, taking advantage of the growing mob, are passing out Ten-Point Program leaflets. As Judge pushes his way through the crush of black folks, two more squad cars pull up.

Logan looks up from Huey's license. "Okay, now, er, Huey . . . So what's your telephone number?"

Huey doesn't buy into the policeman's hassle. "I have confirmed to you my address. That's all I'm required by law to do. We have broken no law, so you have no legal right to detain us."

Logan is flabbergasted. "You got guns, haven't you!" he says, nodding towards Huey's rifle.

"So have you!" Huey points out. The crowd sucks in its breath.

The cops from the other two squad cars swagger over. One of them, Frey, with a permanent sneer for blacks, has already drawn his nightstick.

Back down the block in the Hootenanny, the Bombers are beginning their set. Metro starts the funky drum pulse that is the band's signature and the patrons roar their approval. Vanilla steps to the mike, singing in her raging contralto, "OOOoohh, yes! Oh, Yeah! Don'tcha know!"

ZZZEEECHH! As the electric guitar hits its first lick, there is ear-splitting feedback from the speakers. Vanilla's eyes shoot daggers at Brick working the console, but he doesn't lose his cool. The necessary adjustments made, Vanilla gets down to business, turning her charm on the promoters at the table in the corner. She picks out the most influential one and starts playing up to him. All the while, Metro keeps the beat kicking.

Officer Frey rocks back on his heels, like a boxer moving into position for an uppercut. "What's the matter, Logan?" he quizzes the beefy cop. "These boys giving you trouble?"

Bolstered by the reinforcements, Logan acts tough again. "Well, they were trying to. They all got weapons. And this sassy one here with that rifle has been giving me a lot of lip."

Logan saunters up to Huey and stretches out his hand. "Lemme see that rifle, son. Ain't it . . . "

"No!" Huey snatches the weapon out of Logan's reach. "This is my private property. According to California law, we have a constitutional right to bear arms."

A shout of jubilation bursts from someone in the crowd. "Whoooeee! Them sho' is some baadass niggers!"

The exclamation spurs the other cops into action. Leaving Logan and Frey to eyeball it out with the Panther leaders, they attempt to disperse the crowd.

"Okay, people, move along," the officers begin the familiar litany. "Go on about your business. The show is over. Police business. Leave it to us. Move along, move along . . . " The crowd, docile after generations of enforced obedience, reluctantly begins to move off.

"Brothers! Sisters! Hold on!" Huey shouts. "You don't have to go anywhere. That's the law!"

Everyone freezes. Even the cops stop their shoving. Uncertain what to do, they turn towards Logan.

"What the . . . what the hell are you talking about?" Logan blusters.

Huey, not even bothering to answer the cop, keeps right on running his rap to the people. "This is your business! Stay right here!

You don't have to leave! The man is trying to run his usual fascist bullying tactics on you. The law book says as long as you are a reasonable distance—and reasonable is defined as eight to ten feet to be exact—you've got a right to observe the police carrying out their duties!"

"That's right!" Bobby Seale bellows. *"Y'ALL AIN'T GOTTA GO NOWHERES!!"*

The crowd, emboldened by Huey and Bobby's assurances, regroups and stands fast.

"Talk that good shit, brothers!" someone yells. "Yeah," another voice seconds, "amen to that!"

Logan's round face is flushed with anger. "Is that shotgun loaded, boy?!"

The crowd gasps and holds its breath.

Huey looks Logan dead in the eyes. "It is against the fish and game laws of the state of California," he declares, "to have a live round of ammunition in the chamber of a shotgun or rifle in a vehicle. Pig!"

Pig! The crowd can't believe its ears. Tit for tat, and-a-black-man-at-that, daring to return a cop's insult and call him out of his name.

"Oooh, Sweet Jesus . . . I do believe I have died and gone to heaven," comes a happy affirmation, and then a burst of applause.

Frey is not about to relinquish control. "You refer to an officer as 'officer' when you speak to him!"

Bobby retaliates. "Then don't go referring to us as 'boys'!"

Shouts of "Right on!" and "Tell it like it is!" erupt from the crowd.

The cops draw their guns. The onlookers go quiet and shrink back, figuring at least the brothers with the guns in the hip outfits had given the pigs a run for their money, figuring it was fun while it lasted, figuring the party was over. However, the Panthers don't budge an inch, don't shuffle and don't flinch.

Damn, Judge thinks to himself, *they are for real.*

Logan gets up in Huey's face. "I ask you again . . . is that gun loaded?"

Huey smiles grimly. "Well, it wasn't." He returns the policeman's glare of hate and *CA-LACK!* . . . cocks a round into the chamber. "But now it is!!"

The street goes ape shit. Veins in his neck bulging, Logan starts stammering about the Panthers messing with the Constitution and no matter what it says it couldn't have been meant for the likes of them.

"Supposed to be the same law for one and all," Bobby reminds him.

Logan goes nose to nose with Huey. "For the last time, BOY!" he screams. "What do those guns mean?!"

Huey delivers the party's credo. "They mean, PIG, that the Black Panther Party declares that if you try to brutalize our community we are going to shoot you!"

Judge can't believe his ears. *There it is in a nutshell—right in the fucking cop's face!*

At first the crowd is frozen by Huey's proclamation. Then slowly, the guarded ghetto masks melt, and the reaction goes from stunned disbelief to joy. The mob goes berserk, bursting into cheers and applause. The cops, beaten, climb back into their cars and disappear through the jubilant crowd. As they drive off, a wino goes crazy with ecstasy. "Hallelujah! Hallelujuh!" he sings, whirling like a dervish.

Brick has mastered the console and the Bombers sound great. Vanilla is whirling on stage in the Hootenanny, belting it out. The cafe is in a frenzy.

Vanilla brings the set to a stunning crescendo. ". . . the blues ain't nothin' I can't chaaannge!"

The crowd claps its approval. Vanilla climbs off the platform and rushes over to the bigtime promoter. Puffing on his cigar, he says he personally likes the band but isn't sure he can find a gig for them. Vanilla, who wasn't born yesterday, gets the message. Figuring that she might as well let her looks work for her, she goes out to the parking lot and climbs into the back of the limo with the promoter.

In the meantime, Grove Street is still teeming. Having gotten a whiff of liberation, nobody wants to leave the scene. People wander up and down, hugging whoever they happen to meet, telling and retelling each other about the miraculous Panther confrontation with the police.

Judge passes a barber shop. Peeping in, he sees two battered barber chairs, a couple of basins, a bench, and a circle of smiling old black men celebrating. He waves. They wave back and beckon him in.

"Hey, youngblood," one grins, holding up their bottle to share with him. "You wanta have a swallow with us to celebrate? We flying tonight . . . Amen!"

"Yeah, amen," the others echo.

Judge takes a polite sip.

"Wasn't that something?" one of the old men asks, shaking his head. "Never thought I'd live to see the day! You know the police ain't nothing but the KKK wid badges."

"Ain't no negroes needing no shoes tonight!" asserts another. "We flying . . . Them Panther chillun done give us wings. Have another swallow, son, go right ahead."

Judge dutifully pretends to take another hit, then takes his leave as the laughing barber shop regulars, pleased as punch, "that's right," "amen," and "sweet Jesus" each other.

The evening after the ghetto standoff, Dorsett is hosting a three-man after-hours meeting in his office at Agent Rodgers's request. He sighs, wondering wistfully just what the hell it would take to get Hoover's boy off his back.

Rodgers hands Dorsett a copy of the leaflets the Panthers were circulating the night before at the Grove Street confrontation and asks him to read it aloud.

Dorsett winces. He leans back in his chair, then leans forward again.

"If you please, Dorsett," Rodgers prompts.

Dorsett glances at Brimmer for moral support. Brimmer can only give him a humor-the-jerk shrug. Dorsett makes a minor production getting his specs on his nose, and then, feeling like an asshole, he begins to read. "One: We want freedom. We want the power to determine the destiny of our black community. Two: We want full employment for our people. Three: We want to end the robbery by the white man of our black community . . ."

He breaks off and looks up, aghast. "Christ, next they're going to be asking for reparations!"

Rodgers rewards Dorsett with a big smile. "Exactly! And," he jabs the air with a forefinger, "they couldn't have thought this up for themselves."

"Yeah," Brimmer grunts, shaking a fresh cigarette out of a battered pack. "Sounds like the Constitution to me, maybe with a little Bill of Rights thrown in. Bunch of negroes surely would be unfamiliar with such basic rights as outlined in our nation's most historic documents."

Dorsett frowns at Brimmer. Why couldn't that sarcastic SOB learn to keep his mouth shut?

Brimmer's sarcasm is not lost on Rodgers. "This is no joke, Inspector Brimmer. I fail to comprehend your making light of a serious situation. The reason I requested that the propaganda be read aloud is that we can hear the steady beat of the Communist Party drum in those words."

Brimmer, dipping his head to light his cigarette, smiles to himself. The feds were always trying to find a way to drag the Reds into everything. He thumbs his old Zippo, it bursts into flame. Brimmer lights up and raises his head.

Rodgers begins his interrogation. "Now tell me, Inspector Brimmer, during your surveillance have you seen any outside agitators in the black community? Especially any communists?"

"I don't know if I've seen a communist or not, 'cause I'm not sure what they look like. I have seen black men in berets and neighborhood women feeding kids breakfast. I've seen 'em clean up the garbage and have meetings, meetings, and more meetings. Pretty dull shit, sir."

Rodgers's eyes narrow to angry slits. "These same dull, uninteresting boys in berets have been carrying guns, threatening police officers, and inciting crowds to riot," he says. "Doesn't it bother you that there is a negro gang out there with firearms, inspector? You must realize that the police will be their number one targets! If this deplorable situation continues, I will have to memo Washington on it."

Brimmer starts punching the ashtray with the tip of his cigarette, but he manages to keep his mouth shut.

"They are undermining the United States of America," Rodgers says. Pointing an accusing finger, he continues, "And you, Inspector Brimmer, are not taking your duties seriously enough."

Dorsett has heard just about enough. "Now hold on Rodgers," he protests.

Rodgers, by no means ready to yield the floor, whirls to face Dorsett. "And you, Chief of Special External Affairs Dorsett, if the Black Panthers are to remain in your jurisdiction, some fundamental changes in attitude must be made at once!"

"Like what?" Dorsett growls, his hands making fists below the desktop.

"Like your Inspector Brimmer finding, shall we say, a more active method of involvement."

Near midnight, Dorsett steps out of police headquarters, takes a couple of deep breaths, and starts across the street to his car.

A limousine pulls up next to him. The tinted rear window slides down and Tynan's face emerges from the shadows.

"Evening, Chief," Tynan croons. "Another hard day keeping the streets safe?"

Dorsett quickly checks up and down the street. "What are you doing here?" He is visibly shaken. "I mean, out so late, haha," Dorsett adds with forced joviality. "Out catting around, I suppose."

Always the diplomat, Tynan gives Dorsett a thin grin for his effort. "I like to keep an eye on my clients' investments. One day soon we need to discuss that business expansion we spoke of."

"Look, I don't think this is . . . "

Tynan cuts him off. "That's a beautiful automobile you got there," he purrs, nodding towards Dorsett's new Cadillac. "You'd do well to remember who paid for it."

Tynan taps the partition behind the chauffeur's head and the window rolls back up. The limo slides off into the moonless night.

14

TESTING, ONE-TWO-THREE . . . Witness #9. Name: Alberta Moore . . . Day care center.

. . . Yes, it's my place, I started it myself. Yes, I believe you can move mountains if you believe in yourself. That's the trouble with most . . . well, if not most, a lot of my people. And yes, I was at Grove Street that night, and I've been thankful for being there and seeing what I saw every day of my life since. Those boys believed in themselves. And you know, I'm not talking religion here, but something like that. I started believing in me . . . not all at once of course, but little by little. First I got out of the life and got off what they call substance abuse and later started this day school. It may not look like so much to you, but we get along . . .

CAN YOU TELL ME HOW MANY PANTHERS THERE WERE AND HOW MANY POLICEMEN?

No, I don't remember how many there were—a bunch on both sides. But what I do remember is they were black men, with guns, standing up to white men—police at that—and not backing down. I was so proud. I woulda given one them Panthers some nookie right there if I'd been asked. Shit, I'd given them all some . . . I was one wild young thing back then, like I said. Yes I was—good looker too . . .

The dawn is just starting to push pink against the windows of Judge and Cy's tiny loft. Cy, an Afro pick stuck in the back of his hair, shuffles into the alcove that doubles as the kitchen, rubbing the sleep out of his eyes. Judge, dressed for class, is seated at the table flipping through the pile of Cy's Panther literature. There is a serene quality to Judge, as if he has come to some kinda big decision.

Cy, surprised to see his roommate, wonders out loud, "Kinda early for college class isn't it? Where you been? I haven't seen you for two whole days?"

"Around. Did some walking and stuff, a lot of thinking."

"Gotcha! School work kicking your ass, hunh?" Volunteering a report on his morning chores, Cy holds up a pair of white gloves. "Me, I'm gonna do a little stoplight duty before I go to work."

"I was down on Grove Street night before last," Judge confides. "I saw how you guys handled the cops. I always dreamed about something like that happening. I was proud of you guys."

"Yeah, we were all up on the pigs with our legal shit," Cy beams. "It was beautiful, wasn't it?!"

Judge nods. "Yeah, man, it was." There is a faint smile on his lips. "Look, I was hoping if your old junkheap was running maybe you could give me a lift."

"Running like a top!" Cy assures him. "You got it, brother. Where to? The campus?"

"Naw, brother. Panther headquarters."

Cy is bowled over. "Panther headquarters?!" Pleased beyond words, Cy throws his arms around Judge and gives him a big bear hug. "You joining, my brother! My brother! My Brother!"

"You know how it is, man," Judge grins and hugs him back. "This way we get to hang out like we use to."

Cy and Judge pull up to Panther headquarters. The showdown with the cops has begun to win the black community. Early morning or not, there is a line of men waiting to join, including Rose and McStick sharing a bottle of Bitter Dog.

"Looks like the word's gotten around about the other night," Judge observes, eyeing the recruits.

"Ain't a whole lot of real Panther material showing up though," Cy whispers.

Judge is upbeat. "Well, like Tyrone would say, 'Rome wasn't built in a day.'"

Cy grunts, and they shoulder their way inside past the crowd of brothers rapping shit to each other.

"Man, them Panthers were some bad motherfuckers," one guy is telling another. "Yeah, yeah," someone seconds. "Yeah. They made them cops eat shit. Yes, they did!" a third guy chimes in proudly.

Panther headquarters has been spruced up with a coat of paint. Bobby Seale is seated at a table in front of the old display counter, newly repainted as well, interviewing candidates. Another Panther is passing out Ten-Point Program leaflets and stressing that the Ten Points are mandatory reading for all potential recruits. The brothers on line inside are talking shit to each other too.

"Yeah, I'm gonna tell 'em to just sign me up, then just gimme a gun and point out the cops they want me to shoot."

"Man, I hear that. My momma marched with Doctor King, you know, but I don't know what good it did . . ."

"I hear the Panthers get all the finest pussy . . ."

Cy, with Judge in tow, pushes to the front, making a bee-line for the recruitment table. Judge sticks out like a sore thumb in his university clothes. He's wearing his old Vietnam fatigue jacket, but underneath that he's dressed conservatively in gray corduroy trousers and a shirt with a button-down collar. Tyrone, standing off to the side sizing up the recruits, disappears into the back.

Cy throws his arm around his buddy and announces proudly to Bobby, "My man, Judge, is gonna join up with us."

"Welcome, brother," Bobby enthuses. "Glad to see you. You know if we stand together we can break the chains of oppression. First learn the Ten Points and come back when . . . "

"He knows them already," Cy interjects. "He knows them cold. Better than me!"

"Well, then in that case . . . "

Tyrone comes out of the back. Interrupting, he jabs a finger at Judge. "Huey wants to see you."

Cy and Judge are suprised. "Huey said he had a hunch you'd be coming by," Tyrone grunts in response to the quizzical looks on their faces.

The two pals move towards the back to see what Huey wants, but Tyrone steps between them. "Just him," Tyrone says, stopping Cy.

Judge shrugs a what-the-hell to Cy and walks on into the back alone.

Cy turns to Tyrone. "What's up, brother?"

Tyrone shrugs. "Shit if I know . . . "

Cy holds up his white traffic gloves. "Well, I gotta go. See ya round."

The back room is dim and musty. At first Judge is blind. He stands in the dark, his mind racing. His eyes grow accustomed to the gloom, and there at the other end of the chamber, half-hidden in the shadows, is Huey Newton sitting on a crate and cradling a shotgun.

Huey beckons Judge to join him on a nearby crate. "Welcome, brother. Have you decided to get down with us?"

Judge remains standing. "I'm down," he answers firmly.

Again Huey motions for Judge to be seated. "Your soldier shit is bad, brother. You were a lot of help the other day."

Judge chooses a crate that once held pancake flour. "I'm finished with all that," he says, taking his seat.

Huey is wary. "Mind if I ask a few questions?" He strokes the stock of the shotgun.

Judge is not sure what that means, if anything. "Go ahead," he says. "Ask away."

"Where are you getting the money to go to school?"

"GI Bill," Judge says, then taps his old wound, "plus a disability allowance. We hit a land mine."

Huey frowns, suspicious. "I thought a land mine was supposed to be fatal."

"It was for the two guys in front of me," Judge replies drily.

"You musta been pretty young," Huey probes, still leery. "So how did it go down? You volunteer or something, right?"

"Reform school or something," Judge laughs bitterly. "The court said, 'jail or the military.' My mother chose the Marines. Anyhow, if I stuck around here I'd probably be dead or sittin' on the stoop drinking Bitter Dog with Rose. Why all the questions anyhow?"

"Security has gotta be ironclad! Sister Shabazz is gonna pay a visit. We're gonna be part of her protection."

TESTING, ONE-TWO-THREE . . . Witness #10. Name: Sean O'Connell . . . Newsroom cubicle.

PERSONALLY, DO YOU THINK THE PANTHERS WERE TREATED FAIRLY BY THE MEDIA?

Maybe not . . . We followed orders.

ORDERS FROM WHO? FROM THE POLICE?

Not exactly. However, you do want to stay on good terms with them since, if nothing else, they are a vital source of information on many fronts. Not just crime reporting either, which incidentally is the category they insisted we file any news about the Panthers under. Anyway back to personal, okay? Personally, I think the main thing the Panthers had going for them was style. I don't suppose it's politically correct to use the word "natural" but they had this natural sense of style . . . this flamboyant flair that just seemed to capture the public's imagination.

HOW ABOUT THEIR VERBAL STYLE, THEIR RHETORIC. WASN'T THAT, TO USE THE TERMINOLOGY OF THE TIME, COUNTERPRODUCTIVE?

> Well, the Panthers had two audiences, one white and one black, and they were definitely playing to the black one, often at the expense of the white audience which expects its negroes to be less confrontational—you know, humble. Even though what they said often offended the white audience, it made terrific copy for us in the media. And their primary audience—the black audience—loved them for it. I think what they did was the only logical avenue open to them. When they carried guns and used the language they did, it showed the blacks in the ghettoes that they meant business. When the Panthers called the police "Pigs," it was, as they say, "pay back time." They were simply paying the cops back for all the contemptuous slurs they had had to endure over the years, plus it demonstrated to the black community that they intended to fight fire with fire and stand up to the authorities.

San Francisco Airport, February 21, 1967. When the Punk Panthers fail to rise to the occasion as Larkin promised, the Black Panthers step up to the plate. While the San Francisco Panthers mill around ineffectually, the Oakland Panthers form a protective circle around Betty Shabazz when she comes off the plane. In tight military precision, they guide Malcolm's widow through the crowded terminal, leaving the Punk Panthers, useless in their dashikis and fluffed Afros, trailing behind.

Outside, the Oakland brothers, having planned ahead, have a car waiting for Sister Shabazz plus back-up—another vehicle full of more Panthers, standing by, just in case.

Leaving the Punks to catch up as best they can, the Oakland contingent heads for the first stop on her agenda, the office of *Ramparts* magazine.

While the rest of their team waits below, Huey, Bobby, Judge, and Tyrone stand guard in the waiting room as Betty Shabazz begins her interview in an inner office with a tall, black reporter wearing sunglasses named Eldridge Cleaver. A few minutes later Larkin and his boys arrive and come upstairs. As soon as they realize there is no immediate danger, they make themselves comfortable, leaning and lounging around the room like central casting bodyguards. It isn't long before they lift up their dashikis and begin brandishing their guns.

The reporter asks Sister Shabazz what would she like to say to all the young brothers and sisters out there who would like to follow Brother Malcolm's footsteps?

"I'd say that Malcolm lives in each of us," she replies without hesitation. "We all need to work together for the community." She gestures towards the waiting room. "Like those brothers out there are doing."

Overhearing Sister Shabazz, Larkin starts strutting his stuff. He tosses his pistol back and forth from palm to palm, then twirls it around his trigger finger.

Judge watches him with disdain. Suddenly, a look of disbelief comes over his face, then anger. "Psst, Huey," he whispers, trying to get Huey's attention.

Just then several police cars, followed by a caravan of newsmen, pull up to the curb in front of the *Ramparts* office. Bobby, on lookout at the window, spots the action.

"Pigs, and reporters," he announces. "Looks like we got a little reception on our hands, brothers."

"Let's hit it!" Huey barks, and the Panthers pull their weapons and fall in. Simultaneously, all the Punk Panthers except Jamal put their guns away. Larkin twitters something about not wanting any trouble with the authorities or anything and orders Jamal to put his weapon away too.

As soon as Betty Shabazz finishes her interview, the Black Panthers form a shield around her and escort her out of the office and down the steps to the lobby. Cleaver tags along, and the few Punk Panthers who have gathered up enough nerve to follow hang meekly behind.

The newsmen are waiting on the sidewalk outside the building, microphones and cameras at the ready, but the Panthers stationed below form a human corridor leading to the car, weapons at the ready.

An agressive cop eyes Cy's gun. "What's going on here, son?" he demands. "I think you fellows better come with me."

But Cy, having done his homework, tells the cop that since they have broken no law he has no right to detain them.

The reporters, hoping for another Grove Street confrontation, start shoving and jockeying for position. "There she is!!" one of them shouts as the Panthers come marching out of the building.

Pushing cameras and microphones in Shabazz's direction, the reporters surge forward.

"Please, no photos!" Huey implores. "Sister Shabazz wants to be left in peace!"

Ignoring Huey's pleas, the newsmen try to break through the line of Panthers. One of the reporters manages to pierce the gauntlet.

"Do you fear for your life?" he demands of Betty Shabazz.

Huey steps between the journalist and Malcolm's widow and holds him in check until she reaches the car.

When Shabazz is safely inside, the automobile pulls away. Frustrated at being denied, the journalist takes it out on Huey. He shoves Huey and Huey shoves him back. The reporter takes a swing at Huey. Huey sidesteps and pushes him on his ass. "Arrest this man!!" Huey shouts to the cop in charge. "He tried to assault me!"

"If I'm gonna arrest anyone," the cop threatens, "it's gonna be you!" He takes a menacing step towards Huey.

CLACK! . . . Huey flicks off the safety on his shotgun. "Not today you won't!" he informs the cop.

The Panthers immediately take up battle position, forming a phalanx behind Huey, guns at the ready.

The cops begin to have second thoughts.

Larkin, scared and unarmed, comes running out of the building yelling and waving his hands. "Come on, brothers, we don't want any trouble. Don't point those guns at the officers," he pleads.

"That's right!" the policeman in charge sneers, agreeing with the frightened Larkin, who now hightails it back inside the building. "Be smart niggers like your friend!"

Huey glares at the cop. "He's not our friend," he counters. "I promise you pig, your men draw and this will be a blood bath. It's your call!"

A short eternity passes with the cops glowering at the Panthers and the Panthers scowling right back at them and Larkin and his boys peeping through the lobby window at the stand-off.

The cops back down.

The reporter who took a swing at Huey is still pissed. "Aren't you going to do anything?" he challenges the police.

Nervously eyeing the Panthers, their guns still poised and ready, the cop in charge turns on the journalist and tells him to shut up. "Like he said, asshole," he adds. "They're not breaking any law."

After the showdown, the Panther cars head homeward across the Bay Bridge. In the lead car are Bobby, Little-Bobby, Judge, Cy, Tyrone, and Huey at the wheel.

"You see that jive Punk Panther chief when you said we had a reception community waiting down stairs? He scrambled for cover so fast he dropped his gun," Tyrone laughs.

They go through the toll booth and hit the outskirts of Oakland.

Bobby Seale joins the triumphant recap. "Shit, surprised me they even showed up with guns."

Everybody chuckles and amens to that except Judge.

"Why the long face? What it be Judge?" Cy wants to know. "Nobody got hurt, Sister Betty's safe. This was a good day."

Judge struggles to contain his wrath. "It was empty," he seethes.

"Empty?" Little-Bobby pipes up, confused. "What was empty?"

"That Punk Panther's gun. It wasn't loaded! I checked it out," Judge explains. "I'll bet the rest weren't either."

Now Huey starts to steam. He jerks the wheel violently and makes a screeching two-wheel U-turn to head back to San Francisco. "Let's find out!"

■ ■ ■

Fish are frying on the grill in the backyard of the San Francisco Panthers abode, and music is wafting across the well-kept lawn soothing the guests.

A disillusioned Jamal, holding a drink and wearing a disgusted look, is eavesdropping on Larkin, who is holding forth to one of his lieutenants about what a great victory they have achieved.

Larkin is boasting smugly. "Like I say, brother, we are the vanguard. Today's event proves my prophecy."

Playing lord of the manor to the hilt, Larkin turns to a passing woman and hands her his glass. "Get me more libation, sister," he commands, and then turns back to his ego-tripping. "I tell you," he says nodding towards Eldridge Cleaver, one of the guests, "once Brother Cleaver's story comes out about how we conquered the enemy, faced down those cops and made them . . . "

Larkin suddenly stops his diatribe mid-sentence, his jaw dropping. The Black Panthers are coming around the side of the house.

They march across the lawn straight up to Larkin. Tyrone raises the front of Larkin's dashiki and snatches the pistol out of his waistband. He spins the cylinder. "Empty!" he reports.

Huey is furious. "Malcolm X's widow's life was on the line today. And your guns weren't even loaded!" He makes no effort to mute his rage.

Larkin is defiant. "A gun's a gun, man." He sneers, "It doesn't need to be loaded!"

Huey isn't buying his bullshit. "Tell that to the pigs. Better yet, tell that to Malcolm!"

Larkin tries to play the diplomat. "Just wait a second there, my brother, look at the . . . "

"No, you wait a second!" Huey cuts him off. "You and your 'Punk Panthers' got three choices. One, you join with us and follow our rules. Two, you change your name. Or three, we stop your ass by any means necessary."

Larkin's men line up behind him and the two factions square off. The Panthers are clearly outnumbered.

"Look, pretty ghetto boy, you and your ragamuffins are a long way from Oakland," Larkin smirks. "So just get the fuck out of here before . . ."

WHOP! . . . Huey decks Larkin with a ferocious left. A burly Punk Panther steps in and *WHOP!* . . . Judge drops him like a stone with a karate chop. The other Punk Panthers freeze.

Grabbing Larkin's collar, Huey pulls him up to his knees.

"You're exactly the kind of brother we don't need," Huey tells him, his voice dripping with contempt. "You're exactly the kind of brother who gets others killed. Now, you gonna change your name?"

Larkin's lieutenants advise him to concede, but Larkin doesn't answer. Huey drags him towards the barbecue to sear his behind a little.

"Okay! Okay! I'll do it!" agrees brother Larkin, not ready to join the fish on the grill.

Mission accomplished, Huey drops Larkin like a sack of potatoes and he and the other Panthers back out of the party.

Larkin, down on one knee, rubs his throat and tries to salvage his dignity. "Yeah, we'll change our name, but only for the good of the revolution," he says weakly.

Disenchanted by Larkin's contemptible actions, Jamal puts down his glass and starts up the flagstone path leading to the street. Larkin calls for him to return to the fold, but Jamal keeps walking. "Come back—that's an order!" Larkin shouts, hollering at the wind.

Standing off to the side, Eldridge Cleaver takes it all in.

Back in the ghetto, the Panthers unwind with a party of their own on the rooftop above Panther headquarters. Beer, wine, some fine ladies, the down-to-earth sound of freshly washed diapers and work shirts drying in the wind, and the funky music of the Temptations, the Four Tops, J.B., and Gladys set the atmosphere. Cy and Little-Bobby are showing each other fancy steps and Bobby Seale is holding forth, running down some poetry.

"Two things I do despise, boojie niggas and flies.
The more I see boojie niggas, the more I like flies!"

To add to the sweetness of the moment, the sinking sun has poured a golden molasses color over the party.

Huey steers Judge away from the hubbub to the western edge of the roof. Huey sets his beer bottle on top of the brick ledge and kicks back to watch the sun go down.

"You were all right Judge. No, you were better than all right." Huey turns towards Judge and raises his bottle in salute. "You know what you are, you're what the Party needs. You're smart, you see past just the guns and the berets."

Judge takes a swallow of his beer before answering. "I don't know about all that. But, thanks anyway . . . Salut."

Huey turns back towards the setting sun. "You think you can keep playing the game?"

"Game?" Judge frowns, not following Huey's line. "What game are you talkin' about?"

"You're down, you're really street and righteous, but you come off as kinda square. That can be very valuable to us."

Judge hasn't a clue where Huey is heading. Looking out over the rooftops, he notices the arm of a TV antenna that has come loose and is dangling by the wire, like a body on a gallows.

"I meant what I said as a compliment," Huey assures him. "You think you can keep up the doofus front?"

Judge's mind is flailing all over the place trying to figure out what the hell Huey is talking about. "What front? You mean those clothes I wear to school? I suppose I could dress like that all the time if I had to."

"No, man, I mean everything! Outside and in. Our survival and lives might depend on it. After the other night and then today the word has got to be out on us. Black people trying to stand up for themselves, the Man is not going to take that kind of shit lying down. Sooner than later, the pigs are gonna be trying to infiltrate us."

"You're right, sad but true," Judge sighs. "Yes, I guess they will."

"True, brother, but not sad!" Huey lowers his voice and leans closer. "It's our opportunity! We're gonna double-cross their ass. I got a special mission for you, Judge. How about it?"

"A mission?" Judge never liked the sound of that word, even before the court forced his Moms to volunteer him for the Marines. "A mission? Mind my asking, who I will be working with, the other members of the team, I mean. Who else will be on this here mission with me?"

Huey leans even closer. "No team, my brother." He searches Judge's face as he speaks, not even certain what he is hoping to find there himself. "Just you, man."

Judge is guarded. "Alone? Just me? Me? Why pick me, out of all the other people signing up. Why me?"

Huey hedges, holding back, nibbling around the truth. "Well, for one thing, a mixture of common sense meeting intuition. You know, you being a veteran, going to school, knowin' how to work with the Man."

"Huey, you're losing me again," Judge confesses. "Just what are you getting at?"

"Just like I said, survival. The pigs are gonna try to infiltrate us . . . and we're gonna let 'em."

"How's that?"

Huey finally zeroes in. "Their spy's gonna be our spy. You!"

A pause . . . Finally, the gravity of Huey's proposition sinks in. Judge turns and faces the festivités. The party is rolling smoothly along. Tyrone and a foxy young lady are dancing very romantically. Little-Bobby can't seem to stay away from the potato salad, and Cy is pulling on his fifth beer.

"Me, hunh," Judge turns back to Huey. He is still wary. "I'm curious. You said one reason you chose me was some kinda common sense-intuition thing. What was the other reason?"

The sun goes down, and it's suddenly too dark for Judge to read Huey's face.

Huey's silhouette shrugs. "You fit the profile, brother." He chuckles. "You're exactly the kind of nigger they think they can trust."

Three thousand miles away from Oakland, the Justice Department building sits like a self-satisfied granite giant in the middle of

Washington, D.C. On the fifth floor of the cold government edifice, down a long corridor whose walls are lined with photos of VIPs he has hobnobbed with, through an outer office filled with macabre mementoes of his illustrious career (Dillinger's death mask among them), sits the Uber-Cop himself—J. Edgar Hoover.

Seated behind his massive desk, his large watery eyes scanning teletype copy, he barks orders into his phone. The handsome young aide standing at the far end of the desk fields an urgent call from California. Underneath an American flag, quietly taking it all in, is Hoover's dog.

"You heard me right!" the Director growls into the receiver. "I want additional wire taps on Dr. King's phones!"

The aide covers his phone with the palm of his hand, sidles over, and whispers into Hoover's ear.

Hoover looks up, obviously taken by suprise. "Oakland?"

"Yessir," the aide reiterates, "that's what I'm told."

"Oakland, hunh," Hoover grunts. "Well, we'll just have to see about that, won't we?!"

MEMO/COINTELPRO: CLASSIFIED
RE: UNUSUAL BAY AREA ACTIVITY. ASCERTAIN ORIGIN/STATUS.

WASHINGTON

15

TESTING, ONE-TWO-THREE . . . Witness #11. Name: Refused . . . Darkness.

WHY ARE WE SITTING IN THE DARK? WHAT'S THE MYSTERY? YOU ASKED FOR THIS MEETING.

Why take a chance.

A CHANCE ON WHAT? . . . WHO ARE YOU?

We heard you wanted to know the real story.

THAT'S TRUE, I DO. SHALL WE BEGIN? HOW DO YOU EXPLAIN THE PHENOMENON OF THE BLACK PANTHER PARTY?

That's not your real question, is it? Isn't your real question how did Bobby Seale and Huey Newton, a couple of African-American dropouts preaching power and justice coming out of the barrel of a gun, manage to build a national organization, an army, despite the surveillance and persecution of the authorities from day one?

I SUPPOSE YOU'RE RIGHT.

Of course we're right. Well, you won't find the answers in the doctored files the FBI released under the Freedom of Information Act. There's a lot there they still aren't telling. Not to mention the fact that there is a lot about our resources, even to this day, they never knew about.

ARE YOU SUGGESTING THE PANTHERS HAD SOME KIND OF SECRET WEAPON?

Weapons! Plural . . . A number of them . . . Although their first weapon wasn't much of a secret . . . at least it is pretty plain to people of color. Of course, white people would deny it even exists.

WHAT ARE YOU TALKING ABOUT?

I'm talking about arrogance, brother!

ARROGANCE AS SOME KIND OF WEAPON? I'M AFRAID YOU'RE LOSING ME.

It bought the Panthers time to get their act together.

LET ME SEE IF I'VE GOT THIS STRAIGHT. ARE YOU SAYING THE ARROGANT STYLE OF THE PANTHERS ACTED LIKE SOME KIND OF SHIELD? THAT IT WAS SOME KIND OF SELF-PROTECTING MECHANISM THAT BOUGHT THEM TIME?

No, I'm not talking about the arrogance of the Panthers. I'm talking about the arrogance of white people . . . all white people, when it comes to African Americans. They believe we are stupid.

I'M WHITE AND I DON'T BELIEVE . . .

Bullshit! Sure you do! If you weren't a racist you wouldn't think you could just come in here waltz all around the black community . . . ask some bullshit questions, type up a few interviews, call it a book, and make a pile of money off our backs.

THIS IS A THESIS PAPER!

What makes you think you can come in here and just rip us off? Look, white boy, we're warning you! We want fifty percent of the money of the book . . . or whatever you're doing.

I'M NOT DOING ANYTHING! AND WHO EVER HEARD OF AN AUTHOR GETTING FIFTY PERCENT OF A BOOK . . .

We don't give a fuck what you ever heard of. This is a new day. Slavery is over. I wouldn't advise you trying to rip us off! We demand that half of your book be allocated to us. We're talking fifty percent of the retail price, not any of that wholesale bullshit.

US? WHO IS US?

It's gonna be a nonprofit, nationwide network. We're starting a foundation for the veterans of the Party and eventually a nursery for preschoolers.

WHAT'S IT CALLED?

Never mind that! Look, if you want the facts, from beginning to end and nationwide too, we can be a lot of help. Ask and read all you want to, you'll never get the real truth. There is a lot folks don't know or even suspect. Take Judge for example—I don't think they even mention him once, or the explosion in the garage. We'll be in touch . . .

It's early morning, and Kisha, the nubile high school girl, comes swaying down the sidewalk. Judge, white gloves and all, is in the middle of the intersection at Fifty-Fifth and Market pulling a little traffic duty before heading to campus.

The word is out, and directing traffic has become a cushy tour. A couple of speedsters having been threatened with bodily harm, and no longer do cars and trucks come tearing through the ghetto using it as a drag strip. The few vehicles on the street go gingerly through the intersection and about their business.

Judge grins and waves at his mother, standing on her porch in her housecoat and curlers glaring up the road at him. She turns and goes inside, wondering when he is going to come to his senses and stop all this Black Panther foolishness.

Moms, Moms, sweet Moms, Judge thinks to himself. He believes deep down that she will eventually understand, just like the rest of the black community was starting to do. He belches. Understand or not, good old Moms made him stop by and have some breakfast before going to standing out there waving his arms around like he didn't have a bit of sense left.

While his body sinks into the ballet of directing traffic, his mind floats happily back over the recent miracles. The Panthers were on a roll. The ghetto was starting to come around. A few weeks ago the Panthers couldn't even give an apple away, and now . . . *The recruits were pouring in. Even Jamal, brother-dashiki himself, came in and said he wanted to do something for the community, and if they would have him he'd like to sign up. Next, just when it seemed they were about to be overwhelmed, just when it seemed they had taken on more projects than they could handle—a breakfast program, sickle cell testing, free legal aid, you-name-it—the sisters were there.*

Judge waves a car through and savors the memory of that day. Looking up from running the mimeograph machine at the back of Panther headquarters, he could see past new Panthers bustling about their chores, Bobby Seale at the filing cabinet, Little-Bobby and Tyrone at the table interviewing applicants. The line of recruits snaked out the door, and through the plate glass storefront window he could see the long line of volunteers on the sidewalk waiting to sign up. Suddenly Alma and a veritable platoon of natural-hairdo-wearing sisters of all shapes, sizes, shades, and ages pushed their way in the door and up to the recruiting table.

Tyrone looked up, more than a little surprised. "Alma?" he blurted. "I mean, what are you doing here?"

Before Alma could answer, another sister with red hair and freckles across the bridge of her nose spoke up. "Whatta you mean what is we doing here! We're black, ain't we? And we care about improv-

ing the plight of our people, don't we? Or you figure oppression stops at that thing y'all got dangling between your legs!"

"Or! . . . " interjected a dark-skinned sister, with big silvery earrings and her hands on her hips, "are you going to come on with some mealy-mouth jive about revolution not being a woman's work?"

Judge remembers with a laugh that Tyrone was about ready to freak. "Er . . . Look . . . "

Alma not even let him get his sentence started good. "And we want equality, full-fledged membership!"

"Yeah," added the freckle-faced sister with the attitude, her head rocking from side to side. "None of this okay-sugah-as-long-as-you-stay-in-the-background-washing-my-socks-and-rubbing-my-feet bullshit either!"

Tyrone, ears ringing, looked sheepishly over at Bobby.

Bobby grinned and handed Alma a stack of leaflets. "The Panther Party can dig where you sisters are coming from and there's a lot of work to be done. Read this and if you're down with the Ten-Point Program, go get in line and sign up."

Some of the brothers had felt their manhood imperiled when the sisters started joining, especially since they were given equality. Some grumbled about everybody knowing sisters not really been able to pull they weight. Then during weapons orientation, Alma, with her nurse's dexterity, reassembled her rifle twice as fast as anybody else, putting a damper on the macho crap.

A bemused Judge, smiling to himself at the memories, beckons a car through the intersection. Yeah, it was just like Moms would say, "The lord may not come when you call him, but he's always right on time." Yeah, the black community was starting to see things the Panthers' way. Yeah, black was beautiful, fast, classy, ass-kicking, and name-taking too. The pride of belonging surges through him like electricity.

TESTING, ONE-TWO-THREE . . . Witness #12. Name: Mr. and Mrs. Lefkowitz . . . Living room, cluttered . . . Ancient couple.

He seems to have palsy.

When they first came in, wearing those black berets and leather jackets we thought it was a . . . how do you call it, Poppa?
Shakedown . . . A shakedown.
Yes, a shakedown. I'm ashamed to say it now, but that's what we thought. You know we were in the freedom marchers . . .

YOU WERE FREEDOM MARCHERS, REALLY?

. . . Yes, we went down and even back then we weren't youngsters. It was our second trip south. Miami once, our honeymoon, 1927, before the crash. I talked it over with Poppa and . . . well, we decided we had to go. Albert would have wanted us to. That was what our boy, Albert, gave his life for on Normandy Beach. Freedom. We'd go walking along, singing to keep our courage up. Just imagine, singing allowing you to go on, holding injustice, fatigue, hunger, danger back with a song. The black people in the South taught us.

YOU SAID THE PANTHERS CAME INTO YOUR GROCERY STORE.

They wanted any old food for their breakfast program to feed children. Can you imagine? Children in America, the land of plenty, going to school hungry? What's this world coming to . . .

Middle of the day at Sather Gate, and the entrance to the Berkeley campus is teeming with students. Judge, who has a couple of free periods, is doing his afternoon stint for the cause. He hawks the Little Red Book with one hand and passes out Ten-Point Program leaflets with the other. Off in the distance, Jamal and another new Panther are doing the same thing.

James Brown is blasting away on a portable radio at Judge's feet, keeping him company. "Heeeah, oh yes . . . I'm black and I'm proud."

CLICK . . . Suddenly the music stops. Judge whirls around and finds himself staring into Brimmer's big, weatherbeaten face. The hat, the shirt and tie, the rumpled sports coat smell cop.

"You're Judge, right?" Brimmer says in a low voice, masking his mission with a grin. "Don't panic, brother, I just wanna talk to you—off the record."

Judge shakes his head. "I don't know you. And I got nothing to say to you on or off the record."

"Oh, yes you do, son." Brimmer flashes his badge. "It's up to you, either here or downtown . . . Speaking of records, seems you got in a little hot water a couple years back. Got yourself a little bit of a police record, you know."

"Joy-riding," Judge explains. "I didn't even know the car was stolen. Besides, one, I was a juvenile, so my record's supposed to be sealed and two, a deal was cut whereby I'd enlist instead of going to jail. So you can't use that against me."

Brimmer shakes a cigarette from a fresh pack and takes his time lighting it before he replies menacingly, "I can use whatever I want to. Who knows, maybe the court didn't have the right to offer you a deal? Maybe you still owe the state some penitentiary time. There's always something—or there could be. Maybe against your mother. Now that I think about it, didn't she assault a policeman at that vigil you folks held at that intersection? Of course, this is all conjecture. I'll tell you what . . . let's take a little walk."

Brimmer grabs Judge by the elbow and starts to steer him away. Judge takes a step, then slams on the brakes.

"Let's move it!" Brimmer snarls. "What the fuck's the matter with you? We got a problem?"

"No problem," Judge answers calmly. "I just forgot my radio. Mind if I get it, okay?"

"Yeah, sure," Brimmer says, going buddy-buddy again, suspecting that Judge has pulled his chain to trick him into overreacting. "Want me to help you carry something?"

"No thanks," Judge snaps. *Don't make it too easy for him. It might look suspicious.*

They stroll along until they reach a secluded garden. Brimmer proposes they give it a try. Judge puts his things on a bench, and they meander up and down the rows of petunias and tulips.

Brimmer resumes his pitch. "Look, let's do it the easy way. You help me out every now and then, and I'll make sure your slate stays clean. You don't know it, but these Panther guys are plotting to overthrow the government. The whole black self-defense thing is just a communist cover. I know you didn't realize that when you joined, but now that you're in with them, you could be very useful to your country." Brimmer puts his arm around Judge's shoulder. "Sure, America's got a few problems, but this is the land of opportunity—equal opportunity. My folks were immigrants, came over in steerage, dirt poor. They pulled themselves up by their boot straps."

Judge is astonished—Brimmer is really being sincere. "You

believe all that, don't you?"

Brimmer nods earnestly. "I wouldn't be a cop if I didn't. Without law and order you got chaos, right? Look, we don't expect something for nothing! College is expensive these days. I can help. Whatta you say?"

"I'm listening . . . "

"Do more than listen!" Brimmer warns, turning back into a bogey man. "Call me by Wednesday. At this number." He shoves a card into Judge's pocket and ambles off.

Not sure if he is being watched, Judge plays it casual. He returns to Sather Gate and resumes selling until his next class, and after the lecture he goes home. But bright and early the next morning Judge heads for the church basement where the Panthers run their breakfast program for school kids.

The room is filled with gobbling children loading up for the day. Haze rises from the steam table. Wearing a chef's hat, Huey patrols the aisles with plates of scrambled eggs. In the kitchen Alma is steadying a pot of oatmeal for Tyrone, who is ladling out the porridge.

Judge, trying his best to conceal his excitement, hurries down the steps and snakes his way over to Huey. "They tried to recruit me... like you figured," he whispers.

Tyrone glances over and frowns. He doesn't like Judge being so tight with Huey.

Huey notices Tyrone, and makes a joke to allay his suspicions. "Hungry, hunh, Brother Judge?" he says loudly. "You're a little old to be a schoolboy, aren't you?"

The cloud passes from Tyrone's face. He chuckles and relaxes.

"Cool it, man!" Huey whispers sharply. "You're probably not the only one they've recruited! Stall 'em a little while longer so they'll believe you're for real."

Glancing towards the kitchen, Huey notices that Tyrone is still watching them. He shoves a plate of eggs into Judge's hands and raises his voice again. "Eat up, my man!" While everyone is busy laughing, he murmurs quickly to Judge under his breath,

"Remember, make them trust you."

Then Huey yells across the room. "Hey, Tyrone! You figure feeding our children is gonna make the Man jumpy?"

Tyrone grins, proud to be singled out by Huey. He banters back putting on a Deep South dialect. "Well, black people sho is getting mighty uppity, feeding their children breakfast and shit, taking their destiny into their own hands. Lordy, lordy, what's this world coming to?"

"What's this world coming to?" Dorsett is seated behind his desk chomping on antacids and reading the riot act to Brimmer, who is standing at a very uneasy attention.

"Now we got the coons giving us a pain in the ass! They got guns, drill teams, a breakfast program. They've even got cars following our cars. We're supposed to be the police around here. This shit could be contagious. Are we gonna need the FBI in on this one too? You promised me they'd be history. That was weeks ago!"

"I've got them infiltrated, sir. We're gonna know every move they even think about making."

"Big deal!" Dorsett sneers. "I want more than moves. I want them out of business!"

"With all due respect, sir, that vigil thing got everybody riled up. But things are gonna simmer down. We'll have their asses soon. Just so long as our boys don't do anything stupid to stir them up."

"I hope for your sake you're right. I can keep a lid on our boys, but I can't vouch for every damn department in the Bay Area. Sooner or later some shit is gonna hit the fan. Everybody is getting pretty fed up with these uppity niggers . . . "

Nighttime. Richmond, California, April 1, 1967. Chased by two policemen with their guns drawn, a thin young black man, Denzil Dowell, limps across the suburban road and lunges into an alley. He is panting and out of breath and the officers are gaining fast.

"Hands up!" shouts one of the cops, drawing a bead on Denzil's back. "Halt or I'll shoot!"

Denzil stops and raises his hands.

"Higher! And turn around," the cop shouts. "You ain't going nowheres!"

Denzil does as he is ordered and the police close in.

"I wasn't going nowhere in the first place," Dowell says. "I live around here and I ain't done shit!"

"Ain't done shit, sir!" demands the other cop. "And nigger, don't you move a muscle!"

The cops advance on Denzil to teach him a little respect for white men. Instinctively, Dowell backs up. "I ain't done . . . "

BLAM BLAM BLAM BLAM . . . Denzil shudders and spins from the impact of the slugs. The policemen laugh as if he is only a tin can, and fire a couple more shots for good measure.

Denzil's mother's home is in mourning. The living room is well worn but tidy, with family photos, plastic flowers, and doilies everywhere you look. It is packed with family and friends. Even Reverend Slocum, Mrs. Dowell's old preacher from back in the neighborhood, has come. The shades are drawn against the sun, but even so a few rays manage to poke their way through the threadbare material, reflecting off the gleaming leather of Black Panther jackets.

Denzil's brother George goes down on one knee next to his mother's chair and introduces the old woman to her company. "Momma, these here are Panthers I asked over from Oakland."

Reverend Slocum, standing by the white plaster cast hands of Jesus praying on top of the Philco TV, looks up and comes straight over. "Sister Dowell, these young men are nothing but Godless hoodlums. I know all about you boys going around sticking your nose in white folks' stuff, stirring up trouble."

"You're acting like we killed him, Reverend," Tyrone answers.

The Reverend scowls at Tyrone, but Mama Dowell pats his hand to placate him. She turns her sorrowful face up to the Panthers and thanks them for coming to grieve with her and her family. Then she breaks down. "The police won't tell us nothing," she sobs.

An old neighbor in house slippers and salt-and-pepper wig

protests, "They been shooting black men down around here like niggers was going outta style."

Tears stream down Mama Dowell's face. "My boy didn't do nothing . . . he didn't do nothing." Her head begins to rock, and then she raises her eyes and pleads to heaven, "Lord, cain't nobody do something?"

Huey takes her frail hand in his. "We came to do something!"

Downtown Richmond. On Denzil's home turf, right up in the cops' face, just a couple of blocks from the Contra Costa County Sheriff's office, the Panthers are holding a rally to protest Denzil's murder.

There are plenty of new Panther faces. Some, like Alma and Jamal, Judge recognizes; a lot of others he doesn't really know. All of them are in their berets and black leather jackets and carrying guns, lining both sidewalks, from down at the liquor store at one end up to the beauty parlor at the other. The black community has accidentally on purpose created a traffic jam with their cars just in case the police try to come running in to break up the rally.

Huey and Bobby are up on top of a car. From this perch Bobby directs the Panthers shuttling back and forth distributing programs and leaflets to the crowd, while Huey's voice, amplified by a portable PA system, rings over the gathering.

"The police report says he was shot three times, but our investigation proves that Denzil Dowell was shot six times. And two of those shots were in his armpits! Brothers and sisters do you know what that means?" Huey raises his arms over his head for dramatic effect. "It means they murdered him! Denzil had his hands up!!"

"No more police brutality!" Bobby shouts, working the crowd. "What do we want?"

"Justice!" the Panthers respond in thunderous unison.

Raising a clenched fist, Bobby asks the question again. "What do we want?"

This time the crowd joins the Panthers. "JUSTICE!"

Emotions are running high, and the Panthers are running out of leaflets as the crowd grabs them up with enthusiasm. Bobby beckons

Judge over and tells him to hurry he's got more in his car.

Judge nods and hustles toward the Chevy. He grabs a pile of leaflets out of the back seat. As he straightens up and turns around, he comes nostril to nostril with Brimmer.

Brimmer holds up his badge, this time as a threat rather than a reminder. "Afternoon asshole," he says, wheeling Judge around and cuffing him. "You were supposed to call me a coupla weeks ago!"

Tyrone nudges Huey, and gestures towards Judge being led to Brimmer's car. "C'mon," Tyrone starts to take off. "We gotta give Judge a hand."

"No!" Huey grabs Tyrone and pulls him back. "Its just simple harassment. Can't let it stop us. We got a mission here, brother, we got momentum!"

Meanwhile, Bobby is still working the crowd. "What do we want?"

"JUSTICE!" they shout back as one, whipped into a frenzy.

Reverend Slocum steps forward, his hands raised in a plea for peace. "Amen! The Lord God Almighty be our witness," invokes the preacher. "Let us bow our heads and pray. Oh Savior, we ask only . . ."

The Panthers are in no mood for prayer. Bobby interrupts and raises his fist again. "Black Power!"

The crowd echoes it's rage in a single voice. "BLACK POWER!!!"

Bobby tells Huey he thinks it's time to head for the sheriff's office. The Panthers snap into precise military formation. With Huey and Bobby at the front of the Panthers, followed by the Dowell family and Reverend Slocum, then the crowd, the rally marches on the sheriff's office.

When they get there, a double line of policemen blocks the entrance to the building.

With the crowd screaming "Justice!" and "Black Power!" behind them, Bobby and Huey step up to the deputies.

A musclebound cop steps in front of Huey and puts a big hand in his chest. "You're not getting in here with no gun."

Huey shoves back, but keeps his cool. The crowd sends up a rousing cheer and the cops bristle.

Huey runs down the law to the deputy. "This firearm is being carried in plain view and is therefore perfectly legal according to California statute."

The belligerent deputy snorts his contempt for Huey and the statute. "Over my dead body."

CLACK! . . . Huey jerks a round into the rifle's chamber. A hush falls over the crowd. The police raise their weapons.

Huey is still cool as ice. "That's your call, pig."

The deputy holds his ground. "You ain't coming in here with those guns. That's it!"

Reverend Slocum and Mama Dowell push their way forward, and the Reverend puts his hand on Huey's arm then turns to face the deputy. "We come for justice, not bloodshed," he tells the deputy. "But don't be pushing us too far."

"Please, boys, no more violence," Mama Dowell pleads.

The tense faceoff continues for another moment, then in deference to Mrs. Dowell's wishes Huey and Bobby raise their guns over their heads for the crowd to witness and pass their weapons to the police. Unarmed, they lead the way into the building.

In the office of Captain Pillsbury, the sheriff in charge, the two sides face off again. Pillsbury, flanked by scowling deputies, is seated behind his desk, arms crossed smugly over his belly. Bobby, Huey, the Dowell family, and Reverend Slocum standing across the table from him are the pain-in-the-ass enemy.

Bobby is presenting their grievances. "How can you claim he bled to death? Your own coroner's report says he was shot to death. We demand a grand jury investigation into the death of Denzil Dowell and the pattern of brutality against the black citizens of Richmond."

Pillsbury is more annoyed than ruffled. "The police department has conducted its own investigation and concluded that no misconduct occurred," is his icy rebuttal. "As for a 'pattern of brutality,' the charge is ridiculous."

"Then what do you call four dead black men in six months?!" Huey demands.

The sheriff has an answer ready. "I call it the police doing their duty under the law. You got a problem with the law . . . take it to the legislature!"

Twin light bulbs click on over Huey's and Bobby's heads. They lock eyes and nod.

"You know," Bobby nods, "the pig might just have a point."

The sheriff stands up and points to the door. "Now get the hell out of my office!"

Brimmer's unmarked car sits in front of the peeling doors of a deserted warehouse that began life as a garage in a rundown industrial section of Oakland.

Judge, handcuffed to a chair in the middle of the vast space, looks like he's been through the wringer. Brimmer, smoking vehemently, hovers over him. All around them are rusting machinery, shelving, barrels—the remains of a previous, abandoned life.

"So," says Brimmer, giving Judge a poke with a stubby finger, "we understand each other now, right, Judge?"

"Yeah," Judge grunts sullenly, the taste of blood still in his mouth.

Brimmer uncuffs Judge from the chair. "All right then, you can go now."

Judge wobbles to his feet, acting more shaky than he really is.

"I expect to hear from you soon," Brimmer warns him. "If Huey Newton takes a crap, I want to know how big it was. You got that! Otherwise, I'm gonna come looking for you. And believe me, I won't be as 'friendly' as I was today."

Judge turns to go. "Anything else?"

"Yeah," Brimmer stops him. "Now that you mention it, here's a bit of advice. The Panthers are gonna lose. As soon as the legislature up in Sacramento passes that anti-gun bill, the Mulford Act, you won't be able to walk around carrying them guns and rifles—shotguns either. The question is, Judge, are you gonna lose alongside them—

your future, your mother... Think about it."

Brimmer takes a long drag off his cigarette as he watches Judge limp out. Then he turns towards the other end of the room and nods. Nodding back, Agent Rodgers steps from the shadows.

TESTING, ONE-TWO-THREE . . . Witness #13. Name: Malik Ashanti . . . Vendor.

> Judge? Yeah, I remember him all right! But he never was nobody important. Let's see, as things got really rolling, you had a whole lot of people springing up all over the country. In Chicago, for example, you had Fred Hampton. The police gunned him down in his sleep. Down in L.A., you had Elaine Brown. She eventually was transferred up here. In fact, she ran the Party for a while. I know you white people like to think you invented everything, including women's lib, but you didn't . . .

ACTUALLY, I'D LIKE TO GO BACK TO THIS GUY JUDGE . . . HIS NAME HAS COME UP A COUPLE OF TIMES, BUT NO ONE CAN TELL ME MUCH ABOUT HIM.

> Well, he was just one of the guys around. Always getting in hot water. But as far as I can tell you,he was just sort of a fuck up. Most of the guys, I'd say ninety percent that tried to join, couldn't make it. But still, some kooks would slip through, like this Judge character. Anyhow, our paths kept crossing. I joined the same day he did, and later I was one of the guys assigned to waste him.

KILL HIM!?

> Yeah, one night. But that order was countermanded. We was highly disciplined, so, of course, if your superior's superior changed orders you followed that.

WOULD YOU HAVE . . . I MEAN, KILLED HIM?

Well, it never happened as far as I know. But like I said, we were highly disciplined.

Defermery Park, the major oasis in the Oakland ghetto, is hosting a Panther party, one of their famous barbecue-awareness rallies. It's a beautiful afternoon. Between orators, the band onstage blasts one black hit after another. Amongst the throng are many soon-to-be-famous faces—Angela Davis, Eldridge and Kathleen Cleaver, Elaine Brown, and Stokely Carmichael. Everybody is drinking, mingling, dancing, and getting down.

As the group finishes a tune, the co-founders climb the ladder up to the bandstand. Huey walks to the mike. "Good afternoon. We hope you are enjoying yourself," he greets the picnickers, and launches into a passionate speech. "There is a little business I would like to bring to your attention. It's about the pigs. The pig knows we're organized to protect ourselves. So now the white establishment tries to change the law, tries to make it illegal for us to arm ourselves. We do not intend to be unarmed targets! Now that we refuse to let them get away with the brutality they have been perpetrating on us for centuries, they have come up with this Mulford Act. Now they are trying to make it illegal for us to carry guns to protect ourselves."

Bobby takes the mike. "Well we gonna get on them about that. This is our community and it is a beautiful thing. Now everybody out there, grab some food and have a good time. All I ask is that you save a little for me."

"Let's hear it!" Bobby says, raising a clenched fist. "Power to the people!"

"POWER TO THE PEOPLE!" the crowd shouts.

Huey and Bobby climb down from the stage and the pulsing music kicks in again.

At a picnic table a little off to the side, the Panther cadre is holding a meeting. Bobby has got his plate piled up and his feet firmly under the table going to town on potato salad, cole slaw, Wonderbread, and barbecue. Huey is still loading up at the buffet table.

Tyrone is fussing. "They've been using that 'police guidelines' bullshit as a loophole to abuse black people since dirt was invented. How about Denzil Dowell?"

"They're gonna try and lie their way out of it," Little-Bobby predicts.

Bobby takes a break from his chewing. "They can't!" he assures them. "Not with the statistics we're going to lay on them!"

Huey approaches with his plate. Everybody falls silent, but Huey doesn't seem to notice. He sits down and starts to eat. Bobby deserts his food and starts to pace nervously.

Finally the silence is broken by Winnie, the officer of the day, beginning her briefing. "David Buckley's working a double shift today so he can go tomorrow. Luther Parnell won't be able to leave before 9:30 in the morning," she reports.

"Nine-thirty!" Tyrone snorts. "How come? The revolution don't wait for no one!"

"That's when he gets off from work," Winnie explains. "In all, we've got twenty-nine Panthers going."

"How about the media?" Huey asks.

"TV, papers, they've all been alerted," Winnie reports. "Plus we're carrying that reporter from *Ramparts*, Cleaver . . . the tall, darker brother . . ." She scans the crowd, picks him out, points. "Over there . . . the one that interviewed Betty Shabazz. That'll make thirty."

Bobby Seale, hands clinched behind his back, keeps pacing in front of the table.

Between mouthfuls, Huey proclaims that their trip up to the legislature is going to be a colossal event . . . "We're gonna turn that capitol out!" he promises.

Judge wanders towards the table.

Tyrone blocks the way. "Staff meeting, brother."

Huey signals that it's okay to let Judge approach. Tyrone is surprised and a little annoyed. As Judge goes to pass him, Tyrone pulls him aside. "So what was the deal with you at the Dowell rally, brother?" There is a tinge of jealousy in his voice. "I saw that pig rousting you. You okay?"

Judge has his alibi ready. "Aw, he was just harassing my ass. My driver's license expired."

"Those pigs are grabbing at straws," Huey interjects, then goes back to the details of the Sacramento trip. "If we leave by 9:30, we'll be okay. The Legislature is less than two hours drive. We'll make that before noon."

Bobby is still pacing, and Huey looks up, perturbed and annoyed. "Will you cool it, Bobby! What's up? I've never seen you like this. What it be, my man?"

"What it be, Huey," Bobby blurts, getting it off his chest, "is you ain't going with us! That's what it be!"

Huey leaps to his feet, exploding. "What the fuck are you talking about, Bobby? We're the leadership, you and me. There aren't enough of us as it is!"

"That's just it," Bobby counters. "Look, the pigs don't know how many Panthers there are! But if both of us show up, they might start putting two and two together. We ain't even two hundred strong yet, but we got 'em guessing thousands!"

"Yeah, you got a point," Huey concedes. "I'll tell you what. I'll go! You stay!"

Bobby shakes his head and puts his hand on Huey's arm. "Sorry, brother, you're too valuable. We can't risk you." Giving Huey a hug, Bobby tells him, "We took a vote. It's decided, you stay!" Throwing his arm around Huey's shoulder, Bobby turns him around to face their lieutenants.

All the Panther staff nod. "Yeah . . . He's right! . . . That's how it is . . . "

A painful moment later, and the logic of Bobby's argument seeps in. "Okay," Huey relents. "Makes sense. I don't like it, but it makes sense."

Bobby teases him, "You just stay home and mow your momma's lawn like a nice boy"—an old running joke between the two. "We'll handle them state senators. Come on everybody, enough of this executive shit. Let's take a breather."

"You got that right," Huey says.

As the group breaks up, Huey turns to Judge, who has been trying to catch his eye. "Come on, Judge, let's get a brew . . . I'll treat!"

Tyrone watches Huey lead Judge away. He frowns to himself. Something doesn't quite jive. Thinking dark thoughts, he goes in search of Alma. He finds her at the foot of the bandstand, grooving on the music and looking great in a blouse with a drawstring top and bell-bottom jeans. She gives him a welcoming smile. "Meeting over?"

"A little pause," Tyrone answers. He takes a deep breath and hurries on with it. "Look I need a favor . . . a big one," he says, nodding towards Judge and Huey walking apart from everyone else. "Judge. I got a funny feeling about him."

"Judge? He seems okay. Why don't you ask Cy? He's his roommate."

"It ain't the same, besides he's his best friend. I wantcha to get close to him, you know . . . check him out."

"And just how do I do that?"

"Uh . . . I don't know," Tyrone mumbles, dropping his eyes. "I mean he doesn't seem to have a special girlfriend or anything."

Alma, her back up, glares daggers at Tyrone, and then looks away until she gets herself under control. Finally she turns back. "Yes sir, I guess I get your drift."

Out of earshot, Huey and Judge stroll along rapping.

Elated and all charged up, Huey is talking even faster than usual. "Okay, it's time to go along with that cop," he instructs Judge. "Okay—You agree to spy for the pig. But be careful! They have the technology, the money, and probably a network of informers too. But we got you, Judge. You're our secret weapon!"

"The water's getting deep, Huey."

"It's going to get deeper," Huey warns. "Let me guess. He wants you to keep in touch with him and tell him what we're doing."

Judge nods solemnly. "Yeah."

"And that's exactly what you're gonna do. Except I'll be telling you what to feed him." Huey studies Judge's face. "You all right with this?"

"Yeah . . . I guess. Hey, Huey, any of the other Panthers know about this?"

Huey doesn't answer.

"Yeah," Judge says reading his silence, "this shit is getting pretty thick."

Huey doesn't debate the point. "You got that right, brother! And I got a feeling it's going to get a whole lot thicker."

The doorbell to Tyrone's tiny apartment rings as if it's stuck. Tyrone comes out of the bedroom in pajamas cussing the intrusion on his sleep.

He stubs his toe on the sofa. "Shit! . . . I'm coming!"

He crosses the darkened front room and opens the door cautiously. Alma is standing there, still in her picnic clothes.

"Alma! . . . uh, what's up?" Tyrone's eyes blink in surprise.

Alma gives him a sarcastic little salute. "I came to report."

Tyrone can see she is pissed off. "Yeah sure . . . come on in."

"I searched Judge's place," she begins, very official. "Outside of an old GI footlocker and Cy's stuff, all I saw were engineering textbooks. He seemed pretty normal to me. He's nice."

"Nice?" Tyrone's face burns. "You say you searched his place? He just let you do that, just let you go through his shit?"

"He was in the shower," Alma replies flatly.

"In the shower?"

Alma nods. "I was a little worried about Cy coming in and catching me, so I split before he came out."

Tyrone looks at the floor, feeling awkward as hell. "When you . . . no, I mean when, when did he take this shower? I mean was it before . . . uh, or after . . . I mean . . . uh, you okay?"

"What do you give a shit!" Alma retaliates angrily. "You said it was important. Anyway, that's my report."

"Alma!" Tyrone catches her arm as she starts to leave. "Look, when I asked you to do what you did, it wasn't about not caring. I care, I just didn't know where to turn. There's this clock ticking against black folks. I can hear it in my head. I thought you heard it too."

Alma, her anger gone, nods. "I do, Tyrone. I hear the same clock ticking."

TESTING, ONE-TWO-THREE . . . Witness #14. Name: Dr. Martin Singh . . . Professor's office . . . Pipe, gray goatee.

> I must caution you to please do not try to put words into my mouth. No, Judge did not exactly do what you would call "disappear." All I can tell you is, he did not finish his studies, I mean at least at this institution he did not. I still cannot fathom exactly what your point is. Judge was a serious student, definitely bright. I have never had any reason, then or now, to believe he was mixed up in anything other than his studies. But I do remember him clearly, because of the shrapnel in his body. Something to do with the war. The more delicate electronics equipment would act up if he stood too close.

TESTING, ONE-TWO-THREE . . . Witness #15. Name: Sarah Woodward . . . Federal prison, visitor's room . . . White, middle-age . . . Prison dress, no makeup, glasses.

> Judge? Yes, I knew him, back when we were teenagers. We even had a puppy love thing going. I was a year or so older. I used to tease my dad I was going to marry him when he grew up. He volunteered for the Marines, and I never saw him after that. Nevertheless, since you are here and since he was a black male brighter and more ambitious than this country felt he should be, I bet I can guess what happened to him. Lacking any relevant political ori-

entation, he was duped like so many other black men into believing he could gain acceptance and avoid the stigma of racism by serving as a mercenary for the mother country. Mother country—by that I mean the dominant culture. You see, the United States is actually two nations within the same boundaries. The white one, "the mother country" and the black one, "the colony." Black and white Americans do not really live in the same country. Any ghetto exploited and brutalized under the capitalist's heel is a colony. Realizing that, everything else falls into place. Anyway, since you are here, somewhere along the way Judge must have seen the light.

The governor of California, Ronald Reagan, is standing on the lawn of the state capitol speaking to a group of teenage sightseers, a Future Leaders of America club. Suddenly, the Panthers pull up in their vehicles. They climb out, wearing their berets and black leather jackets and carrying guns.

Chaos erupts. Reagan's bodyguards whisk him away as the Panthers march towards the Capitol.

The reporters, noticing the commotion, go into a feeding frenzy around the Panthers. Backpedaling as he goes, one reporter shoves a microphone in Bobby's face.

"Is this a militant action?" the journalist asks hopefully, nodding in the affirmative at his own question. "Are the Panthers storming the capitol?"

"No! Definitely not!" Bobby replies, shouting directly into the camera. "We are here to send a message. The Black Panther Party for Self Defense calls upon the American people in general and black people in particular to take careful note of the racist California legislature now considering the Mulford Act which is aimed at keeping black people disarmed and powerless while racist police agencies throughout the country intensify the terror, brutality, murder, and repression of black people. Now I have a question for you."

"Uh . . . ," the reporter is startled, "yeah, sure."

"Which way is it to the State Assembly?"

"Uh . . . it's right up there," the reporter answers, still flustered, "on the second floor, sir."

"All right, my good man. Thank you. All power to the people."

The Panthers sweep past the newsman, march up the capitol steps and into the building. The journalists scramble to catch up. It's hard to tell whether there's more Panthers or reporters. As the Panthers march down the hallway, they are surrounded by the press, snapping, filming, and shouting questions.

The Panthers have some questions of their own. ". . . Damn, this sure is a big place . . . Which way did they say the visitor's gallery was? . . . Up there, I think . . . You think!"

Despite all, the Panthers press on, with Bobby Seale in the lead, Tyrone and Little-Bobby right behind him, and Alma and Judge and the rest hot on their heels. Up a grandiose spiral staircase they climb to the second floor, then down a long corridor lined with huge doors. A massive set of double doors has a guard in front of it.

Disoriented, with a circus of journalists and Panthers swirling about, Bobby Seale heads for the guard to get directions.

At the sight of the Panthers bearing down on him, the guard panics. "No! No! This is the Assembly!" he stammers. "You can't come in here!"

"What the hell you mean we can't go in there!" Bobby demands. "We have a right to observe the Assembly in action. You gonna deny us our Constitutional right?"

"You got the wrong door," the guard explains. "You want the visitor's gallery. This is the Assembly floor—it's closed to the public." The guard turns to point the correct door. "You have to go to . . . "

Bobby twists to follow the guard's finger . . . the reporters swing around in the new direction and a crewman smashes into the guard. They both go clattering to the marble floor. The entire entourage panics and goes stumbling backward, smashing the huge doors open and spilling onto the Assembly floor.

From the bottom of the pile, Little-Bobby looks up. He sees arms, legs, camera equipment all over, and tourists gaping down from the visitor's gallery. Swiveling, he sees over at the podium the speaker pro tem, Carlos Bee, standing with gavel in mid-air, mouth hanging open. Security guards materialize . . . they charge forward . . .

The media screams bloody murder. *ARMED INVASION OF LEGISLATURE—ANTI-WHITE PANTHERS STORM ASSEMBLY* shout the newspaper headlines. /"Twenty-nine armed Black Panthers bent on mayhem stormed the state legislature today. Bobby Seale, their leader, declared the Mulford act racist". . . "Governor Reagan declared that such acts of lawlessness will not be tolerated," the radio declares . . . / "According to eyewitnesses the Panthers apparently made a wrong turn and went through the door leading to the legislature floor, mistaking it for the visitor's gallery" a TV announcer reports . . . *TRIAL SET IN MASS ARREST* . . .

TESTING, ONE-TWO-THREE . . . Witness #16. Name: Herman L. Wambaugh . . . Athletic, broad back, brush cut . . . Golf clothes . . . Mahogany bar.

SENATOR, YOU WERE ONE OF THE SPONSORS OF THE MULFORD ACT. IN RETROSPECT, HOW DO YOU FEEL ABOUT THAT?

How did you get in here? This is a private club. Is this some political trick?

NO, SIR. I AM A STUDENT. MY MOTHER'S BROTHER IS A MEMBER.

A student, hunh . . . What's this—some kinda term paper?

NO, SIR. IT IS PART OF MY DOCTORAL DISSERTATION. NATURALLY, SOMEONE OF YOUR STATURE WOULD ADD SIGNIFICANTLY TO MY DATA. SHALL I REPEAT THE QUESTION?

That won't be necessary. The gun laws of the state of California were designed for the convenience of upstanding citizens, not as a loophole for black hooligans. Throughout history in America a gun has served only one of two functions—a little friendly hunting, or to keep law and order. It was a very painful episode for all of us. I am a gun enthusiast myself, but I could not do otherwise than support Mulford.

The day of the hearing, the courtroom is packed with Panthers and press, supporters and detractors. Bobby is on the stand.

The prosecuting attorney is coming on like Perry Mason. "You claim the purpose of your visit was to register the grievance of black people with this . . . uh . . . Executive Mandate from Huey P. Newton, the Minister of Defense of your Panther Party."

"Yes," Bobby answers. "The bringing of a complaint to the governing body is in a long democratic tradition," he starts into his spiel. "Executive Mandate Number One of the Black Panther Party for Self Defense calls upon the American people in general and the black people in particular . . . "

"That won't be necessary," the prosecutor interrupts. "Tell the court, Mr. Seale, are you proud to be the co-founder of the Panthers, an anti-white movement?"

"The Black Panther Party is not anti-white," Bobby corrects him. "You cannot fight racism with racism. We do not hate a person because of his skin color. But we do hate the daily oppression our people are subjected to and have been subjected to for four hundred years."

"Right on, man!" a voice cries out from the gallery. "Tell it like it is!"

Furious, the judge bangs down his gavel. "I must warn you, Mr. Seale—keep your members in check, or I shall hold you and the Panther Party in contempt of court!"

"Begging the court's pardon, that was me." A hippie rises to his feet at the back of the room. "As you can see I'm white, so I couldn't be no Black Panther, but I still recognize the truth when I hear it."

The courtroom goes berserk . . . cheering, booing. The judge pounds his gavel and orders both sides into his chambers.

Bobby, Huey, and their attorneys rise and file into the chambers behind the judge. As soon as everyone is seated, the lawyers go at it tooth and nail. The defense attorney says his my clients broke no law, the guns were not illegal. The prosecuting attorney counters that they will be as soon as the Mulford Act passes. Defense points out that there has been no crime and his clients cannot be prosecuted retroactively, and moves for dismissal.

Prosecution is adamant. "Dismissal! No way . . . There's been too much publicity. The government would look foolish."

The judge's face turns red. "Cameras all around, newsmen camped on the lawn. I'll not have my court turned into a circus!"

Finally, to save face, the prosecuting attorney tenders a deal—three months for everyone with time off for good behavior.

"No!" Huey steps in. "That would mean any Panther already on parole or probation could be charged with a violation and sent back to jail on a previous charge."

The prosecution offers to drop everything against any Panther who has a previous record, and charge the rest with disturbing the peace. Okay, the defense says, he's got a deal.

But the prosecutor raises his hand. "Not so fast—I'm not through yet. It's a deal only if . . . " he points his finger across the table at Bobby Seale, "he agrees to do six months."

The defense is outraged. "You're asking that my client do jail time for what was a simple mistake!"

"Take it or leave it, that's my last offer."

Huey twists in his chair to face Bobby. "You got six months to donate to the Party, brother?"

"You know it, brother," Bobby nods.

FBI Headquarters, Washington, D.C. The familiar no-neck silhouette of Hoover is at the head of the conference table, inspecting his thumbs. Five or six upper echelon staff members sit in servile attendance as the big boss's handsome young assistant briefs them.

"Next . . . the Black Panther Party for Self Defense. They claim to be the voice of the black community. However, analysis of our field report reveals a high level of organizational skill, with . . ."

Hoover sighs, exasperated, and finally looks up. "We've been down this road before, haven't we, gentlemen? What we have here is a classic example of outside agitation. This is obviously an organization funded and masterminded by some communist country hostile to the U.S.! The question is, which one? Who's giving them their marching orders? I want answers. Before we crush these ungrateful coons, find out who their real boss is!"

"That's all gentlemen," Hoover announces, ending the meeting. The staff files out without a word.

Hoover turns to his assistant. "Contact Oakland. Those black bastards could be up to anything."

MEMO/COINTELPRO: TOP SECRET

BLACK PANTHER PARTY ACTIVITIES UNACCEPTABLE. INTENSIFY SURVEILLANCE. IDENTIFICATION ACTUAL LEADERSHIP REQUIRED.

WASHINGTON

■ ■ ■

Huey sits across a coffee table from three Africans in an expensive hotel suite. Two of the nationals wear native robes; the third is in a business suit. The curtains are drawn, and they huddle forward, speaking in conspiratorial tones.

"You have a truly inspired idea," one of the diplomats says. "We are well aware of the many indignities suffered by people of color in America. We, however, are also painfully aware of our enemies' methods."

"Let us think historically, my brother," the African in the business suit counsels. "What will be your government's reaction if you ask the UN to declare that black people in America are political prisoners?" He pauses, then answers his own question in an eloquently sarcastic tone. "'Outrageous,' they will say. 'The United States is all one big happy melting pot of a family!' And they will trot out Uncle Thomases to substantiate their claims."

The first African waves his hand in a gesture of dismissal. "They will claim the Panthers are nothing but a tiny lunatic fringe."

"Your organization is small, my friend," the third diplomat reminds Huey. "Incidentally, how many members do you have?"

Huey does not drop his guard. "Sorry. Brother Malcolm teaches us that, 'Them that tell, don't know. And them that know, don't tell.'"

The diplomats all smile indulgently.

"Yes, of course," the third African agrees. "In my country we also have a saying—'A pebble can easily be brushed under the rug.'"

Huey nods. "Fair enough . . . but how about if the pebble grows into a rock and the rock spreads into a mountain? You can't brush a mountain under a rug."

The diplomats nod and smile and there are handshakes all around.

THUD THUD THUD . . . The early evening air of the ghetto resounds with the heavy stomp of the boots of Junior Panthers carrying broomsticks as they march around a vacant lot. Parents watch proudly while Cy puts the drill team through its paces. Off to the side, Alma and some neighborhood volunteers are converting a corner of the lot into a playground.

Tyrone pulls up with a car full. He yells out the window to Alma, "I'm showing these out-of-town comrades the patrolling procedures. You wanta come along?"

"Go ahead, girl," one of the volunteers urges her. "We 'bout finished for tonight anyhow."

Alma gets in the car and they pull away.

Cy dismisses his troops just as Judge comes sauntering down the sidewalk.

"You got 'em looking good, brother," Judge compliments his friend. "You'd have made a great drill sergeant, did you know that?"

"Thanks," Cy grins. "What's up?"

Judge says what does he mean, What's up? He was the one ask him to stop by.

Cy starts off with about how yeah he guess he's right and about how they kept missing each other, when he gets home Judge is asleep or studying, then finally he comes out with it. "I've been stopping off at this rib joint and there's this stone-fox waitress who always serves me. I kinda go for her. I could use a little help meeting her."

Judge is a little surprised. "I've never known you to be shy, brother," he teases. "If she serves you, you already know her. You don't need me."

"Gimme a break, willya," Cy blushes. "You owe me. I wanta make a big impression. I've helped you out a coupla times. You remember the telephone operator you liked that time? And how about that snooty art student with them gorgeous . . ."

"You mean doing 'The Hero'?"

Cy says, "Damn right! I think I'm in love."

And Judge says, "In that case, come on, let's work on your problem!"

Late that night, Cy sits at the counter of a diner nursing a plate of fries and watching his dream girl, a pretty young waitress named Gracie.

Gracie takes off her apron, slips on a light jacket, and heads for the door. The cook and the dishwasher yell, "Night, Gracie!" and she waves back.

Cy eases off his stool. "I'll walk you to your car," he offers.

"Thanks, I'll be okay." Gracie gives Cy a pleasant smile and a pat on the hand as she exits. "Finish your fries."

Gracie heads for her seen-better-days-ragtop parked in the alley behind the diner. As she reaches to unlock the door, Judge steps out of the shadows, one hand rammed in his pocket mugger-style.

Affecting a menacing growl, Judge orders, "Hey, lady! Gimme your purse!"

Cy appears a la the Lone Ranger. "You lose something, punk?"

Judge swings at Cy. Cy ducks and counterpunches with a jab that decks Judge. Judge gets up and comes back for more. After a brief scuffle, which Cy naturally wins, Judge runs off. Cy turns to Gracie, the damsel he has "rescued." She is obviously impressed by his chivalry.

She gives her hero a dazzling smile. "Thanks."

"My pleasure," Cy says, and gently takes the keys out of her hand. "I'll drive."

Gracie blushes. "Okay," she answers demurely.

When they pull off, Judge comes out of hiding and dusts himself off. He smiles, shakes his head, and watches the car disappear into the night.

On the the other side of the continent it is morning, and an FBI operative named Collins is shaking his head in the crisp dawn to Agent Rodgers, descending the steps of an Air Force transport.

Collins crosses the tarmac to greet him, apologizing. "I'm afraid I got you here on a wild goose chase."

On the way to the safe house, Collins explains that he is convinced they are barking up the wrong tree. Rodgers counters with does he know how much time it means has been wasted. Collins says he can't help that, that he debriefed the Russkie himself, but that Rodgers is welcome to question him himself if that will make him feel better.

After a brief drive, Collins and Rodgers pull into a safe house in the country. The gardener/sentry closes the iron gate behind them.

Rodgers follows Collins down into the basement of the safe house. A balding man, Dmitri Brezkin, the Russian defector, his napkin tucked into his collar, is sitting at a table eating a copious lunch.

"Do we have a Russian translator?" Rodgers asks.

Overhearing, Dmitri looks up and smiles. "That will not be necessary. I assure you, my English is A-OK," he says proudly, dabbing the corners of his mouth with his napkin.

Rodgers, his usual brusque self, gets right to the point. "The Black Panthers . . . What do you know about them, Dmitri?"

"Nothing," Dmitri shakes his head. "As I have told your colleague—Moscow has no involvement."

Rodgers presses on. "Is it possible that some other section of your intelligence organization would have received the assignment?"

"Completely impossible!" Dmitri snorts. "Even so I would have known. Your black chaps must be homegrown. I knew everything! I made it my business to know!"

Later that day, in the foyer of the safe house as Rodgers is putting on his topcoat, Collins apologizes again. "Like I said, I'm sorry I've dragged you across the country on some . . . "

Rodgers cuts him off. "That guy's lying! Defector, my foot! He's a Russian plant!"

Collins frowns. "Everything else he's said has checked out. As far as the foreign boys are concerned, he's legit. They had him for six weeks before they let us have a go at him."

"What the hell do they know," Rodgers spits, unable to surmount his anger. "Damnit, then, who's behind it! Somebody has got to be masterminding these goddamn niggers. They're so organized their crap's starting to spread all over the West Coast."

"All over the country, you mean. Maybe its a 'what' instead of a 'who,'" Collins suggests. "Mass paranoia, collective resentment, or something like that."

Rodgers is taken aback by the idea. "Resentment?" he echoes. "Bullshit! Resentment about what? The coloreds are making enormous strides, for Godsake. But maybe you're right. Maybe it isn't the Russians."

"Yeah, like the Russkie said, probably homegrown, your basic American ingenuity. Hell, they've been here long enough to have learned something."

"Crap! They couldn't organize without help. It must be the Chinese! I always figured it to be the fucking Chinese."

Early morning, Fifty-Fifth and Market, and it's Judge's turn to direct traffic again. Brimmer pulls up and slams on the brakes in the middle of the intersection.

"Get in, son," he barks, reaching back and opening the rear door. "We're going for a ride."

Judge does as he is ordered without comment. Once inside he settles back and waits. They drive in silence until they reach the Bay Bridge.

"Where the hell we going, Brimmer?" Judge finally asks.

"Nowhere," Brimmer answers, lighting a cigarette. "You want one?"

"I don't smoke. What's up?"

"What's up, hunh? Well, you been a little lax in your reporting in to me, Judge. And come to think of it, you never really explained why didn't you tell us about that little storming the capitol party you boys were planning up at Sacramento."

"Yes I did you musta forgot." Judge tries using the offhand approach. "It was, you know, spontaneous."

"Spontaneous my ass!! You boys let the newspaper and television reporters know what you was up to!" Brimmer's voice is trembling with rage. "Let me remind you, wiseass, that you're working for us."

"Yeah, yeah, whatever you say, Inspector Brimmer," Judge replies with an edge.

"Are you fucking sassing me?" Brimmer snarls. "You smartass piece of shit!"

Brimmer takes his portable rotating light and slaps it up on the roof of the car. Twisting the wheel, he jumps three lanes to the rail of the bridge and screeches to a stop. Playing angry cop to the hilt, he jumps out and snatches the rear door open.

"Get out here!"

"Whatta you mean? There ain't nothing 'here,' man," Judge protests. "We're on the Bay Bridge, halfway betwen Oakland and San Francisco. What's with you?"

"Get out of the fucking car!" Brimmer shouts, jerking the handcuffs from the back of his belt.

Slowly, Judge climbs out and offers no resistance as Brimmer cuffs his hands behind his back.

Brimmer is a man possessed. "'Yeah, whatever you say, Inspector Brimmer.' Fuckin'-A right pal, whatever I say. Time you got your wiry head on straight."

Brimmer pushes Judge hard against the railing. He keeps pushing, tilting Judge backward over the railing. Judge tries to keep a grip with his heels, but Brimmer lifts him up and tilts his body downward. Judge's beret comes off. It falls forever towards the blue wall of the bay water, growing smaller and smaller.

"Man, are you crazy?" Judge screams.

"Do you know how easy it would be for you to just disappear?" Brimmer yells above the whizzing traffic. "I could do it right now if I wanted to. What do these cars see, hunh? . . . a white policeman struggling with some handcuffed black guy. Do you fucking understand? Shit, you wouldn't even wash up for weeks."

"Yeah, shit, okay . . . okay, I get your drift. What do you want me to do?"

"That's better." Brimmer pulls Judge back from the brink, but keeps him on the railing. "I want you to move your ass outta neutral! I want a bunch of Panthers served up on a fucking plate!"

"What? A set-up?" Judge is incredulous.

"That's right!" Brimmer starts bending Judge back over the rail to make his point clear. "I want something serious on them, and I want it pronto."

"But . . . but . . . they don't operate that way," Judge protests.

"Fuck how they operate," Brimmer presses. "Just do it—or we

gonna be fishing you outta the bay. Well, you figure out something. I want action. Like your brothers say, 'by any means necessary.'"

"All right—all right . . . Just don't dump me, okay?" Judge pleads. "Back off. I'll do what you need."

"You sure as hell will," says Brimmer, dragging Judge off the railing. He uncuffs him and smiles. "All right then . . . that's better. No hard feelings, hunh? Don't forget, it's your country too."

Brimmer straightens Judge's shirt and stuffs an envelope in the pocket. "Here's a little help on your tuition. Remember—Huey shits one little turd I wanta know. Now come on, son, get back in the car. You got work to do."

20

Morning . . . A class is in session. Little-Bobby and a white teacher stand in front of a roomful of fifth-graders. Little-Bobby asks can anyone tell him what being a Black Panther means. A black boy raises his hand.

"Being a Panther means you get to carry a gun and shoot white people," he answers proudly.

The teacher flinches, and Little-Bobby quickly starts to explain. "The purpose of a gun is not to go around shooting white people."

The little boy tries again. "Shoot other black folks?"

The teacher pulls Little-Bobby aside. "See?" she says in an accusatory tone. "See the poison you're spreading? Guns, guns, guns—that's all they talk about . . . that and shooting each other."

"Beg pardon, ma'am, but Huey's not gonna let no poison like that spread," Little-Bobby assures her. He turns back to the class. "Huey's our Minister of Defense and he teaches us that a gun is not to be taken lightly. It is a tool of self defense."

Noon . . . Tynan takes Dorsett to lunch at an upscale restaurant. Though they are alone in a corner booth, Dorsett still leans forward each time he speaks. "Listen, Tynan," he confides in a conspiratorial tone, "put yourself in my place. There's only so much looking the other way I can get away with. Besides, I gotta draw the line somewheres."

"Look, a little fatter envelope at the end of the month adds up. Who's hurt? I swear, no business with the hard stuff in the white neighborhoods. We'll keep it just with the colored."

Dorsett is still worried. "And when the poison spreads to the rest of the population? What then?"

"What's all this poison-spreading bullshit?" Tynan takes a leisurely, self-assured puff on his cigarette. "Relax, friend, it'll never spread. We wouldn't let that happen."

Afternoon... Tyrone and Cy are strutting down the street in their Panther uniforms.

"So Judge is a busy man, hunh?" Tyrone asks.

"Yeah," Cy agrees. "Between the university and the Panthers, he's been running himself raw."

Tyrone rubs his crotch. "I gotta take a piss!"

"You can use me and Judge's place. We live just around the corner."

Tyrone and Cy turn the corner and run right into the middle of a drug deal. Vanilla and two of her band members are buying dope from Sabu. Spotting Cy, Sabu takes off down the street.

"Go on up to the pad and take your piss," Cy says, tossing Tyrone the keys. "I'll handle this punk. I been kicking his narrow ass since high school."

Tyrone catches the keys.

"If Judge is still asleep," Cy yells, "tell him to get his ass outta bed... meet you guys at the meeting."

As Cy turns to take off after Sabu, the outraged Vanilla blocks his path. "You fucked up my connection!" she yells. "Ohh, I get it—this must be your turf. Okay, we got money. Whatcha got to sell?"

Cy just sighs and shoves her aside. "Beat it, bitch. Can't you see I'm a Panther? Every black man you lay eyes on ain't a dope dealer."

"You fucking Panthers are some square, whitebread brothers! Phony motherfuckers!" Vanilla rages after him. "Shit, you don't even act black!... "

Cy sprints after Sabu, not giving Vanilla's junkie opinion a second thought.

As soon as Tyrone unlocks the door to the apartment, he can hear the water running in the shower. He's about to yell a greeting, but he spots Judge's trousers hanging over a chair. The leak he had to take forgotten, he checks the bathroom door, takes a deep breath, and then hurriedly rifles the pockets of the pants. Finding Judge's wallet, he flips it open, looking for the driver's license. He stops, reads ... He knew it—Judge had lied! But why? Hearing the shower stop, Tyrone puts the wallet back and slips quietly out the door, trying to figure out what Judge is hiding.

Out in the street Sabu is doing some hiding of his own, crouched behind a row of garbage cans, but Cy locates him. He snatches Sabu up by his collar and shoves him against the side of a house. "What the hell you think you're doing?"

Sabu is defiant. "Fuck you!!!"

"No, fuck you! I ain't warning you no more. You killing people, asshole."

Cy gives Sabu a couple of hard shots in the gut and stomps off.

Sabu stumbles out of the alley, holding his belly and trying to catch his breath.

Sergeant Shreck, who has been watching from his squad car, rolls his window down and beckons Sabu over.

Thinking he's busted, Sabu starts to whine. "Aww, man! I ain't done nothing."

"Of course not," Shreck commiserates with him. "Those Panthers are turning into real shitheels, ain't they?"

Sabu is shocked by the kindly cop routine.

"Yes sir," he agrees. "They're motherfuckers, all right!"

"You shouldn't take that," Shreck suggests. "If I was you," he adds, hinting at violence, "I'd stand up for myself. Nobody could blame you for that, if you know what I mean . . . "

■ ■ ■

Evening . . . The Panther meeting is packed. The room is crowded with Panther faces old and new, all attentive and full of purpose. It's quite a change from a few months earlier.

Huey is at the podium, inspired and proud. He is not an especially rousing speaker with his high-pitched voice and pedantic style, and he knows it. Still, the audience worships him because of what he stands for. They nod "That's right, Huey" and "You tell 'em, Huey" whenever there is a pause.

Huey is finishing up his speech. "Look around you, brothers and sisters, new members coming in every day, here and around the country. I'd like the members of our newly opened chapter in New Jersey visiting us from the East to stand."

The visitors stand, their fists raised in salute, and sit back down. They get a hearty round of applause.

"And I'd like to introduce another new member. He is the author of *Soul on Ice*, a respected journalist, and I'm proud to say the newly appointed Minister of Information for the Black Panther Party. Brothers and sisters, Eldridge Cleaver."

Huey steps aside. Eldridge, wearing dark glasses and a diamond in one ear, strides to the podium. He acknowledges the applause and gets down to business.

"Frederick Douglass knew the truth! So did Brother Malcolm. That's why they shot him down. We are hostages, slaves in a capitalist colony . . . and a slave has no obligation to obey a master's rules. Brother Franz Fanon runs it down when he says violence can be a cleansing force. It frees the colonized victim from despair and inaction. It makes him fearless and restores his self-respect!"

Cleaver is electrifying. The audience is silent—hanging on his every word.

"Brothers and sisters," Cleaver continues, "you are all well aware of the chains of slavery, of second-class citizenship that we bear. But there are other more invisible chains, the chains of not speaking your mind. The words left unsaid out of fear of reprisal by the Man. I'm here to tell you that we have a voice!"

Eldridge pauses and gives his listeners a little smile. Huey looks out at the sea of faces—they are mesmerized by Eldridge.

"All right," Eldridge goes on. "I'll prove it to you. All of you repeat after me . . . Fuck Governor Ronald Reagan!"

The assembly smiles and chuckles.

"I'm serious," Eldridge says sternly. "Repeat after me. Fuck Ronald Reagan!"

The audience obeys. "FUCK RONALD REAGAN!"

"Feels good, don't it? Amazing how saying your mind can free your soul. Repeat after me . . . Fuck Ronald Reagan."

Everyone is smiling and elated. Everyone, that is, except a young woman who seems to have fallen asleep in her chair.

"FUCK RONALD REAGAN!" The audience begins to chant.

Little-Bobby notices the woman dozing. "Hey, sister," he says. "You paying attention?"

The girl looks up all glassy-eyed. "Naw, naw . . . I ain't asleep, or nothing, I'm . . . "

"She's high!" Jamal hisses, outraged. "The sister's nodding out! She's a junkie."

"The pigs musta planted her so they'd have an excuse to bust us."

"Another stoolie," Tyrone says, shooting Judge over by the door a meaningful look.

Several female Panthers leap for the junkie, but Alma steps in. "I'll handle this," she says, and she helps the woozy woman to stand. The junkie struggles slowly to her feet. It is a major effort. She is pregnant, and pretty far along.

Alma guides the pregnant girl gently out of the meeting. Judge holds the door for them, then follows outside.

"I'll walk you as far as the corner," he offers.

The night air seems to revive the girl. Her gait steadies, and she shoves Alma's helping hand away.

"I ain't no stoolie!" the girl protests, her words still slurred. "I ain't a stoolie. I just wanta help my people."

"That's what we all want, sister," Judge says.

Alma turns to Judge. "Look, I owe you an apology for leaving so abruptly that night."

Judge doesn't look at her.

Alma tries again. "I guess it's too late to say I'm sorry."

Judge melts a little. "Better late than never." They walk the rest of the way to the corner in silence.

When Judge turns around and heads back, the pregnant girl, fearing danger, starts pleading her innocence again. "I ain't no stoolie, honest."

Tough but kind, Alma explains. "Coming in high like that, you put the movement in jeopardy. The pigs are looking for any excuse to come down on us."

"I just needed a little boost, ya dig?" The girl rubs her stomach. "My baby is gonna grow up to be a warrior. It's gonna be a boy. I want him to grow up to be a warrior . . . not no junkie!"

"Listen, sister, the dope game the Man is running on us is as old as the hills. You ever hear of the Boxer Rebellion?"

"Naw, sister, school me."

"The English were occupying China and bleeding the country dry. The Chinese asked them to leave. Instead, the English brought drugs in, started the opium trade. Drugs, get it? . . . to sap the will of the people. That's what the Boxer Rebellion was about. The Chinese fighting to drive the drug traffic out . . . The Chinese were trying to get the English off their backs. So the English turned them onto opium to keep 'em quiet."

"Did it work?" the girl asks, fascinated.

"Well," Alma goes on, "the English won the first round and the Boxer Rebellion failed. But eventually Chairman Mao came along and drove the English and all the dope out."

"How about us, sister? What round are we in?"

Alma hesitates—she doesn't have an answer. Taking her silence for anger, the junkie stops dead in her tracks. "You ain't gonna hurt me, is you?"

"You're hurting yourself," Alma puts her arms around the girl. "And that baby . . . "

By the time Judge returns, the meeting has broken up and Huey is standing in the storefront doorway giving out patrol assignments. "Little-Bobby, you take your patrol over by the bottom. Cy, you and Snooky take the strip."

Tyrone pounces on Judge. "Where'd you go—Alaska? Where you always disappearing to?" Tyrone grills him. "What took you so long?"

"Brother Judge," Huey interrupts, "get in my car. You're gonna patrol with me tonight."

Tyrone tries to intercede. "Huey, it's too dangerous for you to be doing patrol, especially with Bobby being in jail," he argues. "Besides, we gotta talk."

"Okay," Huey says, "so talk."

"Alone. I need to talk to you alone, Brother Huey."

Huey shakes his head. "Not tonight, we're running late. We'll deal with it tomorrow."

"But . . ." Tyrone starts to protest.

Huey gives him a withering glare as he walks around to the driver's side of his car. Judge brushes past Tyrone to the passenger seat. Before Huey slides into the car, he looks up. "You've got your assignment, brother," he tells Tyrone.

Tyrone watches them pull away, his eyes narrowed to worried, angry slits.

Night . . . Huey and Judge roll through the ghetto streets. They pick up a squad car and trail it a few blocks, making their Panther presence felt, keeping the cops honest.

"I think the sister nodding out in the meeting was a set-up," Judge says.

Huey smiles and nods. "That shouldn't surprise you, brother. The entrenched power structures never go around passing out liberty."

The cops in front of them grow nervous and execute an illegal U-turn to shake the Panther Patrol. Mission accomplished, Huey lets them go.

They cruise along, and Huey turns mellow. "Bobby got six months in prison for taking a wrong turn, but the Panther Party got world-wide attention. Yeah, disciplined niggers marching with guns got everybody's attention all right. You know, the day after we went up to the legislature there were articles in papers about us all over the world! That started me to thinking. We're gonna start our own paper . . . get the truth out to the people ourselves!"

Getting all revved up, Huey slaps the dashboard in excitement. "We gotta keep expanding too. New chapters, everything! Power to the people, brother. We're gonna get the drugs out of the community and all the rest."

Judge, preoccupied with his own thoughts, merely stares out the window.

Huey notices. "You okay?"

Judge nods.

Huey switches the topic. "Remember, if the police suspect you're double-crossing them, you're a dead man."

"And what about the other Panthers?" Judge asks. "Suppose the brothers start thinking I'm a traitor? What then? Who else knows?"

"Listen," Huey tells him. "Forget about the others. Forget everything but keeping tabs on the pigs. We've got to know what the Man is up to. Your shit is vital to us!"

"How vital can what the cops are doing here be?" Judge cross-examines. "What about the rest of the country?"

"This is Panther International Headquarters. Don't you get it?" Huey takes his eyes off the road and locks gazes with Judge. "The pigs will try running their games here first."

Huey turns back to the road. "Look at that playground and that garden," he says with admiration. "A couple of months ago that was a vacant lot. That's pride blooming, in our neighborhood, in ourselves."

A handsome woman in a frayed housecoat spots the car cruising down the street and dashes into the road and flags them down. "You-all them Black Panthers?" the woman clamors, peering into the auto. "If you is," she points up the street, "you better come quick!"

A squad car, it's roof lights flashing, has been driven rudely over the curb and is squatting in the middle of what is otherwise a well-kept lawn. Two big white cops are trying to pry a bony middle-aged black man loose from a pillar of the front porch he is clinging to for dear life. Huey and Judge pull up and slowly get out of their vehicle.

"Don't hurt him officers . . . don't hurt him," the woman in the housecoat runs up pleading. "Just make him stop going up beside my head."

The older of the two cops is enjoying himself. "Now don't you go worrying none, sister," he says, trying to do soul dialect. "We gonna teach this boy a lesson." He pokes the husband with his nightstick and laughs. "We gonna teach him not to go beating up on his woman."

The bony husband can't hold on any longer, and lets go. The older officer starts dragging him across the lawn by his heels towards the squad car.

The younger cop reaches down and slaps the man across the top of his head with the flat of his hand, as if he were punishing a naughty schoolboy.

The wife screams, irate. "You're killing him! I called ya'll to stop him from beating me, not to go killing him!" She raises her arms up to the sky and calls on Jesus for help.

"Release that man!" Huey barks. "If a person is not resisting you cannot use unwarranted force. That's illegal!"

The older policeman lets go of the husband and saunters over to Huey and Judge. "Now you boys butt out," he chuckles, still trying to talk in dialect. "We're arresting him and dat's dat. You want that we should take you bucks down too?"

Huey stands firm. "You wanta try?"

The wife thrusts herself between the police and the Panthers. "I done change my mind, officers. I'm not filing no complaint so you can kill him!"

The husband wobbles to his feet.

"Police brutality brothers, police brutality! Political persecution, brothers! They just doing this 'cause I'm one of you."

The older cop has had enough of the hassle. "Come on, let's get out of here. The coons ain't worth the trouble."

He turns to Huey. "They all yours. You niggers handle it among yourselves."

The younger cop gets the idea. "Don't call us if he beats on your black ass," he warns the wife, "'cause we ain't coming!"

The cops squeal off in their squad car, ripping up as much lawn as possible.

The bony man brushes himself off. "Thank you, brothers. Thank you. We need to keep the honkies out of our business," he says, trying to get political. He wags a finger at his wife and explains the situation. "I warned this bitch about having my dinner ready."

The woman stamps her foot at him. "Nigger, it wasn't ready 'cause I had to stay taking care of my boss's daughter who got herself knocked up!"

Judge focuses in on the husband. "Didn't I hear you say you were a Panther?"

The man grins sheepishly. "What I meant was, I'm with you brothers in spirit. And I'm thinking about joining. Power to the people. Fuck the Man!"

The husband raises a bony fist in the Black Power salute. "You can't even kick your ole lady's behind in peace when dinner ain't ready. We need a revolution. Long live the Black Panthers!"

Huey snatches the man up in his collar. "The revolution is not about you kicking your ole lady's ass! She's not your slave, brother. Male chauvinism is part of the capitalistic society's system of oppressing." Huey shoves the man down. "You lay a hand on her again, and you are going to be praying for those redneck pigs to come and pull me off of your skinny behind!"

The man sits on his butt with his mouth hanging open. He can't believe his ears, but he gets the message.

Huey turns and stomps back to the car. Judge follows him, thoughtful and amused.

"Well, brother," Judge chuckles climbing into the automobile, "sure looks like you've got your work cut out for you."

"Sure have," replies Huey, laughing and turning on the ignition. "But like they say, 'We shall overcome.'"

"Speaking of overcoming," Judge says as they drive off, "I almost forgot. Here!" He hands Huey the money Brimmer gave him. "Another donation from the police."

Huey chuckles. "We got the pigs subsidizing us."

"Yeah, well," Judge grimaces, turning serious. "They want a lot for their money. They're on my ass about coming up with some kind of frame-up. I'm between a rock and a hard place."

"You gotta come up with something. Figure it out. War is hell, brother."

"Look, Huey. You still didn't answer my original question. Who's gonna straighten out the brothers if they start thinking I'm some kind of traitor and get on my ass?"

"Like the manual says," Huey quotes, 'Information is . . . "

". . . disseminated on a need-to-know basis,'" Judge finishes the sentence. "That means nobody knows but you, Huey, right? Maybe Bobby?"

After a long pause, Huey answers. "What it all means is I would rather die on my feet than live on my knees."

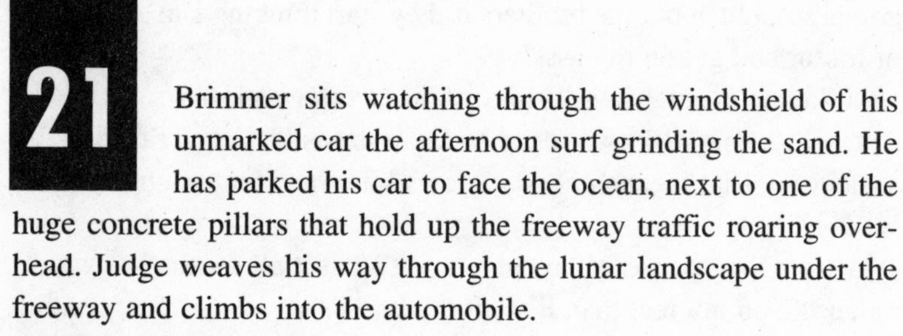

21

Brimmer sits watching through the windshield of his unmarked car the afternoon surf grinding the sand. He has parked his car to face the ocean, next to one of the huge concrete pillars that hold up the freeway traffic roaring overhead. Judge weaves his way through the lunar landscape under the freeway and climbs into the automobile.

"Hiya, Judge."

"How long you been here, Brimmer?"

"Half an hour, thereabouts."

"Well, I'm on time," Judge points to his watch and goes on the defensive. "So don't start no bullshit about me being late."

"I know, I know. I didn't say you were, did I? I just been sitting here."

"Doing what?" Judge ribs Brimmer and points. "Watching the water boogie, or the cars in that junkyard over there rust. Haven't you got a family or something?"

"Not really," Brimmer sighs. "Just me and my cat. You're about the most family I've got these days, Judge."

Judge is embarrased by the glimpse into Brimmer's off-duty world. "Let's get to it," he says, pulling out a piece of paper. He goes into a modified Stepin Fetchit routine, feigning deep concentration as he reviews his notes, but Brimmer doesn't seem to catch on. "Let's see now, the past two days we followed seven police patrols, we monitored four arrests, we got signatures for that stoplight... uh, and we've started to picket the markets in our neighborhood that refuse to hire minorities."

"I know all of that crap," Brimmer cuts in. "Tell me something I don't know."

"The breakfast program for the kids looks like a big hit and we're starting an infant care clinic for the community..."

"I said we know all of that! You're still just a bunch of gun-toting thugs, you ask me. Now what about the plan to discredit the Panthers you were supposed to come up with? You haven't forgotten our little trip to the bridge already, have you?"

Judge looks exasperated. "Like I told you, in the black community the Panthers are heroes. You know why? Because for four hundred years, until the Panthers came along black people have been dialing for help in vain. The Panthers believe in the black community... and you know what? The black community is starting to believe in itself."

Brimmer chuckles. "Just calm down and climb down off that soapbox, willya."

"Look, Brimmer, don't go getting pissed at me because black people are starting to overcome."

"Goddamnit! I said climb off your soapbox!" Brimmer snarls, then eases off. "I admit you folks' community is a lot calmer and cleaner than I've ever seen it. But you're a long way from overcoming shit, son. Hey, how about we get a coffee? My treat."

"Naw, better not, thanks..."

"Don't wanna be seen with me, hunh? I guess you're right. Hell, my brother officers wouldn't be too thrilled to see me hobnobbing with a colored fellow, either. Anyhow, speaking of brothers, if you don't come up with something I can pin on the Panthers soon, both our behinds, yours and mine, gonna be a lot worse for the wear and tear."

Judge risks a probe. "By the way, what ever happened to that 'worst thing for black people stuff' you were talking about that time?"

"Did I mention that? Well, don't matter if I did, because I never heard any more about it."

Judge is not sure if Brimmer is faking or a fool. He shrugs and mumbles how he was just trying to make conversation and lets it go, unwilling to risk exposing his mission.

Brimmer puts a parental paw on Judge's shoulder. "You know something, Judge? I like you."

"Yeah, sure . . ."

"Naw, I really do. I got a kid in Nam myself . . . an officer."

"No shit! What outfit is he with?"

"She . . . she's a nurse. She's with what I think they call a field team. I don't know which one. She doesn't write much. Her mother raised her after the divorce."

"Yeah. Look, I gotta split."

Embarrassed about letting his guard slip, Brimmer is suddenly all business again. "Downtown wants some results, Judge. How you coming with that Panther set-up?"

"I'm working on it. I gotta split . . ."

"Don't let me down. I'm counting on you," Brimmer calls after Judge. Despite the ocean breeze, his words hang heavy in the air.

Cy, finishing up a foot patrol, is strutting down the street making his way back to headquarters to hook up with Judge for a bite to eat. People check out the Black Panther outfit as he goes past, and some even offer up a "right on" or flash the clenched-fist salute. The Panther presence seems to have given the street security and self-confidence. Folks are hanging out, enjoying the early evening air. Bo Diddley's "Oh Baby" grooves from someone's radio.

Rose, staked out as usual on someone's steps, beckons Cy over. "Hey, Cy! What—now you a righteous Panther man, you too uppity to drink with me?"

Cy bursts into a big grin and saunters over. "You know that's bullshit."

"Don't pay no attention. I'm just fucking wid you, man," Rose smiles and passes Cy the bottle. Cy takes a small swig to show that he is down. His face puckers. "Aaaah, man, that's some bitter shit," he complains. "I forgot how nasty that stuff is."

Rose retrieves his bottle with a grin. "Well, just don't go forgetting your friends," he admonishes.

"Ain't gonna happen," Cy promises. He spots Sabu down the street doing something that looks suspiciously like dealing drugs. "Power to the people," Cy says and sprints off to check Sabu out. "Gotta go, stay cool."

"Yeah, power to the people," Rose repeats, making a fist in the direction of Cy's butt tearing down the street towards Sabu.

Judge is alone in the rear of Panther headquarters, running the ditto machine and waiting for Cy to show. Tyrone comes in through the back door and beckons him. "C'mere . . . "

Judge follows Tyrone to the stairwell of the building next door. Midway up the steps in the half light, Alma has a terrified recruit pressed up against the wall in a choke hold. She has a gun in her right hand, and is holding it against the side of his head.

"Signed up 'bout a month ago," Tyrone says, pointing. "He says his name's Matty. I call him spy!"

Tyrone mounts the stairs to Matty and *WHAM!*. . . slams him in the gut.

"The muthafucka gave the pigs the license numbers of every Panther car," Tyrone curses.

"Please, man," Matty pleads, "I didn't do nothin'."

Tyrone grabs the trainee's index finger. "Oh, yeah? Is this the finger you ratted on us with?" *CRACK!*. . . Tyrone jerks the finger backward, breaking it.

Repulsed, Judge turns for the exit, but Tyrone leaps down the steps and stops him at the door.

"What's the matter? You don't like to see a traitor get hurt?" Tyrone hisses. "I wonder why that is?"

Judge glares back. "If you got something to say, Tyrone, say it."

"Anything happens to Huey, it ain't gonna be a finger. I'll . . . "

Another Panther bursts into the stairwell. "Judge . . . It's Cy!" he shouts, his eyes wide with anger and horror. "He's over in the alley. He's been shot!"

Judge shoves Tyrone aside and bolts out the doorway. Tyrone ducks into headquarters, grabs his gun, and charges down the street in the direction Judge has disappeared.

By the time Tyrone gets to the alley Judge is down on his knees, cradling Cy's head in his arms. Cy lies sprawled on the cobblestones in a pool of blood, writhing in agony with bullet holes in his chest.

"Don't die! Don't die!" Judge begs. "Please, Cy . . . Cy . . . Who did this to you man? Was it the pigs? Who did this to you? Oh, shit man, don't go!"

"I'll get an ambulance," Tyrone says, and dashes off for help.

Cy tries to speak, but just blood trickles from between his lips . . .

"Hang on, Cy . . . hang on," Judge pleads. "Who did this to you man? Who did this to you?"

Cy gurgles. He struggles to open his eye. It looks up at Judge, it closes, and he dies.

"You fucking pigs!" Judge's scream, drenched with pain, trails off skyward towards the dull gray Oakland heaven.

Sobbing, Judge lays Cy's head gently on the ground and rises to his feet. Something twists deep within his heart.

The ambulance arrives on ghetto time, twenty minutes late. The medics with their stretcher brush past him. Judge moves through the street like a zombie, his face—contorted with grief, pain, and rage—a reflection of his tormented soul.

Back at the apartment, Judge sits at the kitchen table, his head cradled in his arms crying silently, his shirt still covered with his dead roommate's—his dead buddy's—blood. Suddenly, he raises his head and squares his shoulders. He grabs the phone and dials.

"Brimmer," the voice on the other end snaps.

"Brimmer. It's me, Judge." His voice is grim.

Brimmer is instantly alert. "Judge, hold on, is your phone safe?"

"Who fucking cares? You cops killed Cy."

Brimmer says he is sorry. He means it. He's about to say that he was hoping it would all be over before someone got hurt when Judge cuts him off.

"Just listen—you want the Panthers I'm gonna give 'em to you. I'll give you your fucking frame-up. That make you happy?"

"Now, son, calm down . . . "

Judge grits his teeth. "Son nothin'! Just shut up, shut the fuck up! I'm gonna work with you—that's what you wanted, right? Okay, listen . . . "

The next day . . . The raggedy Panther van crosses an intersection. Two cops waiting in an unmarked automobile on a side street spot it. The police car starts discreetly forward, turning the corner and following the van at a safe distance. "Got 'em!" the detective in the car shouts into his mike.

Using binoculars, Brimmer watches the van come into view from the top of a building three-quarters of a block away from the filling station where the set-up is to go down.

"Here they come . . . I've got 'em in my sights now," he says, starting a running commentary into his walkie-talkie. "He's right on time!"

In the front seat of the van, Little-Bobby is wedged between Tyrone who is driving and Judge squeezed against the passenger door. In the back of the van are three other Panthers.

Judge, seeming preoccupied, keeps checking his watch.

Tyrone eyes him suspiciously. "What's up with you?"

"Nothing. Why?"

Tyrone keeps prodding. "You got something on your mind, brother?"

"Yeah, 'brother.' My best friend is stone dead, remember?"

"Yes, I sorry about that," Tyrone backs off, embarrassed.

"That's all right . . . I sorry, too."

The van is almost abreast of the station. "Shit," Judge exclaims, "I've got to take a leak . . . pull over at that gas station up there, okay?"

The van pulls into the station, and Judge hops out.

"It looks like its going down," Brimmer tells the walkie-talkie.

"Stay in visual contact, but do not close in. No slip ups. I repeat, do not close in. I'm on my way." Brimmer dashes for the exit from the roof and disappears down the steps.

Judge enters the tiny station, which also doubles as a grocery. It is crammed with rows of ghetto essentials from roach-killers to hair straighteners. From behind the counter, piled high with cigarette racks and magazines, an old man's voice greets him.

"Can I help you? If you want gas my nephew will be back in ten more minutes. Same as always."

"Where's your bathroom?"

"Out back, mister." The old man appears from behind the magazines, carrying his head at a strange angle. He feels his way along the counter. "You don't need no key."

Judge's temples are pounding. "Open the register!"

Confused, the old man hesitates, and Judge warns him he is serious and not to fuck around. The old man fumbles with the cash register, and finally gets it open. Judge grabs the money out of the till.

Judge leaves the store, snatches off his beret, and wipes his brow—the signal. He ducks around back to the toilet.

In the van, Tyrone grumbles to Little-Bobby just how long can a piss take?

Little-Bobby, unable to provide a definitive answer to such a cosmic question, just shrugs.

Brimmer, catching Judge's signal, smiles triumphantly and places his flashing red light on the roof. "All right, boys," he barks into his walkie-talkie, "move in!"

A half dozen police cars, sirens blasting, lights flashing, swoop down on the filling station.

The cops jump out, pull the Panthers out of their van, and start slapping them around. Brimmer screeches up and shoves through the ring of cops to stop the manhandling.

"Easy, fellas," Brimmer orders. "Lay off. We need 'em recognizable for the line-up."

The officers loosen their holds, and Tyrone manages to shove the cop he has been tussling with to the ground. Two other cops grab

Tyrone and wrench him down to his knees. Brimmer draws his gun and aims it between Tyrone's eyes.

"Easy, boy," Brimmer bellows, "or I blow your head off!"

"We ain't done nothing!" Tyrone hollers. "Why don't you fascist pigs stop harassing us?"

"Harassing my ass!" Brimmer sneers. "You just stuck up this place. We got a witness. Get on your feet and keep those hands up, or I'll blow you away."

"What kind of bullshit you talking?" Tyrone demands. "We ain't stuck up nothing!"

A rookie cop tugs Brimmer's sleeve. "Sir, there was another one ducked around the back!"

Brimmer plays surprised. "Another one? Are you sure? I don't think so . . ."

"Positive, sir! I'll get him," the rookie volunteers, turning.

Tyrone shouts a warning. "JUDGE . . . JUDGE!"

Brimmer grabs the rookie and yanks him back. "No! You stay here and get these bastards cuffed! I'll get him."

Brimmer dashes around the corner of the station and tries the toilet door. It's locked. He bangs on the door—no answer. He puts his face to the door.

"It's me, Brimmer," he whispers. "You gotta get the fuck out of there, son, fast! They're searching the goddamn premises for another Panther."

Judge unlocks the door and bolts out of the toilet. He tears across the vacant lot behind the store towards the hill Brimmer points him to. When he reaches the hill, he finds it is choked with weeds and slow going.

As Judge starts up the hill, Brimmer takes aim and fires a couple of rounds over his head. At the sound of the shots, the adrenalin-stoked memories of combat rush over Judge. His eyes wide with fear, his legs pumping, he struggles upward through the brambles and garbage. His feet still scratching forward, Judge glances over his shoulder and sees Brimmer standing there, his gun still smoking. As he reaches the top, the rookie comes around next to Brimmer, drops to one knee, and takes careful aim. Brimmer pretends to lose his balance and bumps him. The rookie's shot misses the mark.

Judge disappears over the hill. Brimmer apologizes for being so clumsy, and steers the rookie back to the front of the store.

Brimmer starts shouting orders. "Get a car over here on the double!" he commands. "Take whoever was in that store down to headquarters to ID these punks."

Barely an hour later, a happy Dorsett is holding a press conference on the steps of police headquarters. Reporters swarm around, snapping photos, rolling cameras, and shouting questions up at him.

Dorsett, basking in the camera's glow, smugly addresses the journalists. "Yes, we have a group of the so-called revolutionaries in custody right now, caught red-handed robbing a local business. Today's arrest exposes the Black Panthers for what they truly are . . . common criminals. And as soon as our witness gives us a positive identification, we'll file charges of armed robbery with intent to kill."

"Sir . . . was anybody hurt?" a newsman shouts, sniffing for tidbits.

"I have no further comments at this time," Dorsett replies pompously. He turns on his heel and goes inside, leaving the reporters shouting questions at his back.

Dorsett strides into his office. Rodgers is standing there steaming. But Dorsett is so flushed with his victory that he doesn't even notice that Rodgers is pissed off. Dorsett lets him have both sarcastic barrels.

"Ah, Agent Rodgers, what a pleasant surprise. As you can see, we do have things under control here in our fair city. The FBI doesn't have a monopoly on agents infiltrating enemy organizations!"

"Are you finished?"

"No, Agent Rodgers, I'm not! Once we get these boys put away and the Panthers permanently discredited, I'd appreciate it if you'd leave us to take care of our own business."

"Take care of your own business!" Rodgers disgustedly slaps a thin newspaper down on Dorsett's desk. "Just some hoodlums, hunh? Well, take a look at this! Now they're putting out their own paper!"

Dorsett grabs the newspaper. Across the top, the banner reads *The Black Panther—Intercommunal News Service—25 Cents.* The headline screams *THE TRUTH ABOUT SACRAMENTO.*

"Mary, mother of God," Dorsett gasps. "When . . . when did they start this?"

"They haven't yet . . . it hits the street next week! Luckily we have alternate sources of information," Rodgers gloats. "You promised to finish the Panthers. A year ago they didn't even exist! Now they have chapters sprouting up all over the country. AND THIS!" He angrily snatches the newspaper out of Dorsett's hands and waves it under his nose. "THIS! Mr. Hoover is looking into reactivating the internment camps. He doesn't plan to sit still while either this "peace movement" or this "black power" thing rides roughshod over this nation."

KNOCK KNOCK . . . Dorsett's secretary interrupts Rodgers's tirade. She gives her boss the thumbs-up, and Dorsett instantly transforms from whupped puppy to Mr. On-top-of-it!

"You're right, Rodgers, I promised to deliver the Panthers and that's exactly what I intend to do. Follow me," he commands and struts from the office.

Rodgers follows, stony-faced, unsure. "Where are we going?"

"Line-up," Dorsett answers tersely. He strides down the corridor, head held high, shoulders back. Rodgers, annoyed, trails him by half a step, wearing a quizzical expression.

A reporter loafing in the hallway pounces on Dorsett. "What's up? I got a tip from downstairs that something big might be brewing."

"Stick around," Dorsett banters in an expansive mood. "Who knows, I might give you an exclusive."

The line-up room is divided into two chambers. Dorsett and Rodgers enter the smaller room, where Brimmer is standing over the old man from the filling station. Brimmer beckons Dorsett to a corner to talk to him. Rodgers observes their tete-a-tete from his vantage point just inside the door. Brimmer points through the one-way window separating the two rooms—whatever he is saying, Dorsett is becoming very upset.

The larger room has a raised platform with horizontal lines on the wall. Looking through the one-way window, the witness, seeing but unseen, can identify the suspect in the larger room. Tyrone, Little-Bobby, and the other three captured Panthers are standing at attention on the platform waiting to be identified.

"What the fuck is going on!" Dorsett bellows. "What's the hold up?"

Brimmer, shamefaced, waves his hand in front of the old man's eyes. Nothing . . . no reaction.

Dorsett gives it a try. He swings at the old man, his hand stopping only inches from the old man's face. Nothing again, no reaction.

"This!" Dorsett goes ballistic. "This is your witness? The old man's fucking blind!"

Rodgers grins.

"He just stands in for his nephew at that time every day so he can grab lunch," Brimmer whines sheepishly.

"He couldn't ID his own mother!" Dorsett lashes out. "Who's responsible for this?"

"I got a good idea, boss," Brimmer says.

Dorsett turns on Brimmer. "'No problem, boss,'" he says, his voice dripping with sarcasm as he imitates Brimmer's bravado promise. "'We got a man on the inside, boss.'" He throws up his hands in disgust. "You know what you can do for me? Retire!"

TESTING, ONE-TWO-THREE . . . Witness #17. Name: Al Daugherty . . . Trucking firm dispatcher . . . Mobile trailer.

I don't care to discuss. I did my time and as far as I'm concerned that's that. No one here knows about it and I would prefer to keep it that way. Clear?

I'M NOT INTERESTED IN HOW YOU BECAME A WEATHERMAN, OR WHAT HAPPENED LATER. I ONLY WANT TO KNOW ABOUT THE PANTHERS.

I'm sorry, I can't help you there. We didn't know any more about the Panthers than what we had read in the papers and stuff. We didn't want anything to do with violent, scary black guys in leather jackets.

DID YOU KNOW ANY OF THEM PERSONALLY—HUEY P. NEWTON, BOBBY SEALE, DAVID HILLIARD, FRED HAMPTON, TYRONE, ELAINE BROWN, BOBBY HUTTON, JUDGE . . .

I heard of the first two and the woman, but I never heard of the others.

HOW ABOUT JUDGE? ARE YOU SURE YOU NEVER HEARD OF HIM?

I'm sure. We didn't know that much about a lot of things, but of course we thought we did. That was the problem, we believed our own bullshit—all you need is love and all that. We were just smug little white kids raised with silver spoons sticking out of our behinds. We were all so busy bitching about what we didn't have that we didn't take time to realize what we did have. And of course, we thought we could change the world with a few kisses and some sitar music or something. I remember the first time we went to the induction center. We went waltzing up there with flowers to put down the gun barrels of the National Guard. See this scar? The second time I wore my lacrosse helmet.

DO YOU FEEL THEN THAT THE PANTHERS WERE RIGHT ALL ALONG?

Look—you want your ass kicked? I said I had no comment . . . Look, this is our busy season, okay?

Rose the wino's place is a shack—a cardboard, tar paper, and corrugated tin affair leaning up against the side of a chop-shop in a backyard. The shack is furnished with bottles, years of general filth, and junk scrounged from whomever and wherever.

Dog-tired and dirty, Judge sits on Rose's couch—an old Plymouth back seat scrounged from a wreck. He is nervously dragging on a cigarette and watching Rose's seen-better-days black-white TV. On the screen are a bunch of peace marchers protesting at the Oakland induction center. Hearing a scraping sound outside, he whips out his gun. As a hand takes hold of the canvas covering the doorway, Judge gets into firing position.

Rose shoves the canvas door aside and steps into his castle. "Whoa, there, brother man!" he says, staring down the barrel of Judge's pistol. He raises his bottle with a chuckle. "It's only me and some Bitter Dog."

"Sorry," Judge apologizes and puts the gun down.

"Whatcha watching, anyhow?" Rose asks, joining Judge on the couch. Judge turns towards his buddy.

"Oh shit!" Rose screams, pointing at the TV. "Lordy! Look at that will you! Them white cops kicking their own young folks' ass! Man, what's this motherfucking world coming to!"

The peace marchers, who only a few moments before had been laughing and singing protest songs and waving banners as they converged on the induction center, are now being attacked mercilessly by the police.

Superimposed over the carnage, the words LIVE REPORT... OAKLAND INDUCTION CENTER... LIVE REPORT... OCT 17 1967... LIVE REPORT trot across the screen. The shit is hitting the fan. Local cops, county cops, state troopers, and the National Guard wade into the demonstrators. Tear gas canisters are lobbed into the crowd. A protester who had been using an American flag as a cape is dragged from the induction center steps by his ankles. Scurrying hippies are viciously clubbed... it's all there on the tube.

The TV blinks and another news story flashes on the screen... BLACK PANTHERS FREED AFTER NIGHT IN JAIL. Tyrone and the others are coming down the steps of police headquarters, smiling, undaunted, fists raised in the Black Panther salute.

"That there take the heat off you any?" Rose asks, nodding at the television.

"Don't know," Judge says, stashing his gun away in his belt and rising to leave. "But I'm sure I'll find out. Rose, you did me a solid letting me hide my ass out here." Judge pulls some bills from his pocket.

Rose shakes his head and waves the money off. "Naw, unh-unh, man. I might hit somebody for a little change every now and then, but I don't take no money from friends. It ain't about that. You always been regular, bro."

Judge thanks him. "You're good people, Rose. I'll catch you later."

"Hey, Judge, man . . ."

Judge stops at the door and looks at Rose, who has a pained expression on his face. "What's up, man? What's on your mind?"

Rose pauses, struggling with himself. "Look, Judge . . . I . . . I shoulda told you this before but . . . well, I . . . fuck it . . ."

"Told me what?"

"It was Sabu killed Cy."

"Sabu! What happened?"

"Well, Cy—he was running up the block after Sabu. See, I was sitting on the steps, man. Me and Cy had just had a nip and been talking shit. When suddenly, what the fuck do I know, he spots Sabu trying to do a dope deal or something and takes off after him. Sabu ducks into this alley and Cy goes in, but Sabu musta been waiting, laying for him. Cy never had no chance. Sabu just started blasting away."

As Rose stammers out the story, Judge sees the scene in his mind. *Cy coming around the corner bearing down on Sabu, fire in his eyes. "Sabu, you gotta be a card-carrying member of the stupid family."*

Sabu's smirking face. "Motherfucker . . . I done told you better give me some space!"

Cy coming closer. "Look, Sabu, I warned . . . "

Sabu whipping out a Saturday night special, firing point-blank into Cy's chest . . . BLAM BLAM BLAM . . .

Cy's surprised face . . . blood flecking his chest as he collapses on the pavement, his life draining away and Sabu taking off.

"Where's Sabu now?" Judge growls.

"He's gone like a bat out of hell . . . ain't no one seen him since. Snuck outta town is the word."

"Why didn't you tell me this before?"

"Didn't want folks to think I was a snitch. You know?"

"Yeah, man," Judge replies softly. "I know."

"Stay strong, brother."

"Yeah, Rose, I sure will," says Judge, the searing pain creasing his face as he turns to go.

■ ■ ■

A soiree, big and loud, is in full swing at an Oakland ghetto crash pad. Three different bands are taking turns kicking out the joyful jams to celebrate the release of Tyrone and the other Panthers earlier in the afternoon.

Panthers, locals and out-of-towners, are there along with girlfriends, boyfriends, well-wishers, and plenty of potential lovers. Young people letting their hair down, going about their mating games . . . of course, in a political context.

A new recruit, a lanky local brother, is trying to run his rap on an out-of-town fox.

"So you wanta show me some Oakland hospitality?" the fox says, batting her eyelashes to lead the chump on.

The lanky brother nods.

"Well," the fox replies, turning indignant, "I didn't come all the way from St. Louis to be sharing no sleeping bag with no trainee!"

"Dig it, I may be a recruit today, but you can bet I'm gonna be a Panther lieutenant soon!"

"I bet you can't even recite the ten points of the program," the fox shoots back.

"Well, I got a point you can try ten times! How's that?"

Judge comes in, cleaned up but still haggard. Huey spots him lurking at the fringe of the party and beckons him over.

Huey gives Judge a hug. "Good work, man," he whispers. "Just keep it up. That blind guy gimmick was a stroke of genius."

"I don't think that that pig Brimmer is gonna think so."

Huey grabs a pair of cold beers and steers Judge into a back room away from the party.

"Sorry about Cy, brother."

"Yeah," Judge grimaces.

"You all right?" Huey studies Judge's face. "You look worried. I know they keep threatening you."

"Yeah, like I said the pig's probably pretty pissed, but I'll think of something to cool him out. That's not what I'm worried about. I tried to pump Brimmer about the local cops and feds teaming up on us. He claims he hasn't heard any more about it."

"The cops and feds have been working together for years."

"Gonna get tighter too. Now that the war protesters have been taken care of, we could be next."

"Well, first, they better not count on the antiwar movement being taken out, not just yet. They got balls. I admire them. In fact, they're going to hold another rally at the induction center, and this time I've been asked to speak. Hang in, man. Our shit is starting to move."

"Another rally? Great, I'll be there."

"Not too visible, hear?" Huey cautions. "You've got to lay low until that pig, what's his name—Brimmer? cools off."

"Yeah, Brimmer," Judge replies, still troubled. "He told me he heard there were gonna be a lot of 'good niggers' around. I asked him what he meant by that—dead, or just in jail? He just looked at me funny and said it was going to be something worse . . . a whole lot worse."

"Well, as soon as the pig cools down and it's safe to get close to him, get us some more information." Huey throws his arm around Judge. "Come on, let's get back to the party and meet some of the new ladies."

Just then Tyrone, who has been searching for Huey, pokes his head in the back room. He's startled to see Judge. He glowers at him.

"Brother Judge—you got away clean, hunh?" There is suspicion and contempt in his voice.

Judge overlooks the hostility. "Thanks to you, brother," he responds, trying to clear the air. "If you hadn't shouted that warning, they would have had my ass for sure."

"Yeah, for sure," Tyrone replies.

"What's up, Tyrone. Everything okay?" Huey cuts in.

"Nothing's up, Huey. Wanted to be sure you're okay. I always got your back, remember that." Tyrone scowls in Judge's direction and adds, "You know me, Huey, no kinda slip-ups, no kinda funny shit like that filling station hold-up."

"Naw, don't you worry about a thing. Everything is cool, brother. You hold the fort out there. We'll be out in a minute."

Tyrone leaves. Huey, gratified, turns to Judge. "Man, that Tyrone is a good brother. Always on the case."

Judge frowns, but doesn't reply.

Huey reads the trepidation in Judge's silence. "Don't worry about Tyrone, he's a righteous brother."

"I'm not worried about him. I'm still wondering what Brimmer meant when he said 'worse.'"

"Worse! What could be worse than the situation the black community is in right now?"

"Yeah, but whatever it is, it's coming . . ."

"We can't let that stop us, though. I'd rather die on my feet fighting to be free than live on my knees as a slave. Now come on," Huey says, throwing his arm around Judge again, "let's go meet those ladies!"

Oakland Induction Center, October 20, 1967. At the foot of the induction center steps, a mob of people carrying antiwar banners marches back and forth. On top of a bus a platform has been erected to serve as the speakers' platform. The police, in battle formation and riot gear—helmets, shields, and clubs—just glare at the demonstrators from the sidelines. Maybe the authorities—fearing another wave of the bad publicity generated when they turned the cops loose on the protesters—have decided to cool it, or maybe it's a tactical decision—the crowd is more than twice the size of the one at the last demonstration.

HELL NO . . . WE WON'T GO! HELL NO . . . WE WON'T GO! the crowd chants. Most of the protesters are young and white, the major exception being the contingent of Panthers standing at parade rest in two rows around the bus.

Judge, following Huey's orders to lay low, is not by the bus with the Panther bodyguards. Instead, he is standing in the deepening shadows of a building on a side street, straining to catch the words from the loudspeakers.

And from a vantage point on a nearby corner, Brimmer scans the crowd.

Avakian, a sandy-haired young white guy, winds up his impassioned speech.

"Four days ago, we came to these steps to protest," his voice blares over the PA. "The authorities beat us down, but we are back. We were four thousand then. This evening we are over ten thousand strong! Wrong is wrong. Do you hear that Lyndon Johnson? Do you hear that J. Edgar Hoover? We will continue to protest."

The throng roars its approval.

"We will not let the military-industrial complex co-opt our voice, for we know, as Martin Luther King says, our government is the chief purveyor of violence in the world today."

A huge roar rises from the crowd, and Avakian shakes his fist in the air.

"Yes! We are ten thousand different voices, all unified, saying one thing. That you cannot have an imperialistic war abroad and social peace at home."

Another cheer from the crowd.

"So with that unity, that purpose in mind, ladies and gentlemen, I give you the Minister of Defense of the Black Panther Party, Huey P. Newton."

As Huey stands, a hush descends over the gathering. The squad of Panther protection at the foot of the bus snaps crisply to attention.

The sudden silence nudges Judge's curiosity and pulls him forward. Abandoning the protective shadow of the building to get a better glimpse of what is going on, he slowly eases into the open.

As Huey steps to the mike, there is a polite smattering of applause.

"Thank you for inviting us. The Black Panther Party is proud to be here this evening. We stand with you here before this monument to oppression. Not far from here, Brother Bobby Seale is locked down—a victim of our government's tyranny, a tyranny not only right here at home, but abroad as well."

The crowd, unsure of what is coming, holds its breath.

Brimmer spots Judge, outlined in the fading light, and his eyes go cold.

Judge feels the glare as if it were a live thing on his back. He turns, and there is his nemesis shouldering his way through the crowd. Judge had convinced himself that when the time came he could defuse Brimmer's anger. But now, even though Brimmer is too far away to read the fury clouding his features, there can be no mistaking the terrible anger in the hulking figure plowing towards him.

In an instant Judge takes off, heading for Cy's old jalopy, parked three blocks away.

Brimmer grabs a pair of uniformed policemen, whispers something to them, and then resumes the chase. The local cops jump into their squad car and take off down a street parallel to Judge's flight.

"That same tyranny is at work many miles from here in Vietnam," Huey declares, warming to his subject, "Black men are dying there. White men are dying there. Yellow men are dying there. We're told they're dying in the name of freedom . . . "

Judge, legs flashing from streetlight to streetlight, barrels down the darkening street with Brimmer in pursuit.

"Freedom? Well, now, if their blood's keeping us free, how come so many of us, like Bobby Seale, the co-founder of the Black Panther Party, are in jail? If our soldiers are dying so we can enjoy our rights, how come the police still kill us in the streets?"

Judge glances over his shoulder. Brimmer is losing ground.

YAAHH! An angry roar of approval rises from the crowd.

The squad car screeches around the corner, cutting off Judge's escape.

Judge twists, but can't reverse his field in time. *WHAM!* . . . He runs into the side of the police car and crashes to the asphalt. The cops, guns drawn, drag him to his feet.

Brimmer, out of breath, trots up and snatches Judge from the officers. He brutally pins Judge's hands behind his back and slaps the cuffs on. "Thanks for nothing, motherfucker," he growls in Judge's ear. "That blind man trick you pulled was real cute."

"The question we have to ask," Huey tells the crowd, his voice crackling over the loudspeakers and carrying down the side streets, "is why should the black man go fight the yellow man for the white man? It's that simple."

"Shall we take him down to the station, sir?" one of the cops asks.

"Naw, thanks a lot, fellas," Brimmer replies, giving Judge a knee in the balls for openers. "I'll take it from here."

The cops pull away, leaving Brimmer and Judge alone. Brimmer slams Judge up against a building and punches him in the face.

"The answer is simple too!" Huey delivers his punch line. "We shouldn't!" The crowd cheers.

Judge struggles to protect himself as best he can with his hands bound behind his back. *WHOP WHOP*... Brimmer gives him a couple in the gut.

"The Black Panther Party is opposed to the war in Vietnam! The crowd cheers again.

WHAM THUMP... Patiently, methodically, Brimmer pounds away.

"Our war is here," Huey proclaims, "against unemployment, against the hard drugs in our community, against the fascist power structure that tries to stifle free speech."

BOP... Brimmer slams his fist into Judge's mouth. Stunned, Judge sinks to the pavement.

"Our war is here," Huey winds up, "against a system that beats a black man in his homeland, then sends him to die in a foreign land. That, my brothers and sisters, is our war!"

YYAAAHHHH!! The ten thousand marchers unite in thunderous applause.

Panting and sweaty, Brimmer stands over a bloody Judge.

The rally starts to break up. Like some gigantic broken egg, it streams off in every direction. The Panthers surround Huey and march away in snappy military formation, not disbanding until they reach the first intersection.

Brimmer, hearing the crowd coming, drags Judge into the shadows. He bends down and uncuffs him. "Let this be a lesson," he warns. "No more fucking around! Try that shit again and you're dead meat!"

23

Huey is in the special parking section the rally organizers had set aside for VIPs. He climbs into his junk heap, but before he can get the key in the ignition, Tyrone runs up.

"Huey! Huey!" Tyrone pants. "I'm glad I caught you, man!"

Huey rolls down his window, annoyed. "Tyrone, I'm okay. I told you I didn't need bodyguards to baby-sit me to my car."

"Naw, that ain't it, Huey. Come on . . ." Tyrone takes off, "we caught us a traitor."

Huey jumps out of the car and catches up with Tyrone.

"A coupla blocks down," Tyrone explains as they run. "Pure luck, man. I'd dismissed the squad and was going down the street when I thought I saw that pig who tried to frame us about that hold-up at the filling station coming outta the alley. He musta been back in there talking to him. I've picked out a couple of righteous brothers to help me take care of the rat. They're watching him now. I told them what the deal is and they're down for whatever we gotta do. Just give the word, Huey, and he's a dead man."

Huey has a bad premonition. "Stay cool."

They reach the alley. Two Panthers are standing over Judge, who is slumped forward on the pavement between a dumpster and the wall.

Tyrone points down at Judge. "I think the pig coming outta here was the same one snatched him from the Denzil Dowell rally too.

Just say the word, Huey."

"Things aren't always what they seem, brother," Huey replies drily.

Hearing Huey's voice, Judge raises his head. His face is swollen and he is bleeding from the mouth.

"You don't understand, Huey!" Tyrone protests. "He's a fucking traitor! I saw . . . "

Huey cuts him off. "No! You don't understand! Look at his face!" He squats beside Judge and puts his hand under his chin. "Talking to him? Does this look like the pig was talking to him? Does this look like the face of somebody working with the cops to you?"

"Naw," Tyrone reluctantly admits.

"I'm saying forget what you think you saw! That goes for all of you. That's an order!!"

Huey helps Judge to his feet, and everybody offers to drive Judge home. Judge claims he's all right, that he can drive, and anyhow he has Cy's car. All the Panthers insist on helping him to his car.

The streets are almost deserted. Random clumps of white demonstrators flash the black power salute at them and shout "Right on!" as they straggle past.

When the Panthers get Judge to his car, they start to offer help again. Judge waves them off. "I can take it from here."

Huey feels a tinge of apprehension. "You sure, Judge?"

Judge nods. "Yeah, fine, fine—it looks worse than it is."

The others leave. As soon as they are out of sight Judge lets himself go. He leans woozily across the hood of the car, breathing deeply to try to steady himself.

Another bunch of protesters going past shouts at him from the sidewalk across the street. "Right on!" Judge waves back without focusing on them, and then rests his head on the car.

"Judge! Judge, is that you?"

Judge looks up again, and through the fog in his brain sees Brick jogging across the road towards him. Judge pulls himself together and steps back into the shadows.

Brick trots up. "I shoulda known you'd be here with Huey speaking and everything. How you been?"

"Okay, man. How about you?"

They rap a bit, that combination of close and stilted that old friends who haven't talked for a while use to feel each other out. Judge hopes he sounds normal telling Brick how surprised he is to see him at a rally. And Brick says yeah he still digs action, there was plenty at the first rally and he saved his buddies from annihilation; but more than that, he got to thinking about what the Panthers said about organizing and needing allies and shit, and it was time he grew up; and they were holding a little post-rally party out at his place and he had rented a flatbed truck so there was plenty of room for the trip there and why didn't Judge come on by.

"I got Cy's car."

"How'd you wangle that?"

"He's dead."

"Aww, man . . . Sorry to hear that. He was a Panther, wasn't he? What happened, the cops get to him?"

"Sorta."

Brick points back at his group waiting across the street. "The natives will be getting restless, and I gotta open up the house. You're welcome to come. Anyhow, we gotta hook up sometime soon. You know, talk politics or pussy . . . something like that. See ya."

Judge is relieved when Brick departs, but suddenly he shivers as the fog rolls in over his spirit and he is very lonely.

Brick, leading the caravan, pulls the flatbed truck, loaded with triumphant protesters from the rally, into the drive to his house, and several other carloads turn in behind him. Playing host, Brick hops out of the cab of the truck and is first up the steps. Unlocking the door of the mansion, he ushers his friends inside with a courtly bow.

The group packs into the large kitchen, where Brick has chili on the stove and beer and wine in the refrigerator. When they've filled their plates, everybody more or less ends up in the elegant dining room, whose polished oak table and matching china cabinet were planned with a more formal crowd in mind. The gentlemen's clothing runs from button-down collars to buckskins, and the ladies seem to favor granny dresses.

A four-eyed young man named Alex is angrily wagging his spoon across the table at Douglas, a bearded fellow. "Our organization has seniority over yours!" he insists. "That's why we should lead!"

Stacey, a blonde woman, comes through the doorway from the kitchen and jumps into the conversation before Douglas can answer. "Bullshit, Alex! You guys lost the moral right to lead when you went along with the Democratic platform."

The battle rages on with charges and counter-charges, theories, predictions, everything flying, flopping, and overlapping in a leftist Tower of Babel. Humphrey betrayed us . . . Daley and his machine are going to try to run the convention next year . . . Since when do we have to ask your group for an opinion . . . *FUCK YOU! FUCK YOU TOO!*

Judge doesn't even know he is coming to Brick's until he is halfway up the drive. But seeing the place all lit up and the shadows of people on the window shades, he suddenly remembers the party. Instead of heading for the house, he wanders down across the lawn to the lake, sits down against a tree, and watches the water teasing the moonlight. A ripple here then calm, farther off another ripple. The blue moon chases the waves hither and thither, never seeming to catch on. A few hypnotic blinks of moon here, a few blinks there, like the flashing hem of a flamenco dancer's skirt . . .

Entranced, Judge's mind becomes a time machine taking him back to idyllic summer afternoons . . . three kids diving off a boat and horsing around. Two boys skinny-dipping, one black, one white, and a girl in just her underwear . . . then even further back . . . someday his memoirs, maybe . . .

My eyes were practically leaping out of my head—the soapy water burning and stinging them. I had been daydreaming so hard I hadn't shut them quick enough when Moms shoved me under. She growled that I better quit fooling around and scrub my butt, standing there with her hand on her hip, grinning at how she had managed to sneak up on me. We horsed around a lot. I said since I was almost grown she shouldn't be coming into the bathroom without knocking anyhow. "Well, you better get a move on Mister Ten-years-old-almost-grown," she said, "or you gonna miss the boat!"

The boat was a yellow school bus, all affluent and shiny, volunteered from suburbia for the local Fresh Air Fund to carry tiny disadvantaged behinds. It was a typical Oakland morning, muggy and misty at the same time. Although I didn't have a pipe, I pretended I did, just like my dad, who'd been a cook in the Merchant Marine. The last photo I had of him he was in a pea coat, the collar turned up, the stem of his briar clenched in his teeth, grinning against the cold, leaning on the icy rail with the outline of some frozen seaport retreating in the background like the faces of the mothers lining the curb smiling bravely up at us as the bus pulled away... how many lifetimes ago was that? The driver ground the gears, and then we picked up speed.

I wasn't too psyched about spending two weeks out in the country with nothing to do and white people. I tried to keep track of where I was by the gang turfs we were passing through so I could find my way back when I ran away. After the first half-mile I was at the edge of my universe. I panicked, but I lay in the cut, playing it cool. I looked around at the other kids, all underprivileged masks, glistening with sweat—trying to look fearless, trying too hard to look unimpressed. I figured they were scared shitless like me.

The bus docked in the plaza of a spick-and-span fairy-tale town. Families of white people stood around searching for whoever they had been assigned to open their hearts to.

"Judge Taylor!" I turned and three white people—a man and a boy and girl about my age—came running towards me.

The moment froze in my memory... Behind them there is this drugstore, the sun had come out and the fog had disappeared, there is a post office with this flag up on a pole flapping in the breeze. Brick, Sarah, and their father running towards me, only three or four yards away... Everybody is smiling, their arms outstretched in welcome, like I was some long-lost relative or something. How many worlds ago was that—four? Five?...

"Hey, Judge! When did you get here?" Brick has meandered away from the house towards the lake.

Judge, startled, comes out of his reverie. "Oh . . . Brick! Hi!"

"Welcome home, man."

"Yeah, home . . . Can you imagine what this place looked like to me the first time I saw it?" Judge murmurs softly, his memories still with him. "A palace."

"That's something, hunh? Why didn't you come on in? Can't say I blame you, though. It's a fucking madhouse in your palace tonight, let me tell you. Egos, man, bickering their butts off. If they'd pull together, they could kick ass."

Nodding, Judge turns towards his friend and the moonlight reveals his features.

Brick pulls back, startled. "Jesus! What happened? Those fucking pigs!"

"Nothing—I'll live. How do I look?"

"Look? . . . Like shit! Talk about being between a rock and a hard place. Listen, brother . . . is it worth it?"

"Like I said, I'll live. This shit is not just about me, it's about being able to breathe."

"Whatever it's about, brother, I should be in it with you. My being white shouldn't make a difference."

"It shouldn't, but right now it does."

"Well . . . like you said, you'll live. Wanta come in?"

"Negative." Judge gingerly touches his swollen jaw. "I might just scare the shit out of your friends. It's a little early for Halloween."

When Brick returns to the house, the fuck-yous are still flying hot and heavy.

"Fuck you, Stacey," Curtis, a bony, earnest young man with his mouth full is saying. "We can't break away—you need a party before you can put up a candidate."

Brick pulls a chair up to the table. "I can tell you guys what you oughta do, instead of fighting each other."

"What's that, go off and join the Weathermen like your sister did?" Douglas sneers.

"Leave Sarah out of this, asshole . . . at least she's doing something," Brick says, leaping to his sister's defense.

"Don't mind him, Brick," Stacey says. "He just had the hots for her is all. So what's your idea?"

Brick shrugs. "I don't know. Make a coalition . . . an alliance . . . some fucking thing and start a brand new party that brings everybody together."

The idea appeals to Stacey. "Yeah," she enthuses, "just focus on what we have in common, instead of what we don't! Whatta we all want?"

"Peace!" booms Phil, a long-hair. "No more fucking war!"

"Freedom!" Stacey sings out.

Brick has a flash. "That's it . . . You're the Peace and Freedom Party!"

The idea hits home. Everybody claps.

"Wait a minute!" Douglas tugs his beard. "I hate to be a party pooper, but to put a candidate on the ballot we'd have to have a minimum of twenty-five thousand registered voters—and that's by January."

"We'd never make it," four-eyed Alex concedes. "Even if we could get all of our members to go along, we'd still come up way short." The rest of the group grumbles.

But Stacey refuses to give up. "We gotta try, guys! We gotta try."

"I bet the Black Panthers could mobilize that many voters by themselves," Brick points out.

THE PANTHERS?! . . . Everybody starts fussing.

"Well, why not?" Brick challenges. "They're against the war in Vietnam and drugs and . . . "

"Against drugs!" Douglas interrupts. He pulls on a joint and winces. "Fuck that! Long live pot and acid too. Like Leary says, we gotta explore the labyrinthine regions of the cerebral cortex." Everybody laughs.

"Not marijuana, man!" Brick explains. "The hard shit."

Phil is still skeptical. "Do we really want to be associated with them? Not to mention they're anti-white."

"Anti-white, my ass," Brick replies, exasperated. "The question is do they want us?"

Brick gets up and goes to the door. "HEY, JUDGE!" Brick yells. "Would you guys be interested in joining us in a coalition!?"

24

TESTING, ONE-TWO-THREE . . . Witness #18. Dr. Alvin Warren Fence III . . . Black studies lecture, amphitheater-style hall, three-quarters full, approximately forty students . . . The professor is wearing a kinti cloth blazer and leather fez.

> . . . An old Eurocentric proverb goes, and we have all heard it, "Time will tell." The more colorful slave version paraphrased from a West African proverb is, "It will all come out in the washing." Regardless of which proverb you prefer, the fact of the matter is, time was one thing the Panthers didn't have! Growth was their best defense against annihilation. However, the recruits swelling their ranks were ghetto folk without an overview of oppression. In the vernacular of the ghetto, they just wanted the Man's foot out of their ass—fast!—and to hell with political considerations. Logistically, this led to a bottleneck, and a major problem was the time it took to weed out the spies planted by the Man. Even more interesting for our purposes here is the question, did the Panthers' success beget their own downfall? Did the Panthers' success indirectly bring on the plague of heroin and cocaine? Did their challenging the sys-

tem push the authorities over the edge? Granted the government's arrogance, duplicity, and stupidity were already there, otherwise it would never have done what it did. But, "Aye, and there's the rub of it," as Shakespeare would say—was it the Panthers' defiance that triggered it? Or was it simply the ghetto, once again, bearing the brunt of the establishment's frustration with the forces of change? The resistance to the war in Vietnam, SDS, civil rights, hippies, Yippies, SNCC, PFP. Does it matter? Maybe America was going to wind up a drug culture anyway, without the cops helping.

A sentry with a shotgun sits in the doorway of the layout room of the printing plant the Panthers use to produce their weekly newspaper. Huey, Tyrone, and some of the other Panthers, plus a sister and brother up from L.A., are cooling out inside, waiting for the latest edition to come off the press. They pass a joint around and try to listen to the Bob Dylan album competing with the roar of the huge web press.

In the far corner, the Minister of Culture and his staff, including Alma, are busily working on the next edition of the Black Panther paper.

"Ballad of a Thin Man" comes up and Huey walks over to the record player to hear it better. It's one of his favorite songs.

Huey, grooving to the music and a little high, turns to Tyrone, who has followed him over to the phonograph. "Right there! Listen, hear that? 'One-eyed midget says give me some juice or go home.' That means if the boojies want you to entertain them, then they've gotta pay. Here's the 'geek' part. Geeks are always given the cruddiest jobs, like black people. Dylan's on the case."

"Yeah," Tyrone acknowledges, pretending to understand. He tries to bring the conversation back to his previous topic. "But, listen, Huey—I gotta tell you, I still got my doubts about Judge."

"Remember what Franz Fanon said, brother—'We mustn't be too quick to pass judgment on one another.'"

Tyrone starts to protest, but just then the first copies of the new edition start to roll off the press.

Huey snatches a paper off the roller, not letting Tyrone finish his thought. "Wow—this is beautiful!" Huey says, holding up the paper and beaming with pride. "This is it! The truth, that's what we giving the folks. The truth!"

"We can sure use that down in the City of Angels," the brother from L.A. says. "That's what we need to talk to you about, Huey. The shit's coming to a head down there, with the FBI and all their stooges and stoolies . . . "

"I know what you mean, brother," Tyrone seconds.

At that moment Eldridge comes through the door with a fan-back wicker chair and a six-foot African spear.

"El Rage, so what up with the native stuff?" Little-Bobby says.

"We can no longer let the white media control our images," Eldridge says. He disappears out the door again and comes back with a photographer carrying a tripod and a camera. "We've got to let the people know what we are about ourselves!"

Huey holds up the new edition. "Right on, Eldridge. That's what our newspapers are doing!"

"Lots of our people don't read much, man," Eldridge says, sitting Huey down in the wicker chair and posing him with the spear and rifle. "They need strong imagery to help them out . . . we need a picture."

Huey beckons the other Panthers to join him in a group photo. "Well, this should be all of us then."

But Eldridge shoos the others away and steps behind the camera to check the composition. "Trust me on this Huey—this picture will be worth a thousand words."

Huey shrugs and decides to humor him.

"Speaking of words, the people from the antiwar movement have gotten their shit together and formed a coalition, they're calling themselves the Peace and Freedom Party. Anyway they liked my speech at the rally so much I've been informed that they want the Panther Party to hook up with them. What do you think?"

"I can dig it," Eldridge nods, pleased. "It will broaden our base of visibility and boost our number of speaking engagements."

Huey turns to Jamal. "What do you think, brother?"

"I think that poor black folks are fighting for their humanity, while white folks are fighting for more money. The white kids can cut their hair and join the establishment whenever they want to. We're black forever."

Huey twists in his chair to address the newspaper's editor. "What does the Minister of Culture think?"

The Minister of Culture looks up from the layout he is working on. "I think I don't trust white people," is his terse reply. "What's the deal?"

"They want to start their own political party, but to do that they must have twenty-five thousand signatures by January and they don't have the manpower or organization to pull it off by themselves."

"Pull it off!" Alma scoffs without raising her head from her work. "They couldn't even come close."

"Yeah, so why not let the African carry the load," Jamal sneers. "That it?"

"So what are they gonna give up?" Tyrone comes in. "And what the hell they got that we want, anyway?"

Huey smiles. "I hear you, brother, but negotiations on our various conditions would be a little premature at this point." He turns to Alma, who has been typing furiously the entire time.

"Sister Alma—care to share your thoughts with us?"

"My thoughts?" she says, looking up from her typing. "Well, the FBI is leaning on our printer and he would love some excuse to cancel our contract. The deadline for the next issue of the paper is tomorrow, and . . . " she bursts into a grin, "circulation is up to 125,000 and rising! We're seizing the time!"

Everybody cheers and applauds. Right on!

"Well," Eldridge proclaims, taking advantage of the break. "It's just like Jean Paul Sartre attests, 'We are living at the moment when the match is being put to the fuse.' The question is, is the hand holding that match going to be black or white? Like I said before, joining the alliance might help boost the number of speaking engagements and raise our visibility, plus increase the paper's circulation even more, which is where most of the bread is coming from at the moment."

Huey turns to Tyrone. "What's your view, brother?"

"I'm with you, Huey," Tyrone nods.

All eyes turn back to Huey. He sits there with a slight smile on his face holding the rifle and the spear, thinking . . . Eldridge motions the photographer to start snapping.

In Washington, D.C., Hoover sits at his desk frothing at the mouth. "I won't have it! No more black messiahs!" He looks up from the photo of Huey Newton in the wicker chair on the cover of the latest Panther paper. He tosses the paper on the floor. "Never again!" he fumes.

The next day, Brimmer stalks down the hall at Oakland police headquarters, wondering what the hell is going on.

Everywhere, it seems, there are FBI guys moving in, setting up, making themselves right at home. They are all over the place, sending teletypes, barking into phones. From his new office, Rodgers beckons to Brimmer.

"Brimmer! Could you come in here, please?"

Rodgers, who has had the room set up like a command center, is standing at the head of a conference table. Another agent is standing with his back to Brimmer, studying the chart of the Panther hierarchy outlined on the bulletin board. Dorsett is sitting at the far end of the table, looking like a whipped dog.

"Take a seat, detective," Rodgers orders Brimmer, making no effort to hide his disdain. "This is Agent Pruitt. He will be working with us from here on in."

Pruitt turns to face the room. He is tall, well-tailored, and black.

Brimmer can't believe his eyes. "Agent? But . . . but . . . I mean . . . well, ain't he . . . ," he sputters.

Pruitt permits himself an imperious smirk. "Special people for special problems," he replies impassively in an elegant voice.

"Uh . . . I didn't know the FBI had any . . . uh . . . ," Brimmer stammers.

Pruitt interrupts, sardonic and unruffled. "It is quite obvious there are many things you don't know." He gives Brimmer a curt nod, passes a sheaf of papers to Dorsett, and steps to the head of the table. "Let's move on, shall we?" he says, taking command. "I don't need to say that this department's handling of the Black Panthers . . . particularly Inspector Brimmer's 'undercover operation' . . . has been a complete travesty."

Pruitt nods towards the portfolio in Dorsett's hands. "Those are memos from the commissioner, the mayor, and so on backing Mr. Hoover's decision to put the Black Panthers and their subversive activities under the full jurisdiction of the Bureau."

Dorsett thumbs the file. "Jesus!"

Pruitt continues. "Mr. Hoover does not intend to have our country taken over by communists or their fellow travelers." He pauses briefly for dramatic effect. "As far as Mr. Hoover is concerned, the Panthers are public enemy number one. In short, they have quite simply guaranteed their own demise. We will handle it henceforth."

Dorsett is furious—Brimmer is stunned.

Rodgers, standing a step behind Pruitt, can't resist rubbing it in. "Of course, Mr. Hoover would still appreciate any cooperation you might have to offer."

Dumbstruck, Dorsett simply nods in compliance.

25

TESTING, ONE-TWO-THREE . . . Witness #19. Name: Dr. Jennifer Morris . . .

SO THE PANTHERS ACCEPTED THE ANTIWAR MOVEMENT'S OFFER TO COME IN WITH THEM IN THE PEACE AND FREEDOM PARTY?

Not then, not the first time. Huey said no. He decided we were going to pass on the invitation. For one thing, Chairman Bobby Seale had almost three more months to do, plus organizing signatures would have overextended our manpower resources. Keep in mind we had already initiated so many vital community services—breakfast programs, medical assistance, etc.

. . . MEDICAL, RIGHT? I GUESS THAT WAS YOUR INVOLVEMENT WITH THE PANTHERS?

No, I was just a rank and file member. After my release, I went back to school.

DOCTOR, LOOKING AT THE DIPLOMAS AND AWARDS LINING YOUR OFFICE, I FIND IT HARD TO IMAGINE YOU AS A PANTHER. HOWEVER, IT DOES PROVE THAT ONE CAN TURN ONE'S LIFE AROUND IF ONE WANTS TO.

If that is a subtle allusion to the brother who met with you and demanded a percentage of your royalties, let me say this. Setting aside sexual lust of the oppressor for the moment, in this misogynistic society a black woman is not viewed as an equal threat to the establishment as a black male, and as such therefore benefits more from fruits of opportunity systematically witheld from our men. In fact, that very gender discrimination has often been used by the establishment to foster dissension along sexual lines within the race. Unfortunately, since the black community lacks the means to openly discuss this ploy, the conflict festers.

YOU HAVE THE BLACK MEDIA, DOCTOR.

To survive in our society, the media needs revenue from advertisers—white advertisers. Advertisers who insist on white-sanctioned truth only.

YOU SAY YOU WERE "RANK AND FILE." WHAT SPECIFICALLY WAS YOUR FUNCTION?

I was an organizer. I would go to a place that wanted to start a chapter, help them get on their feet. I was also a drill sergeant too. We had chants that I would use when I taught recruits to march.

HUP-two-three—Know the ten points, if you do not
You do not know, what you are living, or dying for
You do not know who you are, or where you are from
HUP-two-three—A slave hates himself, he hates his skin,
A slave hates his naturally kinky hair
Give a slave a gun and he'll kill his own brother
HUP-two-three—How long are you going to blame your oppressor

How long before you rise from your knees
And become the master of your destiny.

One time we were drilling in an old gym and a fire bomb came crashing through the window. You had smoke everywhere and people running around yelling and then wham! wham! . . . the cops were at the door with a battering ram.

FRANKLY, DOCTOR, SITTING HERE IN YOUR OFFICE, I STILL FIND IT HARD TO IMAGINE YOU IN SUCH CIRCUMSTANCES. DON'T BE OFFENDED—I DON'T MEAN I DON'T BELIEVE YOU.

On the contrary, I understand. Many things I find hard to believe myself. But by that I don't mean my personal circumstance, I mean what the government did. The government turned its Cointelpro forces loose on us. It gave its special Counter Intelligence section the green light to neutralize us. 'Neutralize,' that's the euphemism they used for wiping out our leadership. They started raiding and shooting up Panther offices. Later they moved on to murder. Bunchy Carter and the other righteous brothers down in L.A., Alex Rackley in New Haven, Fred Hampton out in Chicago, they blew him away in his own bed. Did you ever see the photographs? The bullet holes where the authorities strafed the apartment. The pools of dried blood on the floor.

LOOKING BACK, ANY THOUGHTS?

We were right, and so determined and dedicated, I can't accept that we didn't win. I suppose I should say, win yet. We childishly, romantically, underestimated our enemy's capacity.

HOW COULD YOU HAVE BEEN THAT NAIVE? THE UNITED STATES IS THE STRONGEST NATION ON EARTH.

I am not talking about the wealth or machinery or manpower the government had at its command. We had no illusion about that. I am talking about its capacity for evil.

DO YOU REGRET THE PANTHERS NOW?

I would do it again in a second, if that is what you mean. I believed every word and still do.

WELL, ON A PERSONAL LEVEL, THEN . . . ANY REGRETS?

Just a selfish one I suppose.

MIGHT I ASK?

I wish I could have died back then believing the dream was going to come true.

Oakland, October 28, 1967. The automobile rolls homeward through the ghetto streets all deserted and tuckered out by the wee hours of the morning. On the radio Jimi Hendrix is kissing the sky. Huey is at the wheel feeling good, and Gene, the brother next to him in the car having taken himself a bag of fried chicken for the road, is chomping away and chuckling as he relates a run-in with the police earlier in the day. Just cackling and cruising, feeling no pain.

"And I keep saying 'Five' like the Fifth Amendment, you know? And shit these cops are getting pissed. But there ain't much they can do. So dig this, the one who knocked the Panther newspapers I was selling out of my hand in the the first place and kicked 'em up and down the street, gives me a ticket for littering."

Huey notices the cherry-top glow of a squad car in the rear view mirror and pulls over.

Officer Frey, the belligerent baby-faced cop from the showdown on Grove Street comes swaggering up to the car. "Okay, let's see some registration," he orders.

Huey hands him the document out of the car window.

"Well now, Mr. er . . . Williams."

"Williams is not my name, officer," Huey says. "You asked for the registration. The automobile is not registered to me."

"Oh, a smart-ass coon!" Frey jeers. "Well, we'll just have to see about that, won't we? Okay, let's have your license!"

Huey offers his license. Frey grabs it, reads it, and then whips out his gun. Pointing it first at Huey and then at Gene, he warns, "Now don't you boys move a cotton-pickin' muscle!" He goes to his squad car, all the time keeping his gun trained on the Panther vehicle, and calls for back-up.

Frey struts back. "Well, well, well, so what do we have here?" he sneers, shaking the license with his free hand. "The great Huey P. Newton himself. Okay, now, get out of the car, boy . . . slowly!"

Huey shakes a thick law book out of the window at the cop. "California law does not require the driver to leave a vehicle unless he is being placed under arrest."

Frey levels his gun, taking dead aim. "Get out of the fuckin' car!"

Cautiously, Huey climbs out of the car, law book in hand. Frey spreadeagles Huey across the hood of the automobile.

"I am not resisting arrest. Nor am I armed," Huey points out. "Therefore any use of force on your part is illegal."

"Oh, yeah?" Frey retorts. "Well, you can take that law book and shove it up your ass, nigger!"

At that moment, Officer Heanes pulls up in his squad car.

Frey straightens Huey up and prods him towards the shadows with his gun. "Come on, move!"

Heanes, a little anxious, ambles over, fingering his weapon. "Hey, Frey . . . whatcha got?"

"Buddy-boy, we just got ourselves a promotion," Frey says, cocking his revolver and shoving Huey towards the darkness.

Heanes flinches at the sound of the hammer of Frey's gun clicking into place.

"You just keep your eye on the other one," Frey hollers, marching Huey off. "I'll take care of this big-shot coon."

Heanes orders Gene to come out of the car with his hands up.

BANG BANG . . . Gunfire rings out from the dark end of the street. In the gloom Huey and Frey are struggling. Huey swats Frey's gun with the lawbook. *BANG* . . . it goes off again as it falls and they dive for the weapon. *BLAM BLAM BLAM* . . . Back at the cars, Heanes freaks out and starts blasting away at the tussling silhouettes. Gene goes for Heanes. Huey has Frey's gun. He swings around towards Heanes . . . *BANG BLAM BANG* . . . Searing streaks of white and red flash up and down the street. When the shoot-out is over, three bodies lay twitching in the night.

TESTING, ONE-TWO-THREE . . . Witness #20. Name: Billy "BeBop" Benson . . . Two-tone shoes, diamond stickpin.

> How do I know? Well the first part I saw with my own eyes. See, one ambulance came wailing up to the emergency entrance with a shot-up cop, then right after that another with another cop. When the nurse screamed and I came running, I thought it was about a mouse or some shit. No way, it was about Huey. He'd come staggering in through the front door. Hell, the bitch freaked, lost her professional cool, Jack. See, I recognized him immediately because I had tried to join the Panthers but I was high and they passed on me. But I had gotten my habit act together and I was working at the hospital as an orderly to get my bread together to get my ax out of the pawn shop. Anyway we got Huey on a gurney. He had more holes in him than a Swiss cheese, Jack. Anyway we wheeled him in one of the cubicles, blood gushing out of him like one of them geysers in Yellowstone Park. Then we hear these feet pounding down the corridor. The nurse had pulled herself together and called the cops. They come bursting in the room yelling cop killer and shit at Huey laying on the stretcher three-quarters dead himself. They push me and the intern aside, handcuff Huey's arms to the table and start working what was left of the brother over with fists and billy

clubs to finish him off. If the reporters hadn't arrived with their cameras when they did, he was a goner. In fact, nobody expected him to live anyhow.

THIS ACTUALLY HAPPENED?

Shit, yeah—one of the reporters got out a picture before they stopped beating on him. They printed it in the paper too. Maybe it was news to white folks but black folks already knew what had gone down, it wasn't no news to us, Jack. Which brings me to how I know the rest. Black people had tom-toms before you had the information highway. I had this prison guard buddy, who was an ex-musician, played a little guitar, wasn't much good, but claimed he usta play with Johnny Otis. Motherfucker was lying, but anyhow, he was working where they was keeping Bobby. And I don't care what they say black folks do stick together. Bobby Seale had around another month to do on that frame-up about the legislature. Anyway, my buddy slipped Bobby a newspaper around noon the next day. The shoot-out was on the front page. One pig dead and another seriously wounded and this photo of Huey on this stretcher I already told you about. Huey had been shot five times, four in the gut. Only thing Bobby wanted to know was, was Huey gonna live? That was all he kept asking. Well you know the rest anyhow. Huey survived. In fact, they didn't mind about him living. In fact, they were happy. They had 'em a cop killer, see. They figured they had his neck in a noose anyhow and they was going to have a show trial and make an example out of his black ass. They indicted him on Murder One.

26

"Seale? . . . Bobby Seale!"

Bobby, in his dingy prison jumpsuit, is sitting on his bunk in his 7' x 7' cell in the Alameda County Jail finishing the tail of his six months. A black trustee is moving along the catwalk shouting out his name.

"Over here! I'm over here," Bobby answers.

The trustee pulls up in front of Bobby's cell. The white guard at the end of the tier is watching them.

The trustee raises his voice again, so the guard can hear. "All right, brother, get your ass in gear if you wanta get that foot checked out," he shouts through the bars. "You ain't the only one asked to see the doc today."

"I didn't ask to see no doctor," Bobby replies, not getting it.

The trustee keeps shouting. "Sure you did!" he winks and shakes a piece of paper at Bobby. "This slip here says you did!"

Now Bobby catches on. "Oh, yeah, my foot! Shit, I forgot . . . my foot, yeeaah."

The trustee guides Bobby to the waiting room. It turns out to be not much wider than a corridor. Besides the black guard at the entrance they are alone. On one side is the door leading to the doctor's office and on the other side a hospital security cell. The bars of the security cell are covered by a curtain that runs from floor to ceiling.

The black guard glances out the door to make sure no one is coming, then he turns and nods to the trustee. The trustee puts a fingertip to his lips for silence and pulls back the curtain.

Huey is strapped to the bed in the security cell. He grins and gives Seale the black power fist. Bobby returns the salute and the trustee pulls the curtain shut again.

"Thank you, my brothers," Bobby whispers as he leaves.

"Power to the people," the guard whispers back.

MEMO/COINTELPRO: TOP SECRET
NEWTON SURVIVED CONFRONTATION HAS BEEN IMPRISONED AND INDICTED. SEALE RELEASED.

OAKLAND

MEMO/COINTELPRO: TOP SECRET
RESULTS PHASE ONE INSUFFICIENT. BPP MEMBERSHIP INCREASING. INTENSIFY OPERATIONS.

WASHINGTON

Squinting his eyes against the bright sunlight, Bobby steps out of the Alameda County Jail, a free man. He stands there, dwarfed by the gigantic walls of the prison aptly nicknamed Big Greystone at his back. A car pulls up, and the rear door opens. Bobby leans in and kisses his wife and child then climbs into the front with the Panther doing the driving. The Panther asks him what's happening.

"What's happening is Huey," Bobby retorts. "We got to get him out. That's the long, short, and tall of it! Free Huey!"

They drive directly to a high school gym where preparations are underway for a rally. Hundreds of folding chairs have been set up, but only ten or so people outside of the Panthers are in attendance.

A group of the early Panthers, including Tyrone, Alma, Eldridge, and Little-Bobby, spot Bobby coming through the gym doors. Overjoyed, they rush to meet him.

Bobby is shocked. "Where's everybody?" he demands. "I got word through the prison grapevine that everything was going down just fine!"

"It was. We had over a hundred people on the Free Huey Defense Committee alone," Tyrone acknowledges.

"Had?" Bobby comes back.

Grimly, Tyrone concedes, "Yeah, 'had.' Until we chose the lawyer. Name's Charles Garry."

"What the hell has that got to do with anything?"

Tyrone points to a middle-aged white man in a rumpled suit heading across the gym floor towards them.

"That's him," Eldridge says, adding quickly, "that is, if you approve."

"They call him the Lenin of the courtroom," Alma adds.

"He isn't even charging us," Little-Bobby chimes in. "He says he wants justice."

"Fuck the cat's color, can he free Huey?" Bobby rejoins.

"He's the best. If anybody can, he can," Eldridge answers.

"Well, then he's our man."

Bobby steps forward and shakes Garry's outstretched hand, then turns back to the Panthers. "Okay. What else?"

Eldridge says they need allies and fast.

"Anybody got any ideas?" Bobby asks.

Eldridge offers a suggestion. "Well, the Peace and Freedom Party is still trying to enter the presidential race. They still don't have enough signatures and they still want to form a coalition with us."

"President? They ain't about to win that!" Tyrone observes.

"Winning isn't the point," Eldridge retaliates. "It sends a message that the Panthers and the white radicals mean business."

Little-Bobby's eyes are brimming with admiration for Eldridge.

Bobby goes along. "Okay, brother Eldridge, you work out the politics with them. But remember, the focus stays on freeing Huey."

PFP headquarters is in a bustling white business area of Oakland. From the sidewalk everything is upbeat, the front draped with patriotic bunting, but inside the room is full of demoralized workers staring at phones that refuse to ring.

Judge rushes in. Brick, "losing battle" written all over his face, slouches over to greet him.

Judge blurts out his big news. "The Panthers will join!"

Brick goes wild. "They will?!" he beams.

"Well," Judge cautions him, "there are certain conditions."

But Brick is already shouting the news to the rest of the room. "The Panthers are coming in with us!"

Everybody starts applauding.

Oakland, January 10, 1968. The Panthers are holding a rally in front of the Alameda County Courthouse. Panthers and well wishers are spread out across the bottom of the steps. Some are holding aloft banners demanding that Huey be freed.

Bobby Seale, Eldridge, and Stokely Carmichael, an intense, wiry young man in sunglasses, are standing midway up the stairs facing the throng.

FREE HUEY! FREE HUEY! FREE HUEY! the crowd chants.

Uniformed cops glare at the demonstrators from behind the glass doors of the courthouse.

Stokely approaches the mike and raises his hand for silence. A hush falls over the audience.

"I am here as a representative of the SNCC—the Student Nonviolent Coordinating Committee—to declare that SNCC stands shoulder to shoulder with the Panther Party in proclaiming that Huey P. Newton is a prisoner of war."

Carmichael's speaking style is unique—a slow, low-key drawl that underscores the incendiary nature of his message. "Many people say that that's not true. That Huey is not a prisoner of war, or that the Party is exaggerating. But I think it's clear, it's crystal clear that the United States has declared war on black people. She did that when she took the first black man from Africa."

The crowd murmurs its approval, several raise their fists.

Stokely continues. "Now of course, she never came out and said the words, 'I declare war on black people.' She did not do that. Well now, the United States to this day has not declared war on Vietnam, but it is at war in Vietnam. They did not declare war on North Korea but they fought in North Korea. And they did not declare war against the Indians. They just wiped them out. Huey P. Newton, Minister of Defense of the Black Panther Party, must be freed! Period! Free Huey! By any means necessary he must be freed! Free Huey!"

The crowd cheers, a surge of emotion pouring forth. They pick up the chant *FREE HUEY! FREE HUEY!* again, and it rises to the heavens, bounces off a cloud, and ricochets across the continent to Washington, D.C.

"Free Huey!?" Hoover, three thousand miles away on the fifth floor of the Criminal Justice Building, rejoins. "Just who the hell do they think this Newton is?" Hoover turns his chair to face the window. He shakes an affronted finger towards the fast fading winter afternoon and swears an oath. "After the good doctor is gone, and that won't be long, there will never be another black messiah . . . unless we create him!"

Oakland, February 17, 1968. A Peace and Freedom Party rally is underway, the huge hall standing room only. One of the Berkeley antiwar activists is at the podium.

"This is an historic event," he announces. "A coalition of the left, setting aside our differences for the greater good, has formed an alliance with the Panther Party. The Peace and Freedom Party accepts the ten points of the Panther Party as a valid goal for the Panther Party and we agree to assist them in attaining that goal. Furthermore, we believe in the interest of justice that Huey Newton be freed."

The audience greets this pronouncement with stunned silence, then the applause begins, finally rising to a huge crescendo.

The speaker continues. "It is now my pleasure to introduce the Peace and Freedom Party's candidate for Vice President of these United States. Ladies and gentlemen, Eldridge Cleaver."

Eldridge comes to the mike. The audience holds its breath.

"Free Huey!" he says, raising his fist in the black power salute.

The hall leaps to its feet and gives Eldridge a standing ovation.

Overcome with disgust at the welcome Cleaver has received, Rodgers and Pruitt, dressed like hippies, or at least the FBI version, bolt out of the building.

Doing a little snooping on his own, Dorsett spots them heading for the exit. He waddles down the steps after them, and catches them as they stomp around the corner of the building.

"Hey, Rodgers, where's your guitar?" Dorsett tweaks him. "You call that a disguise?" Rodgers glares at him. "Hey, don't get sore—I was just kidding. Mind if I join you? Can you believe it, a convict for Vice President!"

"Well, at least Newton's behind bars," Rodgers replies weakly.

The three of them walk beside the railroad tracks adjacent to the hall. Pruitt is quiet, but Dorsett and Rodgers keep growsing to each other.

Dorsett is still needling Rodgers. "Bobby Seale is back out, and now there's comrade Cleaver. You call that good work?"

Pruitt finally breaks his silence. "Look, gentlemen, let's not turn this into a pissing contest. Their days are all numbered."

"I guess you're right," Dorsett sighs. "Anyhow, there's more than one way to skin a cat."

Rodgers lowers his voice. "Lots of ways, and believe me, Mr. Hoover has a contingency plan for every occasion."

27

TESTING, ONE-TWO-THREE . . . Witness #21. Name: Horace Carter . . . Cabbie.

IT SEEMS THE PANTHERS HAD MORE THAN THEY BARGAINED FOR? CARE TO ELUCIDATE ON THAT?

Come again? Lucy who?

"E-LUCI-DATE." CARE TO TALK ABOUT THE PANTHERS?

As long as the meter's running, I'm cool. I know where you coming from, with that "more than they bargained for" stuff, like they say, "Some folks won't believe fat meat's greasy, or turtles shit in the sand, won't believe a skillet's hot either, 'til their own behind is frying in the pan." But the Panthers and the black community was hip to hard times, so it didn't faze 'em all that much, the authorities turning up the heat. Another thing too the Panthers had organized themselves from the very beginning so that they wasn't no one-man show. That way you couldn't just wipe out the movement by getting rid of one or two of the leaders. The Panthers usta say you can jail the revolutionary, but you can't jail the revolution. No matter how hard the pigs tried to put 'em down, the Panthers was expanding, and their muscle in the black community was growing too. Amen, by leaps and bounds, amen, leaps and bounds.

Panther headquarters is a beehive of activity. Bobby Seale along with a brigade of Panther helpers is manning the phones, which are ringing off the hook. Little-Bobby is supervising the leaflets and pamphlets to be distributed. Tyrone, Alma, and Judge are seated at a table opening boxes and allocating "Free Huey" buttons. Eldridge, on an errand, walks past the table grinning, exhilarated.

"Man, we can't make enough of these things!" Eldridge exclaims, pausing to scoop up a handful of buttons. "We got movie stars calling up asking how they can help. I tell you, brothers and sisters, it's nation time."

Alma turns to Judge. "I wish we didn't need these buttons," she says ruefully. "I'd rather have Huey here with us."

"Yeah, me too," Judge concurs.

Tyrone, looks up sharply. "Are you sure about that, my brother?"

Judge has had it with Tyrone. They both jump to their feet glaring at one another. But before they can go to war, Little-Bobby lets out a whoop of joy.

"Hey, everybody, look! We got visitors!"

In walks Reverend Slocum leading a contingent of his congregation bearing steaming, delicious-smelling trays of food. The Panthers rush to welcome them. Judge takes one look and his jaw drops. There's his Moms, right up front with a macaroni and cheese casserole. They glance at one another, both blush, their eyes meet again, and they smile tenderly.

She holds her casserole out to him sheepishly. "You all been working so much, you know. And doing such good things. Reverend Slocum and me and some of the others thought you might be able to use some home cooking."

Tyrone grins, licking his chops. "Yes, ma'am, we sure can!"

Judge and his mother hug warmly.

Mrs. Hutton, Little-Bobby's mother, points to a "Free Huey" button. "You-all got any more of those?"

Little-Bobby says he will trade her one for a piece of fried chicken, and everybody laughs.

Little-Bobby pulls Eldridge over to meet his mother. "This is Eldridge, mom, this great guy I've been telling you about."

Mrs. Hutton tells him pleased to meet you and Eldridge says she has a wonderful son and Mrs. Hutton grins and then they dig into the food.

Rita lays down the law for her own son. "You gonna come home tomorrow and eat a proper dinner, you hear me?" She points to Little-Bobby. "And be sure to bring that skinny chile with you too!"

Judge and Little-Bobby are finishing dinner as Rita bustles back and forth clearing dishes. Off in a corner the TV plays, its sound turned down.

"Glad to see you boys eat like that," beams Rita, coming in from the kitchen with a deep dish apple pie. "No wonder you're both looking like scarecrows. You don't sleep, don't eat—that's no way to live."

"It's good to be skinny, easier to run from fat cops," Little-Bobby teases. Suddenly something on the TV catches his eye. "Hey, what's that? Look . . . they must be re-running some documentary on Malcolm's murder or something . . . "

They watch the TV for a minute, and then a look of horror creeps across their faces. The deep dish apple pie falls from Rita's hands and smashes on the dining room floor. Little-Bobby stares at the television, frozen. Judge jumps to the TV to turn up the sound, and Rita starts to cry.

The newsman, his normally professional demeanor shaken, reports, "April 4, 1968 is a tragic day for all Americans. Martin Luther King, Jr. was killed today in Memphis, Tennessee."

"Oh no . . . Oh God no, not Dr. King!" Rita moans. "Oh lord, please, not him."

"Dr. King was shot in the face as he stood alone on the balcony of his hotel room. He died in the hospital an hour later. Last night he said this."

A close-up of King speaking appears. "I just want to do God's will. And he's allowed me to go to the mountain. And I've looked over, and I've seen the promised land. I may not get there with you . . ."

Little-Bobby can't believe his eyes. "He never hurt nobody." Tears stream down his cheeks. "And they killed him."

In the corner, the TV impassively shows the scene of the atrocity. Abernathy, Young, Jackson point to where the shots came from as King bleeds on the balcony. Judge puts his arm around his mom's waist to console her.

Suddenly, the screen begins to leap with flames as the cities of America explode in outrage.

Judge rises grimly to his feet. "Come on, Little-Bobby!"

"Where are you boys going?" Rita asks fearfully.

"Panther headquarters, Moms."

In the back room, under a single naked light bulb strung from an overhead beam, the Panther leadership is holding a tense, angry meeting. Flanked by his personal bodyguards, Eldridge stands spewing pure rage.

"No more words! No more goddamn words! No more sit-ins, no more praying for the pig to stop killing us. Later for lying down. Later for waiting to get shot like dogs. Nonviolence died in Memphis. It died with Dr. King. We must retaliate! We've got the fucking guns, it's time to use them."

Eldridge's bodyguards rubber stamp his position. "Yeah, let's off the pig. Off the goddamn pig!"

"Shut the fuck up, motherfuckers!" Bobby screams at the bodyguards, then turns to face Eldridge.

Bobby's eyes have narrowed to angry slits. "Brother Eldridge, I hear you. But I disagree. And you and I both know Huey disagrees too. Yeah, we got the guns, but the pigs got more and the pig has got the National Guard too. We gotta be smart, not just angry. I'm not afraid to fight. But we aren't stupid either. We gotta be smart, not . . ."

"Not what?!" Eldridge cuts him short. "Later for all that!"

"No man . . . later for you!" Tyrone jumps in, seething. "What we gonna do? Forget about Huey and his trial? Start killing pigs. We do that and Huey's a dead man. We gotta stay cool."

Eldridge gets up in Tyrone's face. "What? You giving me orders now?" he challenges.

Tyrone holds his ground, "I'm just telling you what it is!"

"Fuck that. It's time to intensify the struggle. That's what it is!"

Turning on his heel, Eldridge storms out of the room. First Eldridge's guards follow him, and then some of the other Panthers leave as well. The confrontation has driven a wedge through the heart of the Panthers. Little-Bobby's chin starts to quiver. Alma puts her arm around him to comfort him, but Little-Bobby pushes it away and follows Eldridge out into the street.

Shrouded with a deep sadness, Bobby, Tyrone, Alma, Judge, and the remaining Panthers watch them go.

Bobby shakes his head. "Damn!"

The next day, haggard and concerned, Bobby Seale faces Huey across the long table of the visitor's room under the watchful eye of a guard.

". . . Well," Huey is answering him, "Eldridge has got to remember that you are the party's leader. You've got to make him slow his roll."

They look at each other fondly, with deep respect.

Bobby nods and smiles ruefully. "It ain't easy when I'm running all over the country lecturing, trying to raise money to defend your precious ass. You all right?"

"Don't worry about me, man. I'll be okay." Huey raises a clenched fist. "All power to the people."

"Don't worry about you? It ain't the same without you, Huey."

"Remember, you've got to sit on Eldridge." Huey leans forward, his breath forming tiny clouds on the glass partition. "He's gotta cool it."

"El Rage is El Rage, man. You know him."

"Yeah, I sure do."

Bobby returns the salute. "All power to the people."

■ ■ ■

TESTING, ONE-TWO-THREE . . . Witness #22. Name: D. B. Stillwater . . . Proprietor, mom-and-pop store.

> Three young niggers was gonna burn my store down. Had the gasoline cans open and was pouring it on the vegetables and fruit out front until the Panthers came along and made them cease or be deceased. I never could understand that—burning down our own places. We was just doing the Man's work for him, if you ask me. When they killed Rev King and niggers finally realized they weren't going to be able to pray their way to freedom, they sent the ghetto up in flames. I ain't got nothing against burn-baby-burn, but hell don't start with your own place. That don't make no sense. Anyhow at least Oakland didn't go up in smoke.

YOU ATTRIBUTE THAT TO THE PANTHERS' INFLUENCE?

> Goddamn right I do! You know what Hoover did the day after they murdered Doctor King? He went to a baseball game. My uncle in Baltimore sold hot dogs in the stands, saw him with his own eyes. Shows how much of a shit Hoover gave, don't it?

YOU SAY YOUR UNCLE WAS SELLING HOT DOGS? ISN'T THAT USUALLY A YOUNGER PERSON'S JOB?

> Not necessarily, not if you're black and got a family to feed! A job's a job. Speaking of that, you know what the cops usta tell me when I complained 'bout them not doing their job? About letting folks steal my stuff, or worse than that, coming in here sticking me up. They say I wasn't the right complexion for better protection. How can I compete with the white merchant with that kinda bullshit going on? Level playing field my ass. Wanta hear this poem

about freedom I wrote . . . "Malcolm tried it with his fist. Martin tried it with prayer. So the man shot 'em both, for getting too close to getting there!" What happened was, when black people realized the Panthers had been right all along and while Hoover was sitting up there watching the game, gloating and chomping on his hot dog, folks was flocking to join the Panthers. The Party doubled its membership in the two weeks after King was killed. Nobody was backing off either, not the authorities, not the Panthers. But some folks even started figuring the Panthers weren't kicking enough ass, if you can believe that. Anyway the government was feeling its oats and some of the folks and some of the Panthers too were losing their cool, as well. In Oakland it didn't take long, two days after King was killed some more shit hit the fan.

28

Oakland, April 6, 1968. Eldridge and his breakaway Panthers crouch in an alley, armed to the teeth. The squad car they are waiting to ambush comes cruising by on patrol.

"This is for Malcolm!"

"This is for Martin!"

"This is for being motherfucking pigs!"

Guns blasting, the Panthers leap from their hiding spot.

A barrage of bullets hits the patrol car. The cops exchange fire and call for back-up. The squad car bursts into flames. The cops exit the burning vehicle, their guns blazing away. In a few seconds, one blue uniform lies motionless on the ground, the other is crawling for cover. More police cars whip around the corner.

The Panthers scatter. Little-Bobby glances over his shoulder as he runs. Cops are converging on Eldridge, the last to flee.

Eldridge manages to elude his pursuers and dashes down a narrow path between two houses. Little-Bobby makes a U-turn and goes back. He hooks up with Eldridge coming from the other direction. "Come on! Let's go . . ."

Leading the way, Little-Bobby vaults a backyard fence. As Eldridge gets to the fence, *BLAM BLAM* . . . a bullet tears into his leg. He manages to hop and roll over the fence, while on the other side the cops, like big game hunters, are running forward to check out their kill.

"C'mon," says Eldridge, dragging his leg and pointing to an abandoned house.

Panting for breath, Little-Bobby and Eldridge scramble for the cellar door and tumble down the stairs. They hunker down in the basement, sweating and gulping for air. Eldridge checks his leg. Blood soaks his pants.

In a matter of seconds, half a dozen police cars screech to a halt in front of the dilapidated old house. A battalion of cops, heavily armed, approaches.

"Commence firing," a voice shouts.

A fusillade of bullets tear through the thin walls as Eldridge and Little-Bobby crouch on the basement floor. It's a ferocious volley, hundreds of shells pouring through the rickety wooden structure.

The sergeant in charge makes a motion. Tear gas rifles appear.

CRASH! THUMP . . . one tear gas canister comes through the basement window . . . *THUMP* . . . then another. Hacking and partially blind, their eyes stinging from the gas, Eldridge and Little-Bobby crawl along the cellar floor.

"Papa E," Little-Bobby sniffles. "We got to get out of here."

Eldridge is thinking. "Okay," he snaps, improvising. "Take off your clothes."

"What?" Little-Bobby doesn't understand.

"Take 'em off," Eldridge repeats, starting to undress quickly. "Pigs can't shoot a naked man. Where they gonna say you hid a gun?"

Little-Bobby is suddenly shy. "No man, I can't."

Eldridge knows there isn't any other way. "Later for that—just do it!" he pleads, but to no avail.

Hands up, Eldridge and Little-Bobby emerge from the cellar. Eldridge is stark naked, Little-Bobby fully clothed. Instead of grabbing them immediately, the cops, guns raised, back off and form a gauntlet.

"Go on, get in that car, you cocksuckers," orders one cop, pointing towards a patrol car. "And don't try nothing funny."

Eldridge senses trouble. "Stay cool, Bobby, don't resist!"

"Hear that?!" another policeman shouts, gloating triumphantly.

"We got ourselves the other ringleader!"

Moving very cautiously, hands held high, Eldridge and Little-Bobby walk unsteadily towards the squad car. Still dazed and half-blinded, Little-Bobby stumbles. Without warning the cops open fire.

A volley of shots rips through his body jerking it this way and that, finally blowing him apart.

"Oh, my God!" Eldridge howls. In horror, he stares at Little-Bobby's ruined body.

One of the cops approaches the sergeant in charge and produces a pistol.

"He was going for this, Sarge," he says, smiling.

The sergeant nods.

"Bullshit!" Eldridge screams. "You motherfuck—"

WHAM . . . A rifle butt in the back of his head interrupts any further protest. Eldridge's world goes blacker.

TESTING, ONE-TWO-THREE . . . Witness #23. Name: Reggie.

> Actually, the police botched the murder. Did you know that? They heard Eldridge calling out "Bobby" and thought they were killing Bobby Seale, when actually it was Little-Bobby Hutton, the kid. Eldridge was wounded, but they didn't dare murder him afterwards when they had him in the hospital. It would look too suspicious, him dying in police custody only two days after Doctor King was murdered. Plus he was too much of a celebrity in his own right. You see, his book Soul on Ice had become a bestseller. We got Eldridge out on bail, but the pigs kept trying to revoke it. We knew if they got their hands on him again he was a dead man. Before Little-Bobby was cold in the ground we started making arrangements for Cleaver to disappear. Later on if things worked out his old lady, Kathleen, could join him.

YOU WENT TO THE FUNERAL?

> Yes, and looking around the grave as they were lowering the casket down, there were a lot of old faces missing. The pigs were trying to crack down, but it wasn't working, if you get what I mean, because there were more new faces among the mourners than old ones missing.

The Panthers are holding a rally on the Alameda County Courthouse steps. But they and their sympathizers are not the only interested parties.

From an upper window of the courthouse, Special Agent Pruitt looks down on the demonstration. Silhouetted by the light coming through the Venetian blinds, he stands immobile, hands clasped behind his back.

Alma is addressing the crowd. "Can a black man get a fair trial in the United States of America? That right there is the question, and it is not up to the pig to answer it, it's up to us brothers and sisters. Time is running out, for all of us! Huey must be freed! Free Huey!"

The crowd responds. *FREE HUEY! FREE HUEY! FREE HUEY!*

A uniformed black cop approaches Pruitt, who is still gazing transfixed at the rally. Pruitt doesn't notice him immediately, so the cop takes the opportunity to observe the rally himself before giving his report. Finally, Pruitt realizes someone is at his side and turns.

The cop snaps to attention and relates the findings. "Sir, regarding the Huey Newton incident, we have no lead as yet as to who was in the vehicle with Newton. If in fact there was anyone at all."

Pruitt replies with a crisp thank you.

Official business over, the cop relaxes. He gives Pruitt a big soul brother to soul brother smile and nods his head towards the protesters. "I don't know, but in a way you can't help but admiring our youngsters. They're doing a lot of good in the black communities."

"Have you ever heard of the common good?" Pruitt replies frigidly. "The United States is more than a collection of ghettoes. It is an entire sovereign nation."

The cop, caught off guard, blinks as if he has been slapped.

Down below the crowd has switched chants—*POWER TO THE PEOPLE! POWER TO THE PEOPLE!*

"This country was built on principles of democracy," Pruitt lectures. "And in a democracy the majority rules, and we are a minority unless we integrate fully."

The cop frowns. "Whose side are you on anyhow, brother?"

"No officer, you have that wrong. The question, is whose side are you on?" Pruitt turns his back and walks away.

July 15, 1968. Newspaper headlines around the country announce that the Newton trial has begun. Every day, vociferous crowds stand vigil on the courthouse steps chanting:

NO MORE BROTHERS IN JAIL . . . OFF THE PIG!
THE PIGS ARE GONNA CATCH HELL . . . OFF THE PIG!
THE REVOLUTION HAS COME . . . OFF THE PIG!
TIME TO PICK UP THE GUN . . . OFF THE PIG!

Every day of the trial, the courtroom is packed. Every available inch of space is taken.

Jury, judge, and spectators alike lean forward in their seats, mesmerized by the proceedings, hanging on every word as the prosecutor coaxes testimony from his star witness, the surviving policeman, Officer Heanes. Throughout the prosecution's examination, Charles Garry sits at the defense table next to Huey with a slight, strangely confident smile on his face.

The courtroom holds its breath. Besides the testimony itself, there are only two other distinctive sounds in the room. One is the continuous scratching of the reporters' pens as they frantically scribble notes, and the other is the peck peck peck of the court stenographer as she sits robotlike at her small table punching keys and recording the transcript of the trial for posterity.

Prosecutor: So, you would say, Officer Heanes, Huey Newton opened fire, without any provocation whatsoever.

Garry: Objection . . . Counsel is leading the witness.

Judge: Objection overruled. You may answer the question.

Heanes: Yes, sir—he did.

Prosecutor: What makes you so sure? It was a dark night, there was a lot of confusion.

Heanes: Well, sir, I was there.

Prosecutor: That's right, you were—you were an eyewitness. Ladies and gentlemen of the jury, Officer Heanes was there. He saw everything. And he is not on trial. Officer Heanes does not need to lie to save his life. Thank you, Officer Heanes, no further questions . . . Your witness.

Slowly Garry rises. The tension in the courtroom mounts in anticipation of the clash between the main prosecution witness and the shrewd Panther defense lawyer, but Garry declines the opportunity, saying he has no questions for Officer Heanes. The crowd sucks in its breath. With the court still reeling from his refusal to exercise his right to cross-examine, Garry tosses a legal bombshell into the trial.

Garry: Your honor, if it pleases the court, I would like to introduce testimony of a new witness. One who was also there. Another person who also is not on trial for his life and therefore has no reason to lie.

The prosecutor goes red with rage.

Prosecutor: Objection, your honor, who is this man?

Garry: I have just stated that, your honor. This is an eyewitness to the shooting, namely, the passenger in Huey Newton's car.

Judge: Overruled. Mr. Garry, you may examine your witness.

Garry: I call Gene McKinney to the stand.

A murmur ripples through the courtroom as Gene comes forward.

Garry: Mr. McKinney, were you a passenger in the car on the night of October 28, 1967?

McKinney: Yes sir, I was.

Garry: And did you witness the shoot-out?

McKinney: Yes sir, I did.

Garry: From what you saw, did Huey Newton start the shooting?

McKinney: No sir, he didn't.

A shock wave of murmuring runs through the courtroom.

Garry: I see. Well then, Mr. McKinney, did someone else start the shooting?

McKinney: I refuse to answer that question on the grounds that it might incriminate me.

The courtroom gasps in shock and amazement.

Garry: Did you shoot the officers in question?

McKinney: Again, I'll take the Fifth Amendment on that question, on the grounds that it might incriminate me.

The courtroom goes berserk, with the prosecutor screaming, the judge banging his gavel, the jury looking confused, and the posse of journalists stampeding down the aisles.

In seconds, every phone booth in the corridor outside the courtroom is grabbed up by a reporter barking the story in to his news desk.

“The attorney for the defense, Charles Garry, has just thrown a brilliantly conceived monkey wrench into the proceedings. Stop,” one reporter shouts his copy into the receiver. “The monkey wrench came in the persona of Gene McKinney, the missing witness. Stop. In a masterful legal maneuver, Garry, having been granted immunity for his witness’s testimony, placed McKinney on the stand. Stop. McKinney cannot be tried for the murder of Officer Frey and the wounding of Officer Heanes. Stop. However, McKinney’s testimony has cast a reasonable doubt in the minds of the jury as to defendant Huey Newton’s actual guilt. Stop. The once seemingly ironclad case of the prosecution is clearly in jeopardy.”

29

TESTING, ONE-TWO-THREE . . . Witness #24. Name: Darlene Otanji.

I picked up the car where Kathleen'd been told to abandon it. We figured it was more prudent that way. Anyway, the car was this gold color so it wasn't all that hard to spot. After the jury gave Huey manslaughter, which meant he would be out in two years, instead of convicting him of murder, which meant he'd be in for life, and Eldridge jumped bail and got away, the police were really watching us, and on us like white on rice. Eldridge, especially running for Vice President, would have been a dead man if he had stayed in the states. Somehow, inside or out of jail, they would have gotten to him. He was practically walking around with a bulls-eye on his back. But Robert Kennedy was assassinated and they had to wait for the dust to settle before they pulled some more shit. But by that time, Eldridge was in the wind. Anyhow, Eldridge had bought a car with the royalties from the book. It had a phone in it too. He loved that car and before he went underground he told Kathleen to donate it to the Party and that was the last thing she did before she went underground to join him in exile. The pigs they'd knock us down, but we kept getting up. Our membership was growing and each time we'd be stronger and bigger than before. The pigs were freaking out.

Agent Rodgers is on the phone in his command center of an office in Oakland getting an earful from Washington. Rolling his eyes, he imagines himself on the carpet in front of Mr. Hoover's desk, being hauled over the coals by the old man himself.

The truth is, Rodgers's imagination is pretty accurate. On the other side of the country Hoover sits at his desk glowering as Rodgers's blubbering excuses come over the speakerphone. His aide, who has been doing the actual talking under J. Edgar's direction, stands at his boss's side trying not to smirk.

Back in Oakland, Rodgers stands at attention spluttering more explanations into the receiver. "... er ... Granted, sir, the 'Free Huey' thing has become a bit of a rallying cry among the left ... "

Hoover is apoplectic. "Rallying cry!" he explodes, answering for himself. "It's an insurrection!"

"Yes sir, the Panthers have proven very resourceful, sir," Rodgers admits. "They say there's a Panther born every minute in the ghetto. We seem to have underestimated the support of the black community. It's the Panthers' power base."

Hoover sinks back into his chair, looking old. He leans his head back, mulling over what he perceives as his options. Coming to a decision, he shifts forward and touches the mute switch on the phone so that Rodgers cannot hear him. Hoover takes a couple moments more, then looks up at his assistant.

"Well, then we are just going to have to take that power base away, won't we!" he says, signaling his aide to pick up the receiver.

Speakerphone off, the aide lowers his voice to a conspiratorial level. "Mr. Hoover wishes the ultimate contingency implemented."

Rodgers is unprepared. "You mean ... "

The aide locks eyes with his jowly boss for confirmation.

Hoover snatches the phone. "Yes," he bellows. "That's exactly what I mean!"

"Yes, sir, I understand," Rodgers bobs his head servilely.

Hoover hands the phone back to his assistant.

"And Agent Rodgers," cautions the aide. "This conversation never occurred."

> **MEMO/COINTELPRO:** TOP SECRET
> ACTIVATE ULTIMATE CONTINGENCY IMMEDIATELY OAKLAND TO SERVE AS NATIONWIDE MODEL. COOPERATION OF LOCAL AUTHORITY PREFERRED.
>
> WASHINGTON

A sleek power launch leaves the Oakland side of the harbor, heading towards the Bay Bridge and the open water beyond. Squawking sea gulls, riding the early afternoon breeze, glide alongside the yacht, occasionally swooping down to the waves searching for food. Three men sipping coffee are seated in a semicircle at the back of the boat waiting for their host, simultaneously admiring the view and watching a large portable TV. A network commentator is exploring with an expert the possibility that Sirhan Sirhan, Robert Kennedy's assassin, was brainwashed. Their discussion is spiced with actual footage of the assassination.

"Rodgers, this is no good. We shouldn't be here. I won't sit down with this man."

"Drop the comedy, Dorsett. We know all about you. You've been taking the mob's money for years."

"Gentlemen!" Tynan's cultivated rasp grabs everyone's attention. "Forgive me for keeping you."

Smooth as silk, his every movement spelling underworld, Tynan steps on deck from the cabin below. He is immaculately dressed in a white terry-cloth robe and boating sandals.

"May I join you?" he asks rhetorically, seating himself in a deck chair facing the three law enforcement officers and the American flag flying off the stern of the yacht.

He glances at the TV. Kennedy's bodyguards are wrestling Sirhan to the floor. "What a shame, what a tragedy," he commiserates nonchalantly. "My heart aches for that poor Kennedy family."

Tynan lowers the sound. He looks over at Dorsett and gives him a knowing wink.

Dorsett squirms and his cheeks run through every color in the rainbow. Tynan, however is completely at ease. A girl clad in a bikini brings him a drink, then disappears discreetly.

"Odd isn't it, Dorsett? No matter how much we try to deny it, we always seem to find ourselves on the same side of the street." Tynan takes a sip of his drink and settles easily into his chair. "It's almost funny, don't you think?"

"To be quite honest, it turns my stomach," Dorsett refutes him sourly.

"Neither your stomach nor your opinion matters here, Dorsett," Pruitt says pointedly. "What matters is that Mr. Tynan's clients and the Bureau have come up with a solution to our Panther problem."

"One might say the final solution," Tynan adds.

Going into his dumb mode, Dorsett claims he doesn't understand a thing that is going on until Tynan "reminds" him of their previous discussions on the topic.

Turning to Rodgers, Tynan gets down to business. "I assure you, Agent Rodgers, the pacifying properties of heroin are quite remarkable," he sermonizes, beginning his pitch.

"You'd be turning Oakland into a city of zombies," Dorsett interjects.

"Not the entire city, my friend. Look at that, gentlemen."

The elegant craft is passing under the Bay Bridge. The awesome pylons and sinewy steel cables supporting the huge highway overhead glide by. The view is almost unreal.

Breathtaking scenery notwithstanding, Dorsett is still constricted with doubt. "And what if it spreads to the rest of the population?"

Tynan pats Dorsett's knee. "Relax, relax, my nervous friend. I guarantee that that will never happen." He turns his oily charm on Rodgers. "My clients are naturally pleased that your boss has decided to finally entertain our suggestion. Permit me to inquire, why the change of mind?"

"Woman's intuition," Dorsett mutters.

Pruitt answers for Rodgers. "There were certain obstacles, and frankly the Bureau had wished to get by with a less extreme solution."

"Obstacle, singular, I believe," Tynan says, glancing pointedly in the direction of the TV. "But that's all water under the bridge now—right, gentlemen?"

"Are you sure you can control the product?" Pruitt inquires, returning to business. "Can you assure us that it will not get out of hand?"

"Of course. My clients have vast experience in these communities. After all, it is only a question of degree. Giving us free rein in the ghetto will be the final solution to your problem. Look, a junkie's politics are different from yours and mine. Me, I got a little gypsy in me. Let me read the future for you. We sell them the product, along with a few guns to protect their investment. And soon the jigaboos will be so busy trying to buy or push the product that they will be blowing each other's heads off." Tynan pauses and gives Pruitt an insincere shrug of apology. "No offense."

Automatically, Pruitt replies, "This is not a racial matter. It is a question of law and order."

Amused, Tynan acquiesces gracefully. "Of course, of course . . . Anyway, soon they'll be too busy using the stuff or going around shooting each other fighting over turf to be worrying about rallies and protest demonstrations."

"That's the beauty of it," Rodgers says, converted. "They'll do it to themselves."

"Precisely," Tynan concurs. "All we have to do is supply them and step back."

"How soon before it can be on the street?" Rodgers queries eagerly.

"Very quickly. A couple of months at the outside. We'll manufacture and distribute from a local warehouse that used to be a garage. Dorsett knows the place."

"I reiterate. We need assurances of containment, that this solution will be kept strictly in the assigned area," Pruitt stresses, playing strictly by the book. "Dorsett, I want you to delegate someone to keep tabs on the operation . . ." Pruitt locks eyes with Tynan. "No offense."

"No offense taken," Tynan nods back. "Good business procedure."

Dorsett looks from face to face, befuddled. "You talk as if this thing's already been decided."

Pruitt hits Dorsett with an icy glare. "It has!"

Rodgers, reassured by the conversation, steps in to take charge of the mission again. He rises to his feet. Behind him, the American flag is flapping jauntily in the breeze. He gives his bones a big luxurious stretch. "Gentlemen," he says, all smiles, "shall we be getting back? I have a report to make."

Less than an hour later, back in Washington D.C., Hoover's assistant puts down the phone and turns to his master. Hoover's ancient bulldog face is beaming malevolently. He twists in his chair smiling. "Now that's more like it!" he says to his aide, his voice quivering with quiet fervor.

> **MEMO/COINTELPRO:** TOP SECRET
> REGIONAL DIRECTORS ARE URGED TO TAKE ENTHUSIASTIC AND IMAGINATIVE ACTION IN INTENSIFYING COUNTERINTELLIGENCE ENDEAVORS. EMULATE PRODUCTIVE STEPS TAKEN BY BAY AREA IN THESE MATTERS. THE BUREAU WILL BE PLEASED TO ENTERTAIN ANY SUGGESTIONS IN THAT REGARD.
> J. EDGAR HOOVER/WASHINGTON

The chiaroscuro shadows of dusk are falling on the Oakland ghetto as Judge cuts through the alley and starts up the steps to his apartment.

"Psssst . . ."

Judge turns, startled. Something is lurking in the late afternoon gloom under the stairs. It moves.

"Psssst . . ."

Judge retraces his steps. He peers under the stairs and waits for his eyes to adjust.

A voice comes out of the darkness. "It's me, Rose."

"Rose? What are you doing in there?"

"Look, man, what I gotta say," Rose whispers, inching forward into the light, "is just between you, me, and these rats and roaches running around here, you got that?"

"Yeah, man, sure."

"All right then . . . well, Sabu, he's back."

"Motherfucker! Well then I got something to do, don't I?" Judge starts up the steps.

Rose grabs Judge's arm and tugs him back. "Wait, hear me out, there's something weird going on. When Sabu left here he was on his ass, but now he's talking large and living larger."

"Thanks for the info, Rose, I gotta go."

"Judge, man, watch your back. Be careful, man, you gotta have a plan. Sabu's got juice now! Don't go writing no check with your mouth that your ass can't cash."

"I hear you. Don't sweat it. I'll figure out something."

Deep in thought, Judge starts back up the stairs. Rose stands staring after him. Crouching behind a hedge watching the both of them is Shorty, a gigantic bodybuilder, and one of Sabu's henchmen.

Dorsett, beaten to the core, is seated at his desk. He pours himself a shot of Maalox, then spikes it with three fingers of whiskey. He turns his chair to face the wall so that he can wallow in self-pity and sip in peace.

"Working kinda late, aren't you boss?"

Dorsett wheels around and looks up. Brimmer is leaning against the doorpost sucking on a cigarette.

Brimmer spots the bottles. "Jesus! Which is it, a wake or a celebration? You been going at it pretty heavy, boss, for the last few days."

"I'm not sure myself," Dorsett mumbles.

Brimmer invites himself in and pulls up a chair. "You wanta tell me about it?"

"Yeah, sure—you gotta know sooner than later anyway." Dorsett fishes a paper cup out of his desk and passes it and the whiskey to Brimmer. "Congratulations are in order, Inspector Brimmer, I guess."

"What the hell is that supposed to mean?"

"Nothing," Dorsett recants, raising his cup. But his eyes are both fearful and sad and his hand is shaking. "I got a new assignment for you, pal. You're gonna be an overseer."

Judge is lying on his back in bed having a nightmare with his eyes wide open, staring without seeing towards the ceiling . . . The chopper is rising . . . the buddy sprawled in the clearing isn't a soldier at all, it's Cy . . . *BOOM BOOM* . . . the mortar fire is coming closer . . .

BOOM BOOM . . . Judge's door flies off its hinges and Brimmer comes storming in, belligerent, drunk. In a second he's on Judge, snatching him off the bed, handcuffing him.

"Hey . . . what the hell you doing?" Judge demands groggily.

Brimmer tells him to shut the fuck up, just shut the fuck up, and hustles him out of the apartment, down the steps and into the back seat of his car.

They roar out of the ghetto. They pass the outskirts of Oakland and point toward the Bay Bridge.

Judge eyes Brimmer from the back seat. "What's with you?" Judge questions, struggling to keep the apprehension out of his voice. "I've never seen you like this, man."

Brimmer is drunk and getting drunker, but not so loaded that he has lost control. He starts mumbling, "Twenty years on the force. Twenty asshole years." He fishes a pint out of his pocket, takes a deep swig then lays it on the seat next to him. "I've seen same fucked up stuff, Judge."

They pass the toll booths and start across the bridge. Brimmer takes another hit from the bottle. "Done some fucked up stuff too!" He takes another pull, gives the bottle a pat, shakes his head. "Yeah, but nothing like this . . . "

When they get halfway across the bridge to San Francisco he swerves over to the rail and slams on the brakes. He yanks Judge out of the back seat, then uncuffs him.

"Go! Run! Go on! Get the fuck out of here!!"

"What? So you can shoot me in the back, then call it resisting arrest?"

"I ain't gonna shoot you, Judge. Look, it's over. Just run away. Get out. Stay away from Oakland. 'Cause it's all gone. It's done."

"Brimmer you're drunk, man. You're fucked up . . . "

"Yeah . . . Everything's fucked up! Our government, the whole country, me, you, and the Panthers too. You got no idea, do you, what's going on here? This is bigger than you and me. We're just tiny tin soldiers getting shoved around on some big-shot asshole's chessboard. The whole country is fucked up. The Panthers are gonna be history. You too if you don't run like I'm telling you. They're killing you and you don't even know it!"

"Who's going to kill the Panthers?"

"Not who, son . . . what! Drugs, Judge, they're gonna flood the ghetto with dope!"

"Where?"

"They're gonna use that old warehouse I took you to. Judge—save yourself. Go! Get away, just disappear! It's over. You lost. We all lost. It's all over, Judge, save yourself. *GO*!"

Brimmer lurches back to his car and the vehicle weaves off.

Judge, the girders and cables looming behind him, stands there in the middle of the Bay Bridge, with Oakland glowering at one end and San Francisco twinkling at the other, wrestling with himself.

Finally he turns and heads back towards Oakland. *Fuck that shit!* Judge tells himself. *Ain't nothing over.*

The next day Judge pays Huey a visit. A surly guard accompanies Huey through the visitor's room door and to his place at the table where on the other side of the reinforced glass partition, Judge sits waiting.

"Power to the people," Judge greets him fist and all, trying to stall until the guard is out of earshot.

"Power to the people," Huey replies, playing the same game.

"Garry did a terrific job, didn't he?"

"Yeah, great. You could be out in two years, maybe less," Judge comes back, still staying on the innocuous side.

Bored by the banter, the guard finally drifts off to the corner of the room where he belongs.

Huey, taking no chance on being overheard, leans forward and drops his voice to a whisper. "Kathleen—did she manage to get away and hook up with Eldridge?"

"Yeah, we pulled it off," Judge nods. "She made it."

Huey leans back in his chair, relieved. "Well, so cheer up, brother," he beams. "Why are you so down in the mouth? Like you said, I might have to do two years, but at least I'm not dead."

Judge tells Huey that what's about to go down can't wait two years. Huey, all ears wants to know what's up and Judge lays out his suspicions, Sabu being back and living large, plus what Brimmer revealed to him.

Huey sits stunned, absorbing the enormity of the tale. Horror, then despair, march across his handsome features, then determination as he formulates a plan.

"Bobby is in command," Huey whispers. "You tell him any of this yet?"

Judge explains he just put all the pieces together himself, and that Masai and Shirley were getting married today and most of the Panthers including Bobby were at the wedding but Bobby should be stopping off at headquarters that evening just about the time he gets back from his visit with Huey.

Huey leans forward, the vapors of his breath fogging the glass. "It's a test for every ghetto in America, get it? If we let them get away with it, they'll flood every black community before God gets the news. What else did the pig say?"

"Brimmer? Nothing much. He told me to run, to save myself."

"Well?"

"Well, I didn't think that fit my mission description." Judge shrugs, then he chuckles. "Coward wasn't part of the job profile, was it?"

Huey smiles approvingly, and they just sit silent for a moment facing each other, separated by the partition but united by their dedication.

Finally Huey speaks. "We've gotta stamp this shit out quick! Right now!" he goes on grimly. "That's our mission! Tell Bobby I said, by any means necessary, and that goes for you too! Even if it means you blow your cover. The Man is trying to squeeze us into submission. He's so blind in his dogmatism that he's willing to destroy anything to do it, even himself."

The guard saunters back over and points to the clock on the wall. "Time's up!"

"I got you, Huey," says Judge. "I read you loud and clear! I'm on it. Power to the people!"

"Good. Remember, brother, by any means necessary!"

The guard starts to tug Huey away.

"Power to the people," Huey shouts over his shoulder as he is led away.

Judge gives the clenched-fist salute to the closing steel door.

30

TESTING, ONE-TWO-THREE . . . Witness #25. Name: Jerry Howard, Esq.

The government decided to teach the left a lesson it wouldn't forget. They took leaders out of each organization and charged them with conspiracy and fomenting riot at the Democratic convention. I hadn't taken the bar yet, but I was an aide for the defense, so I saw it all. The charge of conspiracy is well known as the "prosecutor's dream" because it requires no evidence of actual meetings, decisions, or implementation of a plan. Several of the people charged in the conspiracy had never even met until Chicago or, in the case of Bobby Seale, before being indicted. The papers dubbed them the "Chicago Eight." Abbie and Jerry were the Yippies, Dave Dellinger antiwar, Rennie and Tom Hayden New Left, so on and so forth, seven white guys plus Bobby Seale from the Panthers. Fucking government. Don't quote me on that. I suppose they threw in a black guy to prove they were equal opportunity persecutors, that way no one could accuse them of discriminating. Of course the government wasn't overly concerned with legalities anyway. They kidnapped Bobby Seale. He was leaving a wedding and they literally snatched him out of his wife's arms. They hijacked him to Chicago, crossing state lines, five or six of them, in itself a federal offense. But, like I said, when it comes right down to it, legality has never been one of the government's biggest concerns.

The pigs were trying to squeeze the community and the shit was flowing faster. One of Judge's textbooks even confirmed what was happening. Bernoulli's hydrodynamics principle says that if a fluid flow is constricted—squeezed—it increases speed. Although the Mulford Act made it illegal to carry a weapon, Judge knows what he has to do. Disciples of Zen might call it destiny, but on the block they call it taking care of business. Judge stops by his place to get something wrapped in oil cloth and hidden under the sink before going to Panther headquarters.

In the meantime, Sister Shirley and Brother Masai have said their "I do's," and Bobby and his family are in a caravan of Panther cars leaving the wedding.

While Rodgers, moving in for the kill, is sitting in a surveillance truck, complete with one way window and wire tap equipment, across the street from Panther headquarters.

And last but not least, Sabu goes looking for Rose to tie up a little loose lip business.

Rose, sitting on his couch with his head between his legs in a heavy Bitter Dog stupor, hears a rustle. He looks up, squinting against the afternoon sun outlining two visitors coming through his canvas door.

The flap drops behind Sabu and Shorty.

"Power to the people, Sabu . . . how you been doing?" Rose jokes, at the same time trying to hide his surprise and pull himself together.

"Solid, brother," Sabu says, pulling out a pearl-handled .38. "You okay?"

Rose squirms at the sight of the gun. "Sure, I'm okay . . . "

"Well, I brought a little something to cure your diarrhea. I hear you been running off at the mouth."

"Come on, man, you know me better than that. Where'd you hear that kinda bullshit?"

Sabu's gold tooth flashes in a lopsided grin. "A bird done told me, a short little bird. By the way, man, how's Stay doing?"

Rose's eyebrows rise as he takes the bait. "Stay who?"

"Stay outta my business!" Sabu says. *BAM* . . . He shoots Rose point-blank in the chest. He walks over to Rose twitching on the floor and pumps two more into his head for good measure.

Shorty raises the canvas door for his boss to exit. "Yeah, power to the people," he snickers to Rose's body crumpled on the dirt floor.

As Shorty is ushering his boss away from Rose's shack, Bobby Seale is being cut off by the cops on his way back from the wedding.

The technician seated at the communications console in the van across from Panther headquarters gets a beep in his earphones.

He listens, then looks up. "I think it's the call you've been waiting for," he says, handing Rodgers a headset.

Rodgers, head bowed, listens attentively. Then he looks up and gives the thumbs-up to the other three agents in the van with him—Pruitt, the communications technician, and the agent at the one-way window.

"It's going down. Right now!" Rodgers announces.

On the other end, an FBI agent is sitting in an unmarked car, his legs sticking casually out the door, finishing a blow-by-blow description of the big catch.

Bobby Seale is being handcuffed and hustled across the street to a waiting car. A posse of federal agents and local police are holding the rest of the wedding party at bay.

"Did it go smoothly?" Rodgers asks.

"Yes, sir. No problem, as smooth as silk. SOP. The lead car cut them off in mid-block, vehicles flanking each side, two in the rear. Exactly as planned."

Bobby is shoved into an unmarked car.

"All wrapped up, sir," the agent reports, watching the automobile roar off. "We now have the suspect in custody . . . over."

Rodgers nods. "Over and out." Handing the headset back to the technician, he slaps Pruitt on the back.

Rodgers twists around and gestures toward Panther headquarters. "We're on a roll. Any activity in there?"

The agent at the console and the one at the window look at each other and shake their heads. "Same two inside, nothing else."

Rodgers looks out the window and spies on Panther headquarters for a moment, then gets an idea.

"Give me a phone and patch me through to them," Rodgers says to the agent at the console, indicating the storefront.

The technician is surprised. "Panther headquarters?"

"Exactly."

BBRRRIIINGG . . . The telephone rings. Alma and Tyrone are alone in headquarters waiting for the wedding party to return. She is typing and he is sitting across from her reading a comic book.

Tyrone picks up the phone. "Black Panther Party."

"Congratulations, asshole!" Rodgers' voice slithers through the receiver. "Huey got off, he should have gotten the chair, but now we got your other boy, Bobby Seale."

"What kinda bullshit you talking? Bobby is at a wedding."

"Not anymore he's not. We're taking him to Chicago on conspiracy charges. You remember the little fracas at the Democratic convention, don't you?"

"Bobby didn't have anything to do with that."

"Maybe not, but we got him for it."

"Who the fuck is this?" Tyrone questions.

"The tooth fairy, and I got a little present for you. You know the guy who helped us get Bobby? One of your brothers, by the name of Judge," Rodgers says and hangs up.

CLICK . . . Tyrone, a furious expression on his face, leaps to his feet. "I'm gonna find that fucking Judge!" He heads for his gun stashed under a floorboard in the storeroom.

In the surveillance van, Rodgers passes the phone back to the technician and lights himself a cigarette.

Pruitt looks at Rodgers, a quizzical expression around the eyes.

"Just stirring things up a little," Rodgers answers Pruitt's unasked question. "Maybe if we're lucky we might even get a lead on where that bail-jumping Cleaver is hiding out," he says with a sly grin.

"That's if Cleaver hasn't fled the country."

"No way. An escape like that takes planning, my friend. Those pickaninnies couldn't organize a barbecue let alone a sophisticated escape."

Pruitt and Rodgers lock eyes. Either Rodgers doesn't realize what he has said, or now that things seem to be going his way, he doesn't give a shit.

Pruitt doesn't challenge the slur. "Who is this Judge you mentioned?" he asks, changing the subject.

"Brimmer's snitch."

"Did you clear blowing the cover on his source with him?"

"That incompetent sonofabitch wouldn't know standard procedure if it bit him in the ass," Rodgers sneers.

Pruitt starts to lecture Rodgers. "Bureau protocol requires that . . . "

"Rodgers!" the agent at the window interrupts. "We have suspicious activity . . . "

Rodgers first turns to the technician at the console fiddling with his dials. "Oh yeah? What are they doing in there?"

The agent looks up from his monitors and shrugs. "Nothing much."

"No . . . over here," the agent on visual beckons. He points through the van window. "Far end of the block. We've got a police car at three o'clock."

"Shit!" Rodgers says. "That fucking Dorsett was supposed to keep his boys clear!" Rodgers almost has to press his nose against the glass to make out the squad car cruising through the dark towards Panther headquarters.

Inside the car are three rowdy cops finishing their shift and grumbling about the Newton verdict.

"Can you believe that lousy jury?" the driver says, nodding towards the approaching storefront. "Letting that fucking Panther get off with just manslaughter."

"Yeah, reasonable doubt my ass," the policeman in the back fumes. "What kinda bullshit is that?!"

The cop in the passenger seat leans out the window and takes aim at the storefront with his index finger. "Fucking cop killer! Newton shoulda gotten the chair."

"Yeah," the cop behind him agrees. "Let's show 'em. Go around the block again."

The driver nods and grunts, "Good idea... Yeah, power to the people my ass!"

"They're leaving," the agent on visual says.

"Good," Rodgers is relieved. "That's all we need—a bunch of local yokels starting something."

"Heads up!... Someone is approaching target area."

Oblivious to the surveillance van across the street, Judge walks through the front door of Panther headquarters.

"Alma—where is everybody? I have to talk to Bobby."

Tyrone enters from the back, slips up behind Judge and presses the barrel of his gun to the base of Judge's head. "Yeah! I bet!"

Judge stiffens at the contact.

Alma comes around the desk. "Bobby? Why Bobby, anyhow?" she digs, half giving Judge the benefit of the doubt, half giving him the third-degree.

"He's the senior officer in charge, that's why! It's important! I got a message from Huey for him."

"Funny you should mention that," Tyrone hisses. "We got a message too. The pigs kidnapped Bobby—no extradition papers, no motherfucking due process, no nothing. They're hijacking his butt halfway across the country to Chicago, but I suppose you knew that."

"Tyrone is next in command. If your report is so important, why don't you tell him what it's about," Alma insists.

Judge's stomach starts to sink. Desperately, he turns his head so he can see Tyrone, still holding the gun on him. "It's about dope! D-O-

P-E, dope, bringing it into the ghetto!"

"What kinda bullshit is that?" Tyrone scoffs. "The ghetto's already got drugs."

Judge tries again. "Not like this. The pigs are gonna let the mob flood us." Tyrone isn't buying it. Judge turns to Alma. "Don't you guys get it! Junkies don't vote! Junkies don't protest, or make waves, or join the Panthers! They are setting up a factory in the old warehouse district! When I told Huey he said we had to stop them . . . right now, before it gets started."

Tyrone snorts. "Told Huey! So how come you know all this? It's some kinda trick, admit it. Why should we believe you?" Judge turns to face him and Tyrone aims the gun straight between his eyes. "You're just some kinda stoolie!"

Fed up with the act, Judge cuts to the chase. "Yeah, I'm a stoolie, snitch, a what-the-fuck-ever you want to call it. BUT FOR US NOT THEM!"

Dumbfounded, Tyrone looks at him like he's insane. "Bullshit!"

Out in the van, the agent on visual shouts a warning. "Rodgers, they're back! Street activity again."

Before Rodgers can get over to the window to see for himself, *BLAM!* . . . the rowdy cops start using Panther HQ for target practice.

The first shot shatters the storefront window. Alma lunges to turn off the light and Judge jumps Tyrone. Tyrone's gun crashes to the floor and slides across the linoleum, and the room goes dark. Judge and Tyrone slug it out by the dramatic beam of light from the streetlamp coming through the shattered window, their silhouettes and shadows tossing around the room.

BLOOM . . . Shotgun pellets rip through the door.

"Did you see that?" the cop in the back seat brags, pulling his shotgun back inside the window to reload. "That was a good one."

"Not bad," the driver admits. "Now it's my turn. Watch this!" Steering wheel in his left hand, service revolver in his right, he reaches his arm across his partner in the passenger seat and takes aim out of the window.

BANG BANG . . . A bad-luck bullet strikes Alma in the arm, spinning her around and knocking her down. The sound of squealing tires comes through the window as the squad car peels off, the moronic cops whooping it up about which one of them is the best shot.

The agent on visual in the surveillance van turns from the one-way glass and cautions Rodgers, "They're going around the block. They could be coming back for another pass."

"Come on," Rodgers beckons Pruitt. He turns to the other agents. "You make sure those idiots don't try it again!" he orders. "We'll hold the fort until you get back!"

Rodgers and Pruitt check their guns and leap onto the sidewalk, and the van roars off after the squad car.

Judge and Tyrone, still locked in mortal combat, struggle to their feet in the twilight of the front room. Tyrone connects with a hard right, sending Judge reeling backward over a chair he can't see in the darkness. Tyrone sprints around the chair to get at him, but Judge, using his feet and Tyrone's momentum, flips Tyrone over his head and sends him sprawling on his back. Judge pulls out his own weapon.

"Stand up," Judge orders.

Tyrone slowly gets to his feet. Despite looking down the barrel of Judge's gun, he is more defiant than ever. "Go ahead, shoot! You can kill the revolutionary but you can't kill the revolution. The ghetto is full of warriors!"

"It won't be for long! That's what I've been trying to tell you. They're going to bury the ghetto in drugs. Listen to me! I need your help."

"More of us want freedom than you pigs got bullets," Tyrone says. Judge is not getting through.

Tyrone continues. "You got the gun, brother. It's your move."

Alma's voice comes from the corner. "No, it's not his move!" The barrel of a gun pokes forward from the shadows pointing directly at Judge. "You shoot him, I shoot you!"

The standoff lasts for one heartbeat . . . two. Then Judge turns his weapon around and holds it out to Tyrone, handle first. Tyrone snatches it and points it at Judge.

"Now it's your move, brother," Judge says drily. "What's our future gonna be? Pushers and gangs preying on the community, junkies scavenging for what's left?"

Tyrone's finger tightens on the trigger. "What the fuck you talking about anyhow?"

"They're setting up a drug factory!" Judge replies.

"Bullshit!"

"What if he's telling the truth?" Alma intercedes. "We better check it out." Fighting off the pain, she drags herself to her feet. "Do you know where they're setting up?"

"I have a pretty good idea," Judge nods, "but I'm not sure I can find the place."

Alma gently places her hand over Tyrone's. He ponders her hand on his a few seconds, then lowers the gun. "Well, you better find the motherfucker, or you're dead meat."

Rodgers and Pruitt are in an alley a few feet from where the van had been parked. Rodgers studies the storefront across the road with his miniature night-vision binoculars.

Pruitt asks him what he sees. Rodgers, frustrated and irritable, snaps back not much, and what did he expect, how the hell was he supposed to keep track of darkies in the dark?

Pruitt lets it go. "They're taking their own sweet time," he says, looking up and down the street for the van to return and give them a hand.

Judge and Tyrone gently help Alma out of the rear of the store and then they snake along a prearranged escape route to the alley. Judge is carrying a can of gasoline the Panthers keep on hand for emergencies. Somewhere a dog starts barking.

Tyrone whispers to Alma to go get some medical help. Alma says the hell with that she is going with them, it's only a flesh wound, she won't bleed to death. Tyrone tells her again to go find a nurse or something and that's an order. Alma agrees, but when Tyrone gets in the front seat, Alma climbs into the back.

"Goddamnit!" Tyrone berates Alma, not turning around, keeping his attention and gun directly on Judge at the wheel. "I told you to go have a doctor or a nurse look at that wound."

"I did. I am a nurse, remember? I graduated last month. I'm going with you."

Judge says they better roll while they still can. Tyrone curses so what the fuck is he waiting for then. While Alma binds her arm with a handkerchief using her free hand and her teeth, Judge starts the car.

Pruitt and Rodgers crouching nearby hear the engine turning over in the alley behind Panther headquarters. Then Cy's big old wreck of a car comes out onto the street.

Pruitt volunteers a guess. "That's them I bet. Where do you think they're going?"

Rodgers flicks his cigarette away. It makes a gentle arc into the dark. "I don't give a shit as long as it's not you know where!"

Pruitt says his car is around the corner. Rodgers breaks into a run. "Let's go!"

31

Judge, Tyrone, and Alma cruise the old warehouse district. The fog off the bay rolls in heavily in the chill air, making their job harder.

Finally, Judge picks up the trail—the glistening oil slick that he noticed when Brimmer took him to the warehouse for that little reeducation session. He remembers how it lasted almost a block, then veered off and disappeared under the rusty corrugated doors of the . . .

There it was! The warehouse . . . with two goons out front.

Not too fast, not too slow, Judge cruises past.

"Those sure don't look like cops, Tyrone," Alma says. "And what the hell they doing standing out there like that in front of an abandoned building in the middle of the night?"

Tyrone makes a quick check for himself. "And they sure ain't from the neighborhood."

Tyrone finally sees it Judge's way. "Sorry about the mix-up, man," He apologizes and hands Judge back his gun.

"It's forgotten, man. Huey said 'do it now.' We have to be quick about it." Judge puts his gun in his belt and continues cruising on down the street. "Looks like they're about ready to start dealing."

"Huey was right, brother," Tyrone says, checking his weapon. "Well, we've got our work cut out for us. It's just you and me."

"Bullshit!" Alma cuts in, flashing her gun. "I'm coming too.

You've got two gunmen outside and who knows how many more inside. You'll need all the firepower you can get."

Tyrone turns to argue with Alma, but Judge stops him. "She's right, Tyrone."

Judge makes a U-turn and steps on the gas.

Alma leans forward. "You got a plan, Judge?"

Cy's old jalopy starts to pick up speed. "Not really, but . . ." As they reach the warehouse, Judge pulls the wheel hard left and barrels across the road. ". . . how about this?" he says, aiming the car for the goons guarding the door. "Two punks less for starters!"

Inside the cavernous old building, Sabu, with Shorty at his side, is strutting around overseeing three other henchmen, his best boys, unpacking the plastic sacks of raw dope hidden between layers of coffee beans in wooden crates.

The warehouse hasn't been fully converted to a bona fide dope factory yet. But a space roughly half the size of a basketball court has been cleared. The rest of the interior is still a jungle of rotten ropes, rusting pulleys, and machines. The only illumination is supplied by workers' lamps strung from the exposed girders overhead. The naked bulbs cast stark, three-dimensonal shadows.

The first big shipment has arrived and the gang's mood is upbeat. One thug asks another if he figures he could get high if he was to drink some of the coffee. Another is dreaming out loud about how he is gonna make so much money he's gonna retire. "You know, Shorty," Sabu chuckles, looking around the warehouse, "America is sure enough the land of opportunity."

Suddenly, there is a tremendous crash, a cross between an oriental gong being struck and an explosion as the car . . . *BLAMA! THUNK!* . . . strikes the building. The huge sliding warehouse door buckles but doesn't collapse completely. It bends inwards, dangling by a cable. The front of Cy's car protrudes into the warehouse with one of the thugs splattered face downward on the hood, harpooned by the emblem on the grill.

Inside Sabu, Shorty, and the three gangsters run for cover.

Outside, the door of the automobile is jammed shut on the passenger side.

The other sentry, who managed to jump clear, pulls his gun and runs towards the car firing wildly. Judge dives out of the driver's side, does a roll, comes up, takes quick aim, and wastes him.

Alma crawls out of the back seat clutching the gasoline can. She and Judge pull Tyrone out of the car from the driver's side. Tyrone is bleeding from a thigh wound.

Alma is worried. "You all right?"

"Yeah, I'll do," Tyrone says. "That was some fancy shooting, brother." He shakes his head, admiring Judge's marksmanship. Yeah, well, Judge says, he's had enough practice.

The trio of Panthers creep forward, guns ready. Inside, the warehouse is quiet. The wind blowing through the door after the crash has set the bare bulbs overhead to swinging, and the shadows from the used-up equipment shift from side to side performing a macabre dance in the gloom.

"Split up, stay low," Judge orders. "Alma, you pour the gasoline. We'll cover you."

Doing a deep duck walk, Alma pours the gasoline in a circle around the pile of drugs in the middle of the cleared space. One of the gangsters on the perimeter raises his head to see what's going on. *BLAM!*... Judge blows him away. A second thug just sticks his gun over the fifty-five gallon drums he is hiding behind and fires blind. Tyrone, leaving a trail of blood, outflanks him and takes him by surprise. The thug twists around, trying to get a shot off at Tyrone, but he is too late. Tyrone fires point blank and the goon tumbles backward into the big sleep and the long shadows.

The shot gives Tyrone's position away, and Shorty fires, trying to pick him off. He misses, and they exchange slugs from opposite sides of the clearing, blasting across the crates and glassine bags stacked on the table in the middle.

Tyrone takes a chance and scrambles for better cover, but his injured thigh makes him too slow. One of Shorty's bullets catches him in the gut. Alma drops the gasoline can and goes after Shorty.

Judge works his way over to retrieve the can, and then crawls over to Tyrone.

Tyrone is sitting behind an overturned workbench bleeding from his stomach.

"How you doing, Tyrone?"

"I'll do, brother, but like I said, I been better."

Judge pushes the can towards Tyrone. "You do the pouring, man. Let's shut this motherfucker down. I'll find Sabu."

Before Judge can move, a bullet blasts splinters from the table an inch from his head.

"You just found me!" Sabu shouts.

Judge makes a run for it. Sabu blasts away at him, and a lucky shot hits Judge in the foot, dropping him to the floor.

In the meantime, Tyrone, leaning back to get his breath, spots the third henchman up in the rafters sneaking along a girder to get a clean shot. Tyrone empties his gun at him. The thug is hit. He screams, flails, and plummets three stories to crash on the concrete floor.

Pruitt and Rodgers are nearing the warehouse when they hear the shots.

"Stop!" Rodgers orders, and Pruitt slams on the brakes.

Rodgers grabs the two-way radio linked with the surveillance van. He says, "Patch me through to Dorsett." Dorsett comes on sleepy. Rodgers gives it to him flat. "Wake up! We've got a big problem."

Inside the warehouse, Judge, operating like a soldier, rolls across the floor. Sabu fires at him. Suddenly . . . *CLICK CLICK* . . . Sabu's gun is empty. Sirens can be heard in the distance. Sabu, in a knee-jerk reaction, pokes his head up. Alma blows half of his left ear off.

Enraged about his boss being wounded, Shorty charges from cover and rushes Alma like an angry bull.

"Alma, watch out!" Tyrone screams.

Alma whirls and plants two slugs in Shorty's big chest. His body barely even shivers. He keeps coming, then slows, then staggers forward reaching out for her, finally collapsing face first at her feet.

Sabu realizes he is alone and retreats deeper into the shadows of the warehouse. Judge limps after him, stalking him from shadow to shadow. The oncoming sirens grow louder.

Pruitt tells Rodgers things could get messy. "This is not something we should be implicated in. May I suggest we leave?"

"When I want your opinion, nigger, I'll give it to you!" Rodgers snarls. "We leave when I goddamn say so! Drive along the side. There's a service road around the back. We can watch from there. Come on, move it! Get the lead out of your ass."

Pruitt squeezes his lips shut, and does as he is told. He drives around to the weed-choked ribbon of earth that was once a service road. From their camouflaged position, they watch the first contingent of cop cars screech to a halt in front of the warehouse.

Inside, Judge has Sabu cornered. The only thing between them is a heavy-duty rack of shelves loaded with a king's ransom of dope.

"Come on Panther man. I know you out there. I know you coming." Sabu steps into a shaft of light. "See? I'm gonna let it go." He raises his hands and lets the gun drop. Judge moves slowly forward, keeping to the shadows.

"I know you out there. I know who you are, brother. I know you like the Man's money as much as me. We can both get paid now. We can be partners. You hear what I'm saying. Ninety-eight and two, brother, me and you."

Judge emerges from the shadows, the gun in his fist aimed straight at Sabu. Sabu waves his hand over the booty on the metal rack separating them, working his way toward the handle of a gun hidden between two bags.

"We got everything, man. We got the cocaine, we got the heroin. C'mon, we don't need to kill each other, black man. We gonna be rich." Sabu leans slowly forward, touching the gun. "The Panthers is over, over... Today is a new... "

BLAM!... Judge shoots him between the eyes. Sabu's body stiffens, for a millisecond it straightens up frozen at attention for an eternity. Judge plants another slug in his chest, blasting him backward. Sabu hits the floor stone cold dead.

Outside the warehouse and the remnants of the door, a small army of policemen are crouched behind a barricade of vehicles. "Come out with your hands up!" the officer in charge bellows.

Judge limps back through the maze of rusting machinery to his friends. Alma is on the floor cradling Tyrone in her arms and begging him to hang on.

Alma looks up, eyes brimming with tears. "We've got to get him out of here," she sobs.

Judge can see death hovering over Tyrone's head, but instead he says, "He's gonna be all right . . . he's gonna be all right. There's a back way out. I saw it the time I was here."

Tyrone is coughing blood. They help him to his feet.

"I ain't gonna make it."

"Yes you are," Alma promises.

"You have until the count of three to surrender!" a bullhorn bellows. "ONE!"

"No, I ain't gonna make it. I'll distract them. Hand me my lighter."

Alma looks at Judge, and reads the truth in his eyes. She fishes the lighter out of Tyrone's jacket, but can't bring herself to give it to Tyrone. Judge gently takes the lighter from her and passes it to Tyrone.

"TWO!"

"You take her and get the hell out of here." Tyrone tries to bend down for the gasoline can, but he can't make it. Alma picks the can up and hands it to him. Their eyes lock, a tragic understanding flowing between them.

"I love you guys," Tyrone gurgles, blood seeping from the corner of his mouth. "You gotta stay alive. That's an order!" Tyrone staggers toward the front door, purposefully spilling gasoline behind himself as he goes. "I'll keep 'em busy."

"THREE!"

Judge tugs Alma into the depths of the warehouse to find the back door. They turn for a last look. Tears stream down their cheeks.

Tyrone reaches the door, pulls himself up to his full height, and tosses the open lighter into the puddle of gasoline at his feet. He raises a clenched fist and steps into the open doorway.

"Power to the people!"

"FIRE!"

As the flames race back towards the pile of drugs, the cops go into a shooting frenzy. A fusillade of shots from the police barricade blast Tyrone, twist him, turn him, blow him down.

Judge locates the back door and eases it open. He taps Alma and makes a sign for her to run for it.

Alma nods that she is ready. "Okay, let's go," she whispers.

"No! One at a time," Judge corrects her, using his wartime expertise. "You go, I'll cover. Remember, stay down."

Alma, staying low, starts pushing her way forward through the tall weeds. The police barrage echoes from the front of the warehouse.

Rodgers, sitting in the car hidden out on the old service road, surveys the siege through his night binoculars. He notices the telltale swaying of weeds moving away from the back of the warehouse.

He pulls his gun. "Cover me!" he says to Pruitt as he slides out of the passenger seat.

Unaware of the danger, Alma continues to shove her way through the weeds toward safety. Suddenly, a gun is pressing against the side of her head. She looks up, and Rodgers is smirking down at her. He takes a step backward and indicates for her to rise with the barrel of his revolver.

"Slowly now. Stand up!" he orders. "One false move and you're dead. Now walk." Rodgers prods her towards his vehicle. Pruitt has gotten out from behind the wheel and waits with his gun drawn. *BLOOM!*... The chemicals in the warehouse go up in a fireball.

"We're gonna take a little ride," Rodgers says as they start up the shallow embankment.

"I don't think so," another voice comes out of the night.

Rodgers, who thinks he is the fastest thing since greased lightning, does a drop-and-whirl, rolls along the ground and in one continous motion comes up firing in the direction of the voice. Judge knows the maneuver. He waits patiently for him to finish his rolling and then shoots him dead.

Pruitt pivots, pointing his weapon in the direction of the shot.

Judge rises from the weeds only a few feet away from Pruitt, point-blank range. They stand there with the drop on each other. Each man knows that if he pulls the trigger, the other will be able to kill him in the instant before death.

Alma stands transfixed, witnessing the tableau. Keeping his eyes glued to Pruitt, Judge turns slightly towards her. "Go," he says, but she doesn't move. In the distance behind them, the warehouse is burning and the cops are running around shouting and the fire department has arrived.

"Leave," Judge urges. "Please . . . for Tyrone . . . for the people!"

With a heavy soul, Alma climbs over the embankment and disappears into the night.

Pruitt inches back to his car, keeping his gun levelled at Judge. Reaching inside with his free hand, he grabs the two-way mike, pulls it through the window, and calls in.

"We have an agent down, presumed dead. Assailant . . . "

Judge's finger tightens on the trigger.

". . . Assailant unknown." Without taking his eyes off Judge, Pruitt lowers his gun.

Judge, his gun still aimed at Pruitt, backpedals down the road. Slowly, the shadows begin to claim him. "I owe you one," he calls. Finally, he is swallowed up by the blackness.

"No, I owe you one," Pruitt whispers.

TESTING, ONE-TWO-THREE . . . Personal. Name: Mr. T-Bone . . . Pier, tackle-box.

FRANKLY, I HOPED TO FIND YOU.

Haven't you finished that project yet?

IT WAS TURNED DOWN BY THE DISSERTATION COMMITTEE. THEY SAID MY DATA WAS SERIOUSLY FLAWED. THEY CLAIMED THAT I MUST HAVE MADE UP SOME OF THE INTERVIEWS, THEN USED ACTORS AND MIXED THEM IN WITH THE ONES THEY COULD CORROBORATE. THEY SAID I SHOULD BE IN THE CREATIVE WRITING

DEPARTMENT, AND THAT I WAS LUCKY THEY DIDN'T THROW ME OUT OF SCHOOL FOR CHEATING.

Sorry about that, I suppose. I coulda warned you. Reality—colored reality anyhow—and white truth don't always see eye to eye. But never mind that—to what do I owe the honor of your visit this time?

STRICTLY PERSONAL, SIR. PERSONAL CURIOSITY. QUESTIONS ABOUT THE PANTHERS, MOSTLY, IF I MIGHT TROUBLE YOU AGAIN.

If you don't raise your voice and frighten my fish away, I suppose so.

WHERE DID THE DRUGS COME FROM?

Good question.

YOU'RE SMILING. DON'T TELL ME YOU DON'T BELIEVE THERE WASN'T A CORRELATION BETWEEN THE RISE OF MILITANCY AND THE RISE OF DRUGS IN THE BLACK COMMUNITY?

Oh, I more than believe it, son, I saw it! Saw it spread, too. Your own folks don't even try and hide it no more. They say in 1970, we had maybe three hundred thousand addicts, and now we got over three million. You ast me why I was smiling, didn't you? Well, I was thinking of that old expression, that's why I was smiling. The one that goes, "God ain't all that crazy about pretty and he sure don't like ugly." No sir, no way. You see, when the authorities acted ugly, when they pumped the dope into the black community to destroy the Panther power base, it didn't stay there like they thought it would, it overflooded the borders of the ghetto and ended up on all America's doorsteps.

SPEAKING OF DRUGS OVERFLOWING, THERE ARE SOME

PRETTY ROUGH RUMORS GOING AROUND ABOUT HOW THE PANTHERS ENDED UP, ESPECIALLY HUEY. I KNOW YOU'RE GOING TO SAY RUMORS MY REAR END OR SOMETHING LIKE THAT.

You just can't stop being white, can you?! You don't know what the fuck I'm gonna say. But before I answer that let me tell your scrawny casper ass this. Before they was eventually crushed, the Panthers ended up with chapters in almost every state of the union and some foreign countries to boot and like I said that with the FBI using so much illegal shit on them that even the government has had to finally come out and own up to it. And despite that you still got some Panthers being held in jail on trumped-up charges. Anyhow, Elaine Brown lives in Paris, Kathleen is a lawyer I believe, Eldridge is around, David Hilliard is here in Oakland, Huey was assassinated in a drug deal in 1989, and Bobby teaches and lectures.

HOW ABOUT HUEY? WHAT'S THE REAL DEAL ON THAT?

Well, all I know is you got them VA hospitals full of weird-ass vets World War One, Two, Korea, Vietnam, but that's okay because you-all done legitimized "battle trauma." But niggers in the street fighting to be free, that's a different story. You gonna say what war? Those beatings, those tortures, those solitary confinements don't count, hunh? Get the fuck outta my face with that whitebread bullshit.

DID YOU EVER HEAR OF SOMEONE CALLED JUDGE?

Rose's friend? Yeh, I knew him sorta. It's a little hazy because that was back in my heavy drinking days.

WHERE HE'S GONE, WHAT HE'S UP TO, IS HE ON THE

RUN? COULD YOU TALK ABOUT HIS PHILOSOPHY, ANYTHING? I WOULD LIKE TO UNDERSTAND HIM.

How the hell you gonna do that? You ain't been black. If you want to understand anything, go over on Fifty-Fifth and Market and take a look. The community finally got that stoplight.

I SUPPOSE YOU THINK I'M HOPELESS.

I already told you about telling black people you suppose you know what they're thinking. You don't know squat about what we're thinking. But you could learn, brother. You can always learn, if you wanted to.